WANDOR'S
JOURNEY

CALIBER®
BOOKS

Also from ROLAND J. GREEN

WANDOR Series
Wandor's Ride
Wandor's Journey
Wandor's Voyage
Wandor's Flight

PEACE COMPANY Series
Peace Company
These Green Foreign Hills
The Mountain Walks

STARCRUISER SHENANDOAH Series
Squadron Alert
Division of the Spoils
The Sum of Things
Vain Command
The Painful Field
Warriors for the Working Day

WANDOR'S JOURNEY
Book Two

For further information visit the Caliber Comics website: www.calibercomics.com

Cover image by: Dubya2x

PROLOGUE

In the thirty-third year of the reign of King Nond II over the Kingdom of Benzos, Bertan Wandor, Master in the Order of Duelists, came to stand before the Guardian of the Mountain beneath Mount Pendwyr. And the Guardian of the Mountain, last of the Five-Crowned Kings, spoke to Bertan Wandor, and set him a testing, thus:

"Go and win Firehair the Maiden.

"Go and win aid from Cheloth of the Woods.

"Go and seek these—the Helm of Jagnar, the Ax of Yevoda, the Spear of Valkath, the Sword of Artos, the Dragon-Steed of Morkol.

"Go among all peoples and through all lands and against all who torment and distress men, wherever you find them barring your passage.

"Go then to the house of him you call father and take up the talisman and watch, while Mount Pendwyr splits with fire, and the hills and woods rise into the sky and are scattered to the sea.

"Go then at last forth to battle and smite those who come against you with all your strength and cunning.

"All such will be your testing. The road is long. The testing is great. May your strength be great also."

And the Guardian of the Mountain returned to the fires whence he came. And Wandor heard these words and rode forth.

Now in Benzos, Wandor was given a task by King Nond, for he won the trust of the king and of the king's strong right arm Count Arlor. And Wandor was likewise given as servant a freedman of the Sea Folk named Berek, and he and Berek swore to each other the sacred Oath of the Drunk Blood.

And Berek of the Sea Folk bore the war name Strong-Axe.

Now in those days Duke Cragor, the Black Duke, sought Nond's throne and Nond's life and wrought evil against all those who might uphold Nond to the outer-most limits of his own power. And those powers were exceedingly great, for the Black Duke was a lord mighty in the land of Benzos, and in his service was the Master Sorcerer Kaldmor the Dark.

In the Viceroyalty of the East, Cragor's hand lay heavy, save in the South Marches. There Baron Oman Delvor held strong for King Nond in honor and with power. And it was to the house of Baron Delvor that Wandor was sent to aid and strengthen that house in all possible ways. But Cragor wished Wandor ill, and in the moment of Wandor's arrival in the Viceroyalty the sorceries of Kaldmor the Dark were unleashed against him. Yet he suffered not, for the Guardian of the Mountain appeared to Kaldmor, and all his sorcerous learning availed him naught, and defeat and humiliation were his lot.

So Wandor came safe to the Marches, and in the castle of Baron Delvor he met Gwynna Delvor, daughter to the baron and a woman of Power. And he found her altogether beautiful, yet he felt no desire for her.

Then came a night when the Earth Voices spoke, and Gwynna received Wandor as a woman receives a man.

And she was Firehair the Maiden.

And she told Wandor of yet another Testing, at the hands of the terrible Yhangi, who rode far and wide across the Plains beyond the Silver Mountains.

So Wandor and Gwynna crossed the Silver Mountains. They did strong battle against the floods of the river Zephas, against hunger and cold, against the wild beasts of the Plains. And by the favor of the gods to the brave and by Gwynna's own Powers they won through to the Plainsmen and were received among them.

But Cragor was an unsleeping foe and wrought further ill

6

against the Marches. His assassins struck down the seneschal of the Delvors, Sir Gar Stendor, and his hirelings and vassals made war against the Marches. But in this war Sir Gilas Lanor swore an oath with the Khindi, the dwellers in the forests of the Viceroyalty. They came forth to serve in the war and wrought much havoc among the servants of the Black Duke.

The spring came and with it the time of Wandor's Testing before all the Yhangi. Wandor came forth to fight against Jos-Pran, War Chief of the Gray Mares, a man filled with pride and distrust. And he defeated Jos-Pran in three combats, yet Jos-Pran was not content.

So Wandor was bidden to ride the King Horse of all the Yhangi. And this Wander did, though none had done it before. And from that moment onward, the Yhangi swore to follow him and do his bidding.

He had great need of them, for in that spring Duke Cragor came against the Marches with a great army. But there was a need to open the South Pass of the Silver Mountains before the Plainsmen could pass to aid Baron Delvor. The Guardian of the Mountain answered this great need, for he made the earth move so that the South Pass lay open to the Plainsmen.

And in the end Cragor's army came to Delkum Pass in the Marches, and there Wandor met it and conquered it. For the Plainsmen came by the tens of thousands, and the *Red Seers* of the Plainsmen overcame Kaldmor's sorceries, and the greater part of Cragor's army perished altogether from the earth and went down into the House of Shadows.

Yet Cragor and Kaldmor the Dark fled in good time from the field of Delkum Pass. Though their strength was for the moment shrunken, yet was their malice toward Nond and all who marched with Nond not diminished. And so they continued their labors for the fall of Nond, while there was peace in the Viceroyalty of the East for the space of about a year.

Now in the spring of the thirty-fourth year of the reign of Nond—

From *The Shorter Chronicle of Wandor*

CHAPTER 1

Bertan Wander bent low in the saddle as his horse neared the crest of the low hill, until the horse's sweat-soaked mane whipped about his face. Somewhere on the other side of that hill should be a dozen-odd of Duke Cragor's bravos. Among them was sure to be at least one archer, perhaps more. Wandor had no wish to see his life and whatever might depend on it brought to an end by a chance arrow.

The fleeing men were the survivors of a force of raiders who had charged out of the mists of the May dawn, lashing the village of Turpath with fire and sword. Fifteen villagers were dead, as many more wounded, eight houses and a barn burned. And there it would have ended, but chance had brought Baron Oman Delver's household to visit Turpath's overlord the night before.

The five mounted Plainsmen on guard duty outside the manor had been on the road to Turpath within minutes after the first smoke coiled greasily, repellently out of the mist. Minutes after the Plainsmen, came Wandor and his wife Gwynna, behind them a scrambled-together force of fighting men armed with what they could snatch up, armored in what they could pull on, some riding without stirrups or even bareback. A few paid for such haste by falling off along the road. But those who kept their saddles headed straight for Turpath and came pounding into the village hard behind the Plainsmen.

Four of the Plainsmen were already dead, also five of the raiders. The rest had spurred their horses away to the north and were clear of the burning village. But hoof marks in the road clearly marked their direction, Wandor's band plunged north in pursuit.

Both parties knew the land well, both were driven by an equal determination—Wandor's men to catch and kill, the raiders to flee and live—and neither's horses were much fresher than the other's. A savage little fight with the raiders' rearguard at Hashor's Ford took six of them and four of Wandor's men. During that fight, the rest of the raiders crossed the little river and built up a lead that it took Wandor half an hour to prune away again.

In the end he came up with them, and more men on both sides went down in a running fight. The raiders found themselves cut off from the only road leading back to their home territory. Only the forest offered them a route home. It was to catch them before they reached that forest, now only minutes away, that Wandor was urging his horse up the bill.

The horse went soaring upward over the bushes at the crest of the bill, nearly losing its footing. A frantic clod-spraying churning of hooves brought it upright again. It plunged downward as Wandor raised his head again and drew his sword.

He cursed as he saw the raiders already reining in their horses and hurling themselves out of the saddles. Only on foot could they hope to make it through the forest to safety. One of the men snatched up a strung bow and nocked an arrow to it. Wandor turned his horse side-on to the bowman. Then he swung himself on to the offside, until only his foot in the stirrup and his left hand on the bridle kept him and the horse in company. It was a Plainsman trick that Gwynna had taught him, except that she still could do it better than he.

An arrow went *weeeeessssssh* overhead, and Wandor guided his horse to the left, heading in toward the forest. If he could cut in between the raiders and the deep forest—

Another arrow gave its hissing moan, and this one struck deep into the horse's neck. The horse screamed as though it were being torn in pieces, rearing up so suddenly that Wandor's grip on the bridle pulled loose. In a split second he tightened his grip on his sword, kicked his foot out of the stirrup to avoid being caught and dragged by the dying animal, and let himself fall to the ground. He rolled as he struck, picking up bruises from the stones in the ground, hoping that the horse would fall where he could roll behind its body without being a target for too long, knowing that was unlikely, hearing another arrow thud into the earth within a foot of his head—

Then a mighty crashing of hooves came from up the hill, instantly drowned out by a volley of war cries as the rest of Wandor's party poured over the crest of the hill at a full gallop. He raised his head to see the last of the raiders leap down from their saddles and scuttle into the shadows of the trees. They left only a dozen-odd horses milling about nervously and looking dubiously at the newcomers.

One of the raiders was a little slow. Or perhaps his quick curiosity rather than his slow feet doomed him. Wandor saw a brief, pale flicker of movement in the shadows. Gwynna, holding a Plainsman horse bow as she rode, must have seen it also. Her arm bent and then straightened, an arrow flickered in the air, and a half-choked cry and a thump among the trees told of a true shot.

Wandor rose to his feet and waved to Gwynna as she cantered down the slope to him. She sprang from her saddle as lightly as one of her own hunting leopards and with the same grace stepped up to Wandor and into his outstretched arms. They closed about her. He traced a line down her back with his long-fingered, muscular hands and wished they were both somewhere else and alone. She lifted her head, and her green eyes flickered upward to meet his. The green leather hat with its gold feather fell to the damp ground behind her. Standing close to him like this, the top of her flame-crowned head rose just to the point of his chin.

After a little, each was sure that the other was still tangible flesh and blood and not a ghost conjured up in the place of one departed to the House of Shadows. Wandor's dry tongue shaped itself to form words.

"Well shot, love. But why so long in coming?"

Gwynna did not bristle because the question was not pitched as a reproach but only as an inquiry, the inquiry of a soldier seeking to find out what had happened. But there was a slight edge to her clear voice as she replied, "Why so far ahead? You were pushing on as though you had the King Horse himself under you. We foundered three of our mounts, keeping as close as we did."

"Fortunately it wasn't the King Horse," said Wandor, with a glance toward the body of his mount.

10

"No," said Gwynna. "It wasn't. It might have been you instead. Why leave the King Horse to gorge himself fat and service the Delvor mares while you charge into every little skirmish fifty yards ahead of your nearest supporters? Our plans won't fall to pieces if the King Horse dies. But what about you?"

What about me indeed? thought Wandor. This was not the time to reply that a good commander always leads from in front, although he believed that to be true. His mentor, Sir Warin Marklor, fallen to teaching the apprentices in a House of Duelists but still with a Knight's instincts, had taught him so. And there was King Nond himself, who (when young and strong, not the great swollen creature who sat in Manga Castle today), had led the charge that won the Battle of Yost and given the Viceroyalty of the East to the Kings of Benzos. Baron Oman Delvor had seen Nond riding in the lead, had indeed foundered his own horse trying to keep up with his king.

Nor was it the time to confess the chill that entered into him each time he saw Gwynna riding pell-mell into a fight. No horse ever foaled could throw her deliberately. But a few horses had found what she asked of them more than they could do and still keep on their feet. And what of the spears, swords, arrows, and clutching, clawing hands of enemies who would glory in her body dragged naked behind their horses as much as they would in his?

Those enemies might well be right. Although the Guardian of the Mountain had spoken *to* him and only *of* her, yet she was part of the great plan. More important than anything the gods might conjure up in the course of the games they played with mortals as the pieces, she was part of his mind and heart and soul. Could he push on to whatever goal loomed at the end of his road without her beside him?

Instead of either of these for-the-moment unsayable things, Wandor only nodded gravely and tried to look contrite. "I'll try to stay closer to the others. But today it was maddening. A dozen of them about to get away after carrying out a raid practically under our noses."

Gwynna sighed. "What else could we have done? With the Khindi aiding us properly, we could make every patch of forest a death trap for the enemy. But they seem to have forgotten everything they ever swore to Sir Gilas. Now they say that our quarrels are not theirs and sit around their village campfires. And Cragor's raiders can give us the slip any time they dive into the forest."

She was beginning to get angry now, a condition that Wandor had seen often enough. When that anger was directed at him, it made him as wary and as cautious as a hostile army could have done. "And those wretched peasants are still too afraid of the Khindi to follow the raiders into the woods. The peasants know forest craft; they have bows and dogs. They could track the raiders well enough, but will they? Since Cragor's invasion collapsed last year, they've clung as close to their hearths as though Kruga Hearthmistress had fastened each one there with a chain around his thick ankle!"

Wandor was tempted to point out that the peasants had much that needed doing after the invasion in the way of rebuilding and replanting. But Gwynna was in too full flight to give any hearing to that notion. She stormed on. "And just now Turpath has lost a fifth of its people dead or maimed, and there are orphans and widows and the spirits of the dead crying out for vengeance, and yet I'll wager the survivors won't stir a step farther, from their hearths than before, Oh gods, protect us from the cautious and give us some men who are fools enough to charge headlong after an enemy whenever he shows himself!"

"Like me?" said Wandor quietly, as Gwynna paused for breath. She saw the smile spreading across his face; then her own face turned the same color as her hair. She dropped her glance and pressed her face into the leather of his riding tunic.

Gwynna was released from her embarrassment and Wandor from the need to say anything more by the approach of Berek Strong-Axe. The huge Sea Folker was faithful to the last degree in following Wandor into any battle where the Master to whom he had sworn the Oath of the Drunk Blood might go. But the massive draught horse he had to ride had more strength and endurance than speed. Only if a battle lasted a good long while did Berek ride up in time to do more than help count the bodies, succor the wounded, and collect the booty. These tasks he did conscientiously and as conscientiously reported the results to his Master.

Now he came up to Wandor, looming nearly a head taller, and bowed slightly. A grim smile played across his red-bronze face, not yet overlaid by a summer's tan. "Mistress Gwynna, the man you killed seems to have been the leader of the raiders. At least," he added, "he was the only man among them wearing a Master of Arms clasp."

"That makes twelve of those louts we gathered in," said Gwynna almost absently.

"Yes," said Berek. "And almost all their loot and most of their gear and all of their horses, although some of the horses will not be much use again. It has not been a bad trade, except for the villagers."

"No," snapped Gwynna with another flash of temper. "It hasn't. But we're not traders bargaining Ponan furs against Chongan silks. We're fighting a war!" She turned on her heel and strode back to where her horse stood peacefully cropping the short spring grass. Wander and Berek stood in silence and watched her mount.

The strain on all of them was growing as the endless petty warfare grew less petty, more savage and costly. Perhaps Gwynna was fortunate in being able to relieve the strain with these thunderstorms of anger.

For the moment, Wandor was most conscious of his empty stomach. Breakfast would be waiting at the manor. And though a Chongan ascetic might find reasons for putting off getting to that breakfast, Wander could not.

The manor cook was known throughout the Marches as a man who had to be kicked out of bed in the morning and dragged into the kitchen by his heels. But on this morning the uproar of the raid had served just as well as his master's boot usually did.

Breakfast was smoked ham and winter sausage, dried apples and plums, chunks of pale-yellow cheese and whole loaves of gray country bread, the sadly dried-out remnants of last year's crop of walnuts, washed down with ale and brimming bowls of goat's milk so fresh it still steamed in the faint morning chill as the serving maid placed it on the table. The lord of the manor was still in Turpath counting up the damage and those in need of aid. Wander, Gwynna, and Baron Delver had the lord's end of the long table all to themselves.

They also had time to relax, and even eat to repletion. That meant a few mouthfuls for Gwynna, a healthy meal for Wandor, and for Baron Delvor a mass of food almost large enough to sate King

Nond himself. They were preparing to rise when the door swung open with a crash and Sir Gilas Lanor strode in. His breeches were dark with saddle sweat, while his absurdly youthful face had lost some of its youthfulness behind a layer of stubble and grime. His expression was so grim that none of the three at the head of the table needed a single word to tell them to follow him outside, away from unwanted ears.

Outside he led them in silence away from the manor house, past the outbuildings, out through the gate of the wooden stockade, out even beyond the piled stone for the lord's planned stone wall. There he sat down on a moss-green slab, took a deep breath, and said, "Duke Cragor is hiring mercenaries."

Baron Delvor puffed up his red cheeks and began indignantly, "You dragged us all the way out here to tell us—" before his daughter put a firm hand on his arm and he sputtered away into silence.

Sir Gilas shook his head. "I know. He's been hiring them on and off for the last ten years. But not like this. A message just arrived with Count Arlor's signature and seal. Cragor is hiring every available free-lance he can get, and he's buying up the contracts of every one with an employer willing to sell. He's even picking up men right and left from the households of the nobility. Every petty lordling seems to be contributing half a dozen."

"What about the great houses?" Sharp voiced, from Gwynna.

"Arlor says nothing in the letter." Sir Gilas shrugged. "Those who want to see the House of Nobor fall and the strong monarchy fall with it will be on Cragor's side when he needs them. Working openly with Cragor would be too dangerous for them now."

"Unless—" began Wandor, then stopped for a moment before continuing. "How is Cragor supposed to be paying these men? Mercenaries tend to want their money in advance, particularly in a venture like this. If they don't get it, the captains usually won't assemble men they can't rely on paying—or controlling. There aren't many captains like Master Besz who can keep a thousand men in hand even when he hasn't had a contract for months!"

"So far Cragor seems to be using mostly his own money," said Sir Gilas. "Arlor mentions rumors of Chongan money and agents trickling in. But he is careful to call them rumors."

Wandor nodded, but the greater part of his mind was

14

elsewhere. Count Arlor was King Nond's best and most reliable assistant, trusted above all others and deserving that trust. Wandor would give him the same trust.

So the Black Duke was massing a large—and expensive— army of mercenaries. Where *was* the money coming from? As husband to Crown Princess Anya, Cragor had always received a generous allowance from the Royal Treasury of Benzos. And there were his own estates beyond that and no doubt some secret contributions from fellow nobles. But considering what mercenaries inevitably cost, to assemble and maintain an entire army of them would beggar even the Black Duke within a few months.

Unless—and here he had stopped and fallen silent—within a few months Cragor expected to have wealth far beyond his present level. Chongan gold? Certainly the twelve great city-states of the far South had it in abundance. But their leaders, and even more their transient "Kings," tended to be cautious about investing it in foreign intrigues.

No, what Cragor must expect to have open to him within those few months could only be the Royal Treasury of Benzos. Which meant that he was about to move against King Nond, kill him, massacre his supporters, and shove the wretched Anya on to the throne of Benzos over her father's body. Then Cragor would be king in Benzos in all but name. He would be free to mass his forces and hurl them across the Ocean, into the Viceroyalty of the East, against Nond's stubborn supporters here in the Marches. Wandor sighed. The victory at Delkum Pass had been expected to set Cragor back a year—and it had done just that. But now that year had passed, and the Black Duke was on the move again.

"Cragor is getting ready to strike," said Wandor flatly. He watched Gwynna and Sir Gilas nod. The Baron shook his head, but not in denial—in utter weariness. The words hung in the air like the sour smoke of a funeral pyre.

Otherwise it was a spring air, with no trace of winter chill undercutting it. The smell of leaf mold and spring flowers and damp grass came to Wandor on the breeze. As an apprentice in the Trorim House of Duelists, such spring breezes had always drawn him outward, beyond the houses of the little city huddled among the dark Hills, into the forest that lapped against its walls, to drift across country for days at a time.

His fellow apprentices had called him moon-struck if they felt kindly toward him. And they had talked of his dirty Sthi blood coming out and drawing him back to his people if they did not. Sir Warin Marklor had frowned at those latter, predicting that they were laughing at one who would surpass them all.

Had Sir Warin been gifted with foresight? Wandor knew he had indeed surpassed all his fellow apprentices from the Trorim House. But could Sir Warin have had the remotest notion of what strange road his favorite apprentice was to walk to go so far?

CHAPTER 2

Evening, with fading daylight still washing over the stone of Randul Castle. The plains a thousand feet below had already sunk into purple shadow as they rolled away toward the east on either side of the burnished silver of the River Avar. A brisk, chill wind blew from the northwest, from out of the Hills. The banner of the House of Cragor stood out board stiff against the pale gold and pink of the western sky, black fanged gryphon's head on a red field whipping above the keep.

The ancient square keep stood almost on the cliff's edge. Between its base and the low east wall that ran along the cliff lay a small courtyard. From that courtyard a short flight of crumbling stone steps ran up to the top of the wall. Here in the lee of the keep a man could stand protected from the wind, to stare out over the plain and assemble his thoughts into whatever shape he wanted or needed.

Duke Cragor stood against the parapet, leaning cautiously against it. The mortar was rotten everywhere in the castle. It had stood on its cliff in the wind and the weather since far back in the Years of Darkness. Who had built it was no longer recorded even in the legends of the peasants who looked fearfully up at its dark bulk from their cottages far below. Some murmured of spells worked at its building or human blood mixed with its mortar to keep it standing so long.

Cragor ignored peasant murmurings on this as on all other matters. But he would gladly take advantage of other people's superstitions to aid his own schemes. As long as the peasants believed Randul Castle reeked of sorcery, they would keep far away from it.

There would be less chance of prying eyes to watch his own comings and goings and those of his men.

Some of those men were coming tonight with another man who might—no, *would*—add the final touch to Cragor's plans. A Fire Priest of the barbarian tribes of Ponos, the chill land of forest and tundra and icy rivers that stretched away to the north of the Kingdom of Benzos. The Ponans had once raided south many days' hard riding, almost to the Avar itself. They could not or would not conquer, but as they swept through on their shaggy ponies, they left a trail of ashes and tears behind them.

It was to bar the Ponan raiders from their land that the first Hond kings of Benzos had created the Royal Army—the standing regiments of cavalry and infantry, the experts at siegecraft and victualing and all the other arts needed to sustain an army. That had been just and right and proper, for the glory of those kings and the expansion of the Kingdom of Benzos. Now it reached far to the north of the Avar, and castles, farms, and even flourishing towns stood where there had once been a wasteland. For two centuries the great houses of the nobility and the petty barons, the Free Knights and Masters of Arms, all had sent their best armor and horses to equip the Royal Army, their sons to command it, their gold to sustain it.

And to strengthen the instrument of their own destruction. Ignorant and shortsighted, when they had thrown down the child-king Minto, last of the Rarils, and raised to the throne Duke Porel of Nobor, they had thought their position secure for all time. For was not the new ruling House their own creation? Cragor had read the chronicles of that time two centuries ago, smiling with grim amusement at the precisely recorded folly of his ancestors.

King Porel himself had merely further strengthened and polished the weapon. More and more of the Free Knights took the king's service and joined the Royal Knights. More and more the commanders of the army saw themselves as servants of the king. The ever-more prosperous free yeomen, bowing to no master but the king, came forth in ever-increasing numbers to fill the ranks of the army. The independent Order of Knights shrank, and the once mighty bands of mercenaries shrank.

Porel I reigned thirty-seven years and died in bed, as befitted a king known as "the Peace Lover." He left to his son Porel II a bulging treasury, the finest army in the civilized world, and explicit instructions as to what to do with both. The first thing Porel II did was build Manga Castle—Manga the Impregnable, which had sheltered him as it now sheltered King Nond. A secure refuge built, Porel II launched his army against the nobles.

Cragor's jaw muscles tightened beneath his black beard as he recalled the stories of the years that followed. Porel II was "bleeding those who have themselves most wrongfully and disloyally bled our subjects"—a famous phrase. And blunt, too. Porel II had never been mealy-mouthed. With an army such as his, there had been no need for tact.

For twenty years rebellious nobles—and "rebellion" was an easy accusation in those days—did bleed. Or burned or suffocated or drowned, depending on what Porel's torturers and executioners felt like doing to a particular victim.

Eventually Porel II died with an assassin's arrow in his lungs. But by that time nearly all the nobles unwilling to see the Kings of Benzos rule as well as reign had preceded him into the House of Shadows. And he left a son, the first by the name of Nond, to finish what he had begun.

For six generations now the Kings of Benzos had ruled by their own strength—not, as it should be, by the will and consent of their nobles. The Kingdom had grown great, to be sure. Nond II himself had launched the armies of Benzos across the Ocean and carved out a virtual new kingdom in the Viceroyalty of the East. But Cragor knew that Benzos would have grown still greater if those of blood and birth had not been driven to skulk on their estates. Mighty as they were, the kings were served only by swarms of base-born clerks, a handful of nobles with the morals of harlots, and those Knights who had chosen self-advancement above loyalty to their Order. So the gods had called on him, Cragor, fifth Duke of that House, the Black Duke, to sweep away the barriers to Benzos's new greatness and rise up the Kingdom. They had given him a mighty opportunity to take advantage of King Nond's necessities, and he had grasped that opportunity. Now he would sweep away that great fat hog of a king who wallowed in Manga Castle, long past wielding power yet not willing to share it with those who could. Sweep him away, place his cringing daughter on the Leopard throne, and in all save the name be king himself. Cragor threw his head back and spread his arms wide as he stared out across the plains toward the east, toward Benzos itself. From here the world seemed a shrunken, dwarfed thing, crawling with little creatures that he could reach out to clutch, watching them wriggle, hearing them scream, snapping them between his fingers.

A gust of wind sneaking around the keep tore at his red-lined black cloak and flipped it up over his head. Cragor struggled out of the garment, cursing savagely. The moment of exaltation was shattered forever.

Perhaps just as well. There were yet too many details in his plan that needed to be worked over with a cool head and a steady hand. The Ponans were among those details.

Their raiding parties could not meet regular Royal Army soldiers in the field, nor take any but the most modestly fortified towns. But those same raiding parties still kept more than a quarter of the Royal Army of Benzos permanently stationed in the north to fend them off.

Single clans or the following of a single war chief were the most the Ponans had ever sent south. Suppose they now came down many thousands strong? How much more of the Royal Army would this suck north? Another quarter, perhaps? And yet another quarter was stationed in the Viceroyalty of the East, too far away to affect Cragor's plans in Benzos itself. This left—how many?—to prop up Nond's throne. Apart from men assigned to garrisons far in the south along the Chongan border—ten thousand, at most. Not all of them fighting men, either, although among them would be some of the Household troops, the finest of all. Against these Cragor could rely on throwing at least thirty thousand men. That should be enough.

It would be a wretchedly ill-timed jest of the gods if they weren't enough. Cragor had scraped his coffers down to the last green-tarnished brass penny bit and poured their contents into the open, clutching, greedy hands of, dozens of mercenary captains. Well-filled coffers they had been, for Cragor had put little of his immense wealth into personal splendor. The great town house in Benzos existed only because he found useful a suitable frame in which to display his wife.

Cragor had subdued Anya herself to the point where she would not have protested at living in a peasant's hovel or even a dungeon. But there were those—King Nond among them—with different notions of what was due a Princess of the Blood.

Well-filled coffers once, empty ones now. The payments to the mercenaries and the money set aside to underwrite the bargain with the Ponans had sucked the last gold from them. The agents of Pirnaush of Dyroka, the current "King" in Chonga, assured Duke Cragor of His Omnipotence's best wishes for the new rule in Benzos, and neither gave nor promised a single silver *qual*. Other forms of assistance they had mentioned—vaguely—but not what Cragor needed most. To be sure, "King" Pirnaush needed ample gold to prop up his own shaky status. But the tone of the refusals suggested there might be more in the fat Dyrokan's mind than simple prudence and thrift.

In Benzos the great houses had certainly been lavish with sympathy and promises of support—after Cragor had moved. They were very careful to make that last condition clear. Would the Ponans also insist on waiting for him to make the first move?

And then what? Strike with what he had against a solid mass of royal soldiers or delay further? Delay further, lose supporters, and have the mercenary captains soon coming around with their hands held out again for more money, money he would not be able to give them? Mercenaries had revived to almost their old strength during the past ten years—and were showing almost their old hunger for ready gold. Cragor threw his arms wide again, this time smashing his knuckles into the stone. He swore at the pain, then turned to descend the stairs to the courtyard.

As he reached the courtyard, the wind brought him the sound of approaching hooves. The gate guard's voice shouted a challenge. It was hard for him not to dash around the keep into the main courtyard like a boy on his way home from school. By the time he had calmed enough to walk at a dignified pace into the courtyard, the gate had squealed open to let the horsemen through. Stable hands and house servants ran up to help them dismount.

All four riders were dressed in the green homespun and roughly tanned leather of the local foresters. In this area that disguise could pass almost anywhere without question. But the Ponan was unmistakable to Cragor's trained eye. A full head shorter than the others, bowlegged from a life spent largely on pony-back, broad dark brown face with squashed-in nose and wide-set black eyes, almost everything below the nose concealed by the square-cut beard that marked him as a Fire Priest. Except for priests and chiefs, it was a rare Ponan who bothered trying to trim the wire-tough hairs of his beard into any sort of shape or order.

As the man dismounted, Cragor stepped forward to greet him, hands raised and palms outward in the Ponan gesture of honor. "Welcome to the castle, Blessed One."

The Ponan nodded curtly. "The Brothers of the Flame sent me. I have traveled far. I am hungry and thirsty." Cragor could not tell whether this abruptness was the result of ignorance of Hond speech or the man's natural manner.

He turned to one of the servants. "Is the guest chamber ready?"

"Yes, Master."

"Blessed One, if you will follow me..." He gestured toward the open door of the hall. Then he had to almost run to catch up with the priest. Those bowed legs could carry a man over the ground at a surprising pace.

Once seated before the fire, the priest fell on the wine and the venison laid out for him as though he had not eaten for a month. When the jug and the plate were both empty, he took off his tunic, then bent and unlaced his boots. Cragor wished the man had left them on. The Duke did not know how often Ponans washed their feet, but once a year seemed a generous estimate. He picked up his own wine cup and sipped at it, then put it down. His stomach was too knotted with tension and suspense to cope with wine.

The priest rubbed his hands together, combed lice out of his hair and threw them into the fire, then spat loudly several times on the carpet. Cragor managed not to wince. Then the priest reached into the leather pouch on his belt and took out a smaller black fur one. From that he took a necklace of shimmering red stones and hung it around his neck. Then he turned to Cragor, who, swallowed and sat up straighter as he noticed that the priest's whole manner had changed. Along with the necklace, he seemed to have also donned a new and unexpected dignity.

"Cragor," said the Fire Priest. There was a long pause. Cragor was sweating from more than the heat of the fire. "The Brothers of the Fire have met in Council at the House of Fire. Each has said what he wished to say about your offer. All now speak through me, for the People."

Cragor nodded. Split into tribes and clans, the Ponans yet all acknowledged the dignity of the Fire Priests and made them the negotiators when trade was sought or diplomacy needed. And once the Brothers of the Flame had met in Council and reached a decision, every rider of every remote clan or tribe would consider himself bound by that decision—unless and until the Priests changed their minds. This they did often enough. Cragor managed to put that last thought out of his mind for the moment and return the priest's stare.

"You have offered gold," the priest continued. "A hundred thousand gold crowns now, a hundred thousand more when you rule in Benzos. That is great wealth."

"It is no more than you de—" began Cragor. His efforts to be courtly were cut short as the priest raised a hand. "Gold is good. We will take it. And also we will take land. All the land that was our fathers', as far south as the river you call the Nifan. That must be ours, also."

For a long moment Cragor felt as if he had been kicked in the stomach by a mule. He swallowed, conjured up a mental map of the kingdom, then swallowed again. To pull the northern frontier of Benzos back to the Nifan would mean pulling it back more than a hundred miles, abandoning scores of thousands of people to the Ponans. What would be said if this were the first act of Queen Anya's reign?

"What if I do not want to throw so many of my people into your hands?"

"Then we can see you do not want our help, either." The priest's face split momentarily in a chilly smile. "Consider what has been done to us and how much we have lost. Then think again whether we ask too much."

Cragor thought. They were asking much, certainly, but too much? Particularly when their aid was the difference between probable success and certain failure? But would giving away the land of Benzos

23

merely bring him to disaster a little later?

It might if he did indeed give it away. But did he have to—really? The Ponans would be occupying the land in any case after they stormed down from the north. All they wanted was formal recognition of their right to it. And that was a scrap of paper that he could tear up once he was securely in power. "Once he was securely in power." A beautiful phrase. Then Queen Anya could proclaim a mighty war against the treacherous barbarians to drive them from the sacred soil of Benzos. There was nothing like a foreign war to unite people behind you, and here would be one ready-made and popular to the last degree. Two birds brought down by the same arrow. The tension inside Cragor eased so suddenly that he almost burst out laughing.

But he kept his face sober and continued to stare at the priest. Now it would be that smelly savage's turn to wait! The silence went on. Cragor would have liked to see the Fire Priest begin to fidget, but finally gave up hoping for it.

"I accept. Blessed One," he said. A broad smile spread across his face as he rose and held out his palms to the priest. The Ponan rose and pressed his palms against Cragor's.

"So be it," he said. "And now I wish to sleep. We may talk more tomorrow."

Cragor's shaky legs managed to take him out of the chamber, up the stairs, and down the corridor to his own rooms before they gave up. As he collapsed on the bed and bawled for wine, his mind was working furiously, flicking ideas from side to side like beads on a Chongan counting frame. Messages to the important people. The principal mercenary captains, his Grand Chamberlain, the regimental commanders of the Royal Army that he had won over. A special message to Baron Galkor in the Viceroyalty of the East—keep things quiet and wait for the help that will be sent as soon as possible. Meanwhile, take no risks. And *hope* that Kaldmor the Dark would soon finish whatever unearthly business he had in the Hills and be ready to cross to the Viceroyalty as soon as possible.

Cragor grimaced at the thought of Kaldmor the Dark. He disliked both mediocrity and sorcery, and the little man in the purple robes was a mediocre sorcerer. But there was an unmistakable aura of sorcery still hanging over the Viceroyalty. And there had been an open and terrifying display of it at the Battle of Delkum Pass. Keeping things quiet in the Viceroyalty undeniably needed a sorcerer. Not an especially good one, for the moment—so Kaldmor the Dark would do well enough—for the moment.

Cragor rolled off the bed and rose to his feet "All the fiends carry off you slow-footed idiots!" he roared. "Where's my wine?"

CHAPTER 3

Count Arlor would have gladly spurred his big roan gelding along the High Road to Manga Castle at a full gallop. Indeed, he would have willingly traded it altogether for Bertan Wandor's King Horse or even for the legendary Dragon-Steed of Morkol. But after a night of rain the High Road's stones were treacherous with slimy mud. He could only jog along at a trot and hope that King Nond would wait in patience, his massive back to a good solid wall. Not even in Manga Castle was the of Benzos safe these days.

The count wore a much-patched brown leather jerkin with a hood and faded dark-red breeches that disappeared into battered riding boots. It was not well to look too prosperous riding alone along the High Road these days, even between Benzos and Manga Castle. So he dressed to be taken for a small tradesman down on his luck or a journeyman of some craft drifting from town to town in search of work. Under those outer garments, though, he wore a steel cap and a shirt and breeches of fine link mail. The stout club that dangled from his saddle would split apart with a sharp tug to expose a slim-bladed sword. And sheathes in boot tops and along forearms held a quartet of Costurn fighting knives.

Arlor pulled his hood tighter to conceal everything except his eyes. The morning fog was lifting. Perhaps there would be enough sun today to begin drying the fields. It had been a wretchedly chill and sodden spring. After last year's spotty harvest there had been little enough seed grain, and far too much of that had already rotted in the ground. There would be famine before the summer was over—already was famine in some of the northern areas, toward the Ponan lands. Arlor thought of the sumptuous breakfast doubtless awaiting him at Nond's table with a twinge of guilt. Should he suggest a more frugal table to the king? He should, but it would be a waste of time. Fatalism grew on Nond more each day like some creeping vine. He behaved more often than not as though the fate of Benzos lay in hands other than his own.

With the lifting mist, familiar sights and sounds reached Arlor from the farm cottages along the road. Small barefooted boys squelched through muddy front yards to empty night-soil jars. Their older sisters squatted with buckets beside cows, while the banging of wooden bowls told of mothers ladling out porridge. He recalled seeing the same sights on early-morning rides past the cottages on his father's estates.

Visibility was a mile or more now. In the distance he could see the cluster of white and yellow wooden houses and shops that was the village of Manga. The farms along the side of the road were giving way now to taverns and inns. Some of these had been here as long as Manga Castle itself, raking in silver first from the men who built it, then from the men who garrisoned it, offering both the same things— sour wine, flat beer, aging trollops on the last leg of their progress down to the waterfront houses in Avarmouth or even overseas to Chonga. An inn on the right seemed to be open already. Doing a brisk business, too, judging from the number of people around it.

Abruptly Arlor dug his heels into the horse's flanks and dropped one hand toward his disguised sword. The people around the tavern door were surging back and forth, arms rising and falling, amid curses and women's screams and the thud of feet. The gelding surged up to a canter, bearing down on the crowd. They scattered like a flight of birds, leaving a man lying on his back by the front steps of the inn. His clothes were half ripped off and stained with mud and blood. More blood was running from his smashed nose.

Arlor reined in and threw back his hood, then exposed his sword. He glared down at the people as they slowly drifted back toward him. "What is going on here? You flout the King's Justice practically under his nose?"

27

"To the fiends with the King's Justice and you, too, you damned pimp!" came a woman's voice from the back of the crowd. A gray-haired woman nearly as tall as Arlor himself shouldered her way through the crowd dragging a younger woman with her. The second woman was carrying a bundle wrapped in a shawl. "Where was the King's Justice when my daughter's baby died of hunger? That toad there—" she jerked a sausage-like thumb toward the man on the ground "—was hoarding grain. Grain that might have kept the little one alive. Nobody paid any attention to it. So we're going to show him, and you, too."

"The Royal Gendarmes—"

"Take bribes just like everybody else," snapped the woman. "The bastard was bribing them to stay out of his storeroom. Well, he can't bribe us!" There were animal growls of agreement from the rest of the crowd. Somebody flung a clod of mud hard at the neck of Arlor's horse. It struck, and the beast jerked under him.

"Go on," yelled the woman. "Go on and stuff your face at the king's table. But take a look at this before you do!" She jerked the shawl away from the bundle and thrust it up at Arlor.

Hands and feet like the claws of a bird. Twig-thin legs. Skin the color of dusty wax. And a belly swollen melon-round with starvation. Arlor looked down at the dead baby and felt the saliva welling up in his mouth. If he stayed here another second, he was going to be sick. He thought of reaching for his purse, to throw down a handful of coins, then realized the futility of the gesture. In silence he dug his spurs in. The gelding plunged through a gap in the crowd and away up the road, hooves scrabbling for footing on the wet stone. From behind him came curses, the woman's savage laughter, and a shower of stones, turds, and clods of mud.

King Nond contemplated the four-egg omelet steaming on his plate for a moment, then dug his silver spoon into it to scoop out a massive chunk. Arlor looked from the king's bearded jowls down to his own plate, where a slightly smaller omelet looked back at him. Then he looked away. His stomach would normally have been clamoring for food. This morning, however, it was silent. The count looked up at Nond with a momentary blaze of anger and resentment. Then the anger faded away, to be replaced by concern. Did insensitivity and a cast-iron stomach carried so far mean that Nond's mind was finally beginning to disintegrate?

Now the king shifted his gaze from his empty plate to Arlor's still-full one. Then he raised his eyebrows until they almost merged with the steel-colored hair still growing thick across his forehead. "You are not hungry, Count Arlor?"

"No, I'm not."

"I believe you. But do not let it become a habit." The king shoved his plate away and reached for a massive silver mug of beer. "You will not bring that baby back to life by starving yourself. You will not keep any others alive. All you will do is impair the functioning of your own excellent brain. If you think that I at least am becoming too senile and gloom ridden to have any further need of your brain, consider that you yourself may need it. Then reconsider the wisdom of impairing its functioning by a useless feeling of guilt."

A House Master of the Order of Duelists could not have plinked a point more accurately through an opponent's guard. Arlor winced, stared at the king and then down at his plate, and began on the now-cold omelet. Nond's lips curled faintly behind his beard.

Eventually the servants vanished with the plates and spoons, Nond leaned back until the carved oak chair creaked under the strain and crossed thick-fingered hands across his paunch. "Count Arlor. How safe is the Viceroyalty of the East now?"

The question took Arlor on the hop. His wits went sprawling for a moment while he scrabbled together what he knew on the subject. To gain time he asked politely, "Safe for what, Your Majesty?"

"As a refuge for me," said Nond quietly.

If that remark had been intended to hasten the count's reply, it did precisely the opposite. Even the nimblest brain takes a little time to recover after going sprawling twice in one minute. Finally the count sighed and said, "If you want an honest opinion—"

"If I wanted any other kind, would I endure you?"

"Very well. The Viceroyalty is not a safe refuge. Baron Oman Delvor and Sir Gilas Lanor—"

"And Master Bertan Wandor." With emphasis.

29

"And Master Wandor," said the count. "These men control the Marches fairly well, except for raids. And they have an alliance with the Plainsmen, for what that's worth. But they don't have the organized strength to penetrate into the coastal areas. Those are held or at least patrolled by Cragor's supporters and the royal garrison. Part of the garrison is still loyal, but Cragor has apparently won over a good number of the officers."

"Even after murdering Sir Festan Jalgath at Delkum Pass?"

"Yes, Your Majesty. Cragor has spread the story that Sir Festan wanted to lead a revolt in the Viceroyalty. So Cragor very loyally slew him."

Nond's face worked like dough for a moment; then he surged out of his chair, face blazing red as if it had been sunburned. "By the gods, I will see Cragor *die*. I will see him die even if I have to watch from the House of Shadows. Whatever I have done by accident or error to make Cragor's path easier, the gods still owe me that! And I will have it!" One hand reached out to the heavy beer mug. The muscles cording the back of the hand stood out for a moment. Then the mug dropped to the table with a thump, as flat as if a smith had hammered it out on his anvil.

Nond dropped back into his chair with a groan that the chair echoed. Arlor looked at him for permission to continue, but it was Nond who spoke. "Count Arlor, the Viceroyalty may not be as safe as we could wish. But it is still safer than Benzos itself, or even Manga Castle. Would you not agree?"

The count nodded.

"Then we must take ourselves to the Viceroyalty. No matter where I am, if I am alive, I can give Cragor a great deal of trouble. But if I die here, like a snared rabbit..."

Arlor nodded again and rose. Some of the tension had gone out of him now. He looked at the king's face, still flaming red, and then down at the crushed mug. Nond's wits were not failing, any more than his hands.

CHAPTER 4

Wandor turned to see Gwynna and her two hunting leopards reach the roof of the keep. The musk of the big cats and her own perfume drifted across to him. They mingled with the odors of stables and roasting meat rising from the courtyard.

He embraced her gently out of respect for her clothing. She wore a snugly fitted tunic of dark blue silk with ermine trim at wrists and throat and a deceptively long and flowing white skirt. The skirt was slit almost up to her waist on either side, and as she moved. Wandor could see her red riding breeches and kidskin boots flicker and flash through the white. In such garb she could grace a dinner table or a palace, but she could also run, ride, and fight. A further concession to her father's, rear-guard battle for respectability was not wearing her sword at dinner. It was a good thing her father did not know how many of the throwing knives Wandor had taught her to use lurked in convenient places.

Wandor wore plain black wool, fine-combed and fine-woven, from head to boot top. He had been a Duelist who filled his thin purse with nothing but his skill at weapons for too many years to abandon plain dress. He also wore his sword. The fate of Sir Gar Stendor, struck down in the keep of Castle Delvor itself, was much in his mind. There was no safety except in a constant readiness to fight.

Gwynna backed gently away from his embrace and turned to stare off toward the south. A faint crinkling of her forehead that only Wandor could detect told him she was frowning. She shook her head.

"They're late."

"There could be any number of reasons for that."

"Perhaps. But I still don't like it."

Jos-Pran, Zakonta, and some fifty Plainsmen—or Yhangi, as they called themselves—were due at Castle Delvor for dinner that night, dinner and a discussion of plans. Wandor had ridden the King Horse of the Yhangi and married Gwynna Firehair. That was enough to make all the Yhangi do him honor little short of worship. He was their king in all but name and could call on them to follow him anywhere against any foe.

But demigodhood does little to solve the practical details of preparing and waging a campaign. Regardless of whom they might be following, the Plainsmen's horses would need fodder, their quivers would need refilling. Hence the council tonight. Wandor expected no miracles from it, however. It would merely be one more stone in the wall that was rising—all too slowly—against Duke Cragor.

Even from the top of the keep one could not see to the borders of the lands given by King Nond to Baron Oman Delvor thirty years before. It took two days' riding to cross those lands from east to west, three from north to south. From all directions the hills rolled toward the castle, and marching over them like an infinite army was virgin forest in a dozen shades of green, blurring and softening the outlines of the land.

Except on the north, though, the army ceased its march some miles from the castle. The first bands of peasants who had risked the leap into the unknown that settling in the Viceroyalty had been at first had cleared the land, They had turned the trees into cottages, barns, stables, and fences, brought crops out of the rich topsoil. Now a second generation lived in those cottages, and from the number of babies Wandor had seen, the third generation was well started. Wandor looked south again. A faint blue haze of wood smoke was creeping across the fields as fireplaces went to work on the evening meal.

Abruptly he stiffened. A thicker cloud of smoke was coiling up from the edge of the forest, rising into a tall, thick column in the feeble breeze, glowing bright red against the forest greens. Gwynna's eyes met his in startled comprehension.

"The warning signal for Khind attack! The Khindi haven't

been helping us lately, but certainly—" She stopped as Wandor pointed.

Horsemen were pouring out of the forest and turning into the Delvor lands, on the road that ran straight up to the castle. Wandor narrowed his eyes, trying to recognize them across the miles and through the dimming twilight. Plainsmen. Signs so subtle that he could not have described them in words told him that they were moving at a gallop not out of exuberance, not out of eagerness to reach the castle and their dinner. There was danger behind them.

He turned to Gwynna. "Our guests are arriving, and I think trouble with them." As if to underline his words, the alarm bells and gongs began to clang and boom. Behind them on the roof of the keep more red smoke swirled up from the warning beacon kept fueled and ready. Gwynna slapped wrists, ankles and waist to make sure all her knives were still in position, then followed Wandor to the stairs.

The Plainsmen could hardly have drawn rein all the way from the edge of the forest to the castle gate. By the time Wandor and Gwynna had scurried down the gloomy stairs and out into the courtyard, the gates were already squealing open. A moment later Jos-Pran led his band into the courtyard.

The War Chief of the Gray Mares would not have looked excited or frightened if he had been told that the world was going to end in ten minutes. But as he swung himself down from the saddle and approached Wander and Gwynna, his square brown face showed something less than its usual stolid calm.

He clasped hands with both of them and openly surveyed Gwynna's waistline. Then without any social remarks he said flatly, "We were attacked by Khindi on our way here."

By now Wander was getting reasonably accustomed to such surprises. He did not wince, shudder, cry aloud, or change color. Rather wearily, he said, "Did you lose any of your men?"

Jos-Pran shook his head. "None of the arrows came anywhere near the men. We lost four horses only."

Gwynna shook her head. "Then it wasn't a serious attack. Otherwise most of you would be dead on the road. I've seen a Khindi archer pick off a squirrel on a branch at a hundred yards."

"Well and good," said Jos-Pran. "But then what did they

intend to do with all those arrows? I do not believe that even Khindi think to frighten Yhangi by firing a few hundred arrows over their heads."

"No," said a voice from behind Jos-Pran, and he turned to see Zakonta standing there. Something had put her under a strain also. The wide mouth was, drawn tight, and the dark gray eyes narrowed in concentration. "But then not all people are as brave—or as stubborn— as the Yhangi. The Khindi could be sending a message to the baron and Wandor that their friendship not be taken for granted. Perhaps they want more in return for their aid than you have offered them. Remember, your castles and farms stand in the middle of lands that once were theirs alone. It should not surprise you that they balk at losing warriors in quarrels which are not truly theirs."

"Zakonta," said Gwynna impatiently, "you know better than any of us what is at stake here. Without the Khindi we have very little chance of defending the Marches against Duke Cragor. Are the Khindi so blind that they can't see the difference between Cragor and my father as overlords?"

Zakonta shook her head. "Not the more intelligent ones. But the intelligent ones are as rare among the Khindi as they are everywhere. Rumors of the Black Duke's crimes and a chance for loot are not enough to call forth most of the Khindi or keep them in the field."

Wandor suddenly sensed that Zakonta did not wish to talk further of this matter in the open courtyard with a hundred ill-assorted pairs of ears within hearing. It would lead her on to things she wished to say only in private. He spread his hands in a welcoming gesture. "Come, friends and guests. Our house is yours. Greetings and Honor, Jos-Pran and Zakonta."

"Honor and Greetings, Wandor and Lady Gwynna," they replied, and followed Wandor toward the keep.

"Very well, then," said Gwynna. "Is there anything that will bring the Khindi out and keep them on our side?"

Wandor looked past the fireplace to where Zakonta lay nestled in Jos-Pran's thick arms, her face for the moment unreadable in the subdued glow of the dying fire. He thought for a moment of how this scene would have shocked the late Sir Gar Stendor. The daughter of House Delvor, reclining before the fireplace in the Trophy Room, pillowed half on cushions and half on her husband, a plainly dressed House Master of the Order of Duelists, on the rug before the fireplace one of the Delvors' finest and savage Plainsmen, a War Chief and a *Red Seer* at that, similarly taking their ease. Between the two couples on the rug before the fireplace one of the Delvor's finest silver trays, and on it jugs of fruit spirits, sweet wines, dried fruits, candied nuts. And fifty more Plainsmen now bedded down in the barracks of the men-at-arms, after gorging themselves from the castle larder. Sir Gar would have been appalled, for he had worshiped at the shrine of the proprieties as much as at those of any of the Five Gods.

At Gwynna's query, Zakonta sat up, gently pushing Jos-Pran's arm away from around her waist. She clasped her hands in her lap and licked her lips. Then she nodded.

"What is it?" Wandor and Gwynna spoke almost together.

A long silence. Gwynna sat up and stared at the woman who had been her mentor and guide in the use of her own Powers. She was also beginning to fidget. Waiting was always hard for Gwynna. Then:

"The Helm of Jagnar," said Zakonta.

Gwynna smiled briefly. "You told me that was only a Khind legend. No one can say for certain if King Jagnar ever existed."

"He existed," said Zakonta in a voice as matter-of-fact as if she had been giving a recipe for bread. "When I was teaching you, Gwynna, I called a great many things myths and legends that are not. I did not know then how much you would need to know, and the less one knows about some of the things that are in the Seer Book, the easier one sleeps at night. But now..." Her voice trailed off, as if the reasons for Gwynna's needing to know the truth now were either self-evident or unutterable.

"So Jagnar the Forest King really lived," said Gwynna. "And did he really lead the Khindi against the Empire of the Blue Forest?"

"He did," said Zakonta. "And with the help of Cheloth of the Woods, he overthrew it. But—"

"Cheloth of the Woods," said Wandor slowly, half bemused. He shook his head. Zakonta stared at him. He could not have more

35

thoroughly broken into her speech if he had started singing a bawdy song.

Gwynna stared at him, also, then quickly tightened her arms around him and laid her cheek against his. "What about the Helm, Zakonta?"

"Jagnar died in the overthrowing of the Empire, but Cheloth saw to it that he had fit burial. Cheloth took the Forest King's helmet with him to the Temple of the Dwarf God in the capital city of the Empire. He cleansed the temple and filled it with spells of preservation and beast-magic."

"Beast magic?" interrupted Wandor. "Such as the Beast Worshipers of Yand Island use?" He swallowed. The notion that he might have to accept the aid of a sorcerer versed in such notoriously unwholesome arts did not appeal to him.

"There are other Beast Magics besides that corrupt and perverted form used on Yand Island," said Zakonta briskly. "The Empire of the Blue Forest itself had some, Cheloth still others. It was those he used in the Temple of the Dwarf God. It is said that he sleeps amid those spells yet. He lives, though, and will wake when a man seeking his aid approaches him in the proper spirit. What that is, not even the Seer Book has anything to say."

"The Empire of the Blue Forest fell nearly two thousand years ago," said Gwynna flatly, "Cheloth cannot still be alive."

"Cheloth of the Woods was not a man," said Zakonta. "He was of his own kind. We do not know all that he could do or be."

"Do we care?" murmured Wandor as he rose to his feet. He drifted to the window and stared out, past the sentries tramping back and forth along the wall, out into the dark countryside. He shivered, "It's started again," he said, half to himself.

"It never stopped," came Gwynna's voice from beside him. "I know, you hoped it was now a straight battle of human wits and skills." She put her arms around him again and raised herself on her toes until her green eyes glowed in the darkness in front of his. "I wanted that as much as you did. But it couldn't be that way."

Wandor shook his head. He wondered if she were telling the truth. She had lived half her life or more in this world of spells and witchcraft and men made pawns and toys by powers older than the hills and forests outside. She was at home there, and at times it seemed she gloried in it. He did not. He approached it with halting, reluctant footsteps, like a child on his way to school—and sometimes with a schoolboy's resentment at being less than completely his own master.

"No," he said at last. "I suppose it couldn't." His arms tightened about her. She said nothing, but after a while her lips came up to meet him in the darkness.

CHAPTER 5

It was time to lay down the spade and pick and return to the true tools of a sorcerer.

Kaldmor the Dark poured water from the canvas bottle in the corner of the cave over his dirt-encrusted hands, then picked the mud out from under his fingernails with a silver knife. Out here in the Hills, one could only fight a losing rear-guard action against dirt. Kaldmor would have cheerfully offered half a dozen of his most potent spells in return for one that could produce a hot bath.

Then his expression sobered. These were dangerous thoughts if one was beginning a sequence that might—could—would reach out to Nem of Toshak.

Nem of Toshak. Last, greatest, most terrible, and most successful of the High Masters of Toshak, the Twilight City. The—could he be called a man?—the *being* who led the High Masters of Toshak in their great war of spell and counter-spell that brought down the last of the Five-Crowned Kings and brought an end to the Ancient Days.

Melded by his own spells and those of Cheloth of the Woods into the fires beneath Mount Pendwyr, that last king nonetheless lived on as the Guardian of the Mountain, protector of Bertan Wandor. If the Guardian ever concerned himself with the matter, he could smash Kaldmor out of existence as a man swats a fly. Kaldmor's vanity was not great enough to blind him to that fact

Hence the long solitary trek into the Hills and through their gloomy forests to this cave on a hill so remote and inaccessible that even the Sthi, the little dark Hill People, seldom came near it. Stumbling along on feet softened by many years of life in the mansions and palaces of the mighty. No spells to speed the journey or even to heal the blisters that sprang out before the first day's journey was over. He could not risk alerting the considerable magicians of the Sthi to his presence before he reached his goal. Nor could he risk waking unwelcome echoes from these hills by promiscuously casting his own spells. Here in the Hills the fragments of magic worked by a hundred generations of sorcerers clustered as thickly as bees in a swarm.

And then many hours of work with spade and pick, grubbing in the dirt floor of the cave to which the ancient map had led him, as though he were a common laborer excavating for a new drain! But once more there had been no choice. The tomb of Nem of Toshak was surrounded by physical barriers as well as magical ones. No sorcerer who disdained dirt and sweat could hope to penetrate all of them, nor could any ordinary man relying on crude material force. Only by alternating spell and spade in a precisely defined sequence could one have a chance of even calling to Nem, let alone receiving answer or aid. Nem of Toshak had despised any sorcerer unwilling to dirty his hands. So he had devised this sequence to ensure that only the most worthy sorcerers would have a chance to communicate with him.

That was a thought that made Kaldmor stop and frown. For the first time since the day forty years before when he discovered his own Powers he felt a stab of humility. Was he a "most worthy sorcerer"? Assuming he carried out the remainder of the sequence, would Nem's spirit respond to him even then?

He shrugged and squared his sloping shoulders as best he could. He was here on the spot, and assuming inevitable failure would be a folly greater than assuming inevitable success. Besides, Cragor needed Nem's aid. Cragor need it? He, Kaldmor the Dark, needed it even more. Never mind Cragor's political dreamings and schemings. If the Five-Crowned Kings reigned again, they might warp the whole Spirit World so that not one dark sorcerer or wizard would be left with enough power to light a fire under a pot of soup. That was enough reason for his pushing onward.

He turned toward the mouth of the cave and spread a

darkening spell across it. Now no one outside could see the light soon to be filling the cave. Then he hobbled to the back of the cave where his pack lay, opened it, and began laying out his instruments.

Rain was coming on again as Count Arlor rode out of the side street. The stars were vanishing from the sky over Benzos, and the first tentative mutterings of thunder drifted out of the west. A rising breeze stirred the muggy air and made the torches along the Avenue of Nond the First stream out in long pale-gold flares.

They were coming up the Avenue toward the gate now, two thousand horsemen, the last of the Royal Army contingents ordered north to cope with the onrush of the Ponans. Two entire regiments of heavy cavalry, with baggage wagons, remounts, portable smithies— everything needed for waging war in a land where sources of supply were few, those left un-ravaged by the Ponan raiders still fewer.

The officers of the lead regiment were riding in a cluster at the head of the line. Arlor recognized several and remembered one in particular. Count Ferjor of the Tenth Regiment, who had encountered Bertan Wandor on the latter's first day in Benzos. The count had given Arlor a vivid picture of Wandor standing in the middle of the burning Khind quarter slaughtering Cragor's bravos. A portrait of one good fighting man well drawn by another such—and the count had no notion that Wandor was anything else.

He is fortunate, thought Arlor as he watched the count's plumed helmet disappear into the darkness. We would all be far happier about this matter of Master Bertan Wandor if there were not so many unearthly things lurking around its edges and occasionally springing out into full view. At the Battle of Delkum Pass, for example. The terrible head coalescing out of the smoke and swaying forward toward the advancing Plainsmen, and then Gwynna and Zakonta conjuring up the sphere of light and hurling it against the head.

The last of the horsemen had passed. Now the Avenue was filled with the lumbering carts of the baggage and supply units and the auxiliaries. The eyes of the teamsters were fixed grimly forward, hands frozen tight on the reins. There was none of the excitement that was part of Arlor's image of an army going off to war. No pretty girls throwing flowers, no street urchins darting under the horses at the risk of their lives in order to snatch things from the baggage carts. The column was marching north almost in silence, like the priests of Alfod the Judge filing into their temple for a First Judgment celebration.

The last of the carts rumbled off into the darkness, leaving behind them a litter of droppings, spilled straw and grain, and odd bits of clothing. Arlor's horse picked its way cautiously through the debris, then jumped forward.

Arlor headed south at a canter, through the deserted streets. Even here, amid the homes of the rich, where bands of revelers drifting from party to party had once kept the night filled with noise and light until dawn, there were now few who cared to be outside their locked and barred doors and windows. The footpads and assassins roamed freely in Benzos now, and other less nameable fears hung over the city as well.

Kaldmor's apparatus lay complete on the floor of the cave. Its instruments had increased the weight of his pack to something that would have made a seasoned infantry man groan and sag, let alone a middle-aged sorcerer of unblushingly indolent habits. And these were only symbolic representations of the true elements of Kaldmor's spell-working devices. The laws of magic said a proper symbol was supposed to generate the same power as the original object, if handled by a reasonably competent sorcerer. But Kaldmor still could not help wondering if in these grim Hills his powers would be adequate—or function without bizarre and ugly side effects.

His four golden pots with crystal lids were now tiny golden bottles with lids no larger than a lady's fingernail. The brown and mummified human hand could only have been that of a newborn child. The black candles were no larger than Kaldmor's little finger, their holders of fine iron wire instead of massively solid metal. Everything was shrunken save the great staff, a foot taller than Kaldmor, gold-sheathed at the foot, silver-sheathed at the head. That was his, linked to him in such a way that no mere symbol could maintain the link.

He stripped himself naked, shivering for a moment in the dank

41

chill of the cave before his mind could bring his body to heel. Then quickly he drew his pentagram around the deep hole he had dug in the dirt floor of the cave. Next a quadrilateral of the four golden bottles within the pentagram. From each of the bottles he shook a few grains of powder into his left hand and mixed them thoroughly. Then, with the staff in his right hand he stepped to the edge of the hole, opened his left hand, and watched the mixed powders sift down into the darkness. The hole was twelve feet deep. The powders gleamed for a moment in the pathetic light of the candles—shimmering red, sooty black, cobalt-tinged blue, a deep green like a fine emerald—and then vanished.

Kaldmor carefully stepped back one pace at a time until he was outside the pentagram. He found it hard not to keep on backing. There was a ridiculous feeling in him, a feeling that somehow increasing the physical distance between himself and the pentagram would increase his protection against whatever might appear within it. He subdued the feeling with an effort and began his chant.

His chant rose to fill the cave and echo from the walls. As the chant rose, a blue mist also began to fill the cave. It was a mist that eddied and swirled and swayed as though sudden gusts of wind were tearing at it. Slowly it thickened, crept in a dense column to the edge of the hole, and began to flow steadily down into it.

CHAPTER 6

The night was clear, and the road was dry and empty. So this time Count Arlor came up the High Road to Manga Castle at a pounding gallop. He would almost rather have ridden more slowly. This might be the last time he rode out from Benzos to the castle. Certainly it would be the last time until King Nond was restored to rule over Benzos. Nond or—who? The king was old, and a natural death might take him before he could return to rule the land. Call it—until Duke Cragor was defeated. That Arlor would see, that Arlor would help bring about, or he would deny the gods and their justice.

He had made the trip on the average of once a week every year of the last ten, in all seasons and weathers, on all matters of business for Nond. He had carried news, he had carried messages, he had carried jewels and delicate goldsmith's work to adorn bleak chambers. Once he had led a pack horse carrying a freshly painted portrait of Crown Princess Anya. It had taken all his will to bring that portrait to its destination rather than turn aside and make for his country lodge, to hang it in his private chambers where only he could gaze on it.

But tonight would be the end for all that. In an hour Captain Thargor's *Red Pearl* would row up the channel from the Avar to the water gate of Manga Castle. In two hours Arlor and King Nond and a few trusted servants would be aboard the ship, in three on their way down the Avar. By morning they would be passing Avarmouth. And by noon they would be out of sight of land, bound away for the Viceroyalty of the East, facing only storms, shipwreck, and the Sea

43

Folk.

It had been ten days since the last contingent of the Royal Army had marched north out of Benzos. In that time Nond's already-shaky rule over his capital city had begun to break apart like an iceberg hitting a tropical current in the Ocean.

Behind Arlor glowed signs in the western sky of what was happening—the red glare of fires in Benzos. If a wind sprang up before the fires had burned themselves out, Cragor might lead his mercenaries into a capital lying in smoldering ruins. A deliciously grim irony—Cragor reaching out to pluck the long-dreamed prize and seeing it go up in smoke at the moment of plucking. No doubt his own agents had set the earlier fires. But now they were being spread by men with no loyalty to anything except their own desire to loot, burn, and kill.

A yellow glow ahead of him now, sweeping toward him out of the darkness. Arlor reined his horse back to a canter and stared at the inn spouting flames from half its windows. A crash, and a large portion of the roof dropped into the flames. Fed by the fresh air, they now roared high up above the roof, as high as the tops of the trees in the rear court.

Arlor had seen the inn on a damp morning six weeks ago surrounded by a mob of starving and furious villagers. Had they beaten the innkeeper to death after they had driven Arlor away in humiliating rout? Or had justice—if it was justice—waited until tonight to catch up with the man? And should Arlor try to summon aid? No. If disorder had reached down and found a victim so close to Manga Castle, there was no time to spend trying to rout out firefighters.

Arlor put spurs to his horse, and the flames of the burning inn slipped away into the darkness behind him.

Captain Thargor made sure that both sword and dagger moved easily in their sheaths before he came on deck. For the first time he was going armed as he brought the *Red Pearl* up the channel to the water gate of Manga Castle.

And there would be a good crop of other firsts for him and for his ship tonight. For all that he had sailed on royal charters and royal commissions a score of times, he had never carried King Nond himself. He had never had to swear a solemn oath to speak no other ship from the moment he left the water gate to the moment Nond set foot on the shore of the Viceroyalty. That galled his sailor's conscience. But the world was turned so topsy-turvy, perhaps these days a sailor's conscience was a luxury. At least he had his life and a good ship under him, and his fortune was in good gold crowns locked in the vaults of Bisgror Brothers in Avarmouth. He would do his best to ride out the storms blowing from the land, as he had ridden out those blowing from the sea for thirty-five years.

He gave a final tug at the mail shirt under his wool tunic, opened the cabin door, and went out on deck. He looked sourly down at the planks. In the bright moonlight the stains and dirt on the normally well-scrubbed wood showed far too clearly. That damned landlubber of a high-nose count had been stubborn and determined, not caring how much he outraged a sailor's instincts.

"Don't spruce up your ship, Captain Thargor. Leave her dirty. Make her look like the oldest, the most disreputable tramp that ever went begging a cargo around all the ports of the Ocean." Thargor had winced then, and he winced now at the memory. But he had obeyed.

He had also obeyed by hand-picking his crew, weeding out anybody who couldn't be trusted to keep his mouth shut. They would be crossing to the Viceroyalty shorthanded because of that. Should he have filled the gaps with some of his old shipmates? Not unless he wanted to mark them for Cragor's vengeance and Cragor's long reach.

Thargor walked forward, past the men tramping back and forth with the thirty-foot sweeps carrying the ship up the channel. Normally ships that could manage the channel were hitched to ox teams and towed up the channel to the water gate. But teamsters could talk in their cups and would talk under torture, so tonight the *Red Pearl* would do without them. Thargor hoped the gods would send him a bit of wind for the run downriver. His crew would reach the Ocean flat on their backs if they had to man the sweeps all the way down the Avar.

The ship slid through the raised drawbridge over the channel and into the basin that fed the castle moat. A great silver patch of moonlight shimmered in the middle of the basin. But its sides lay in deep shadow, with no light or movement showing.

None showed from the castle, either. It squatted inside its moat like a huge growth on the face of the land. The *Red Pearl* drifted in to the stone jetty by the water gate. No one caught the heaving lines. Not a soul was visible to show that the castle had not been abandoned and left to its horde of ghosts.

Thargor snapped orders, and the men at the starboard sweeps lifted them and swung them up until they came down with a bang on the jetty. Two young sailors ran monkeylike along the still-dripping sweeps on to the jetty. They caught the hawsers as they sailed through the air and made them fast around the stone bollards. Not a speck of dirt anywhere on the jetty, Thargor noted. The master of the water gate was a retired naval officer with a good sailor's love for keeping things all neat and clean.

The *Red Pearl*'s crew heaved her in until she was fast against the jetty. When the echoes of the stamping feet and plashing water had died away, silence clamped down on the basin and castle harder than ever. Thargor looked up at the castle again. A yellow light now gleamed in one window of the keep.

When Count Arlor entered, Nond was sitting in his great carved oak chair. He seemed to be staring fixedly at the guttering stub that provided the only light in the chamber. Arlor had seen that chamber ablaze with a dozen of the finest wax candles, two feet long and as thick as a man's arm. Nond had always liked to have light and warmth about mm.

"Your majesty."

"Yes." The voice was low, but not lifeless.

"The *Red Pearl* is at the water gate. The crew is loading your gear now. Perhaps you should consider going on board now?"

"No doubt," said Nond. He heaved a sigh, then pushed down on the arms of the chair. The heavy oak creaked and groaned under the strain. He rose and stepped out from behind the table, the deep hooded eyes swinging from side to side as they surveyed the chamber.

"I've brought your sealskin cloak, sire. And your weapons belt."

"Thank you, Arlor. But I wonder if it will do any good to me or anyone else for me to go armed? Oh, well, I'm subjecting myself to enough inconvenience as it is. A few pounds of steel on my belt will neither make nor mar." He took the robe from Arlor and put it on unaided. He fastened it with a plain brass and steel pin, then buckled on the belt with sword and long dagger. He stood in silence for a moment.

In that moment it seemed to Count Arlor that another face looked out from behind Nond's massive cheeks and jowls. The face of a young warrior-king, riding in triumph to celebrate his conquest of the Viceroyalty of the East. It was the face that had struck the heart of a five-year-old boy, brought by his father to watch the parade.

The moment passed, thirty years returned in one crushing instant, and Nond smiled the weary smile of the aging king he was. "Let us go, Arlor."

They went down the stairs of the keep to the level of the Great Hall. There two guardsmen joined them, as well as one of the understewards. All three would be going with them in the *Red Pearl*. All three carried bulging bags of clothing and glittered with mail and weaponry. And all three Arlor knew to be both skilled and swift with their blades.

With three more men around them Arlor felt a little better as they hurried down the winding stairs as fast as Nond could move. That was faster than Arlor would have dared hope. But echoes of their hurrying footsteps from the damp walls of the passage tightened his nerves like the joints of a man on the rack. Half a dozen times he whirled, hand on the hilt of his sword, seeking to surprise whoever he was certain he heard following them. All he ever saw was the corridor stretching away into a darkness disfigured more than broken by patches of light from the torches in brackets along the wall.

Finally they reached the iron gate at the end of the passage. Arlor took the key from the understeward and shoved it into the lock. The lock opened with a small squeal, and the gate itself swung open with a much louder one. They stepped out on to the jetty.

The first thing Arlor did was take in a deep breath of damp, river-scented air, then let it out in a tremendous sigh of relief. The second thing he did was see Captain Thargor approaching. Beyond the captain the hull and masts of the *Red Pearl* rose black against the moonlight. From her decks came clatters and thumps, as the last of her cargo was stowed away.

Thargor raised his hand to his wide-brimmed hat. "All ready for sea, my lord count. Is this the last?"

Arlor grinned. "It is, captain." He turned to Nond. "Time to go aboard, Your Majesty." Nond turned silently, stared at the ship for a moment, then nodded. He stepped out of the archway, on to the open jetty.

Before Nond could take two steps, a sudden splashing noise from below the edge of the jetty made Arlor whirl. This time his sword sprang free. As it did, a head rose above the edge of the jetty, dark against the gray stone and the moonlit water. Then a hand came up over the edge, something gleaming dully in it. The hand snapped up sharply and what it carried gave off a sharp metallic *tching*. Something else went *pfffooomp*, into Nond's cloak.

All this happened in the time it took Arlor to raise his sword to fighting stance and take one step forward. He was still holding the foot-long iron gate key in his left hand. He got rid of it in the most useful way—a straight throw at the man's head. It struck a glancing blow and bounced off into the water. But it slowed the man just enough so that Arlor was on him and over him as he leaped out on to the jetty. Another object was gleaming dully in his right hand.

Arlor's blade slashed down across the man's right wrist. Before Arlor could strike a second time, the man's leg muscles knotted and jerked, carrying him five feet sideways in a single leap. His eyes swiveled to take in Nond, standing as if frozen by magic; then his left hand darted in under the white cloth around his neck.

"Move, you old—!" Arlor bellowed at the king, then launched himself forward. As he moved, so did Nond. But the assassin was moving, also, red flames shooting from all over his body in foot-long jets. By all that seemed right in nature he should have been blind, but like a Ponan fire sprite pursuing a human soul, he closed unerringly on Nond. The king was backed against the wall now, unable or unwilling to move farther.

The assassin was barely a yard from Nond when Arlor hit him with the sheer impact of his two hundred pounds moving at full speed. Caught in midstride, the assassin went sprawling on to the stones. The flames spewed up more savagely. He tried to rise, scrabbling blindly with hands and feet, his face now completely enveloped in flame. Then he gave a rasping scream and fell to the jetty, kicked convulsively twice, and lay still. An unmistakable smell of charred flesh rose into the night.

For a long moment the three men—Nond, Arlor, and Captain Thargor—were as silent and as still as the corpse at their feet. Then Arlor's knotted stomach hurriedly unknotted itself. He made it to the edge of the jetty barely in time to give his dinner to the fishes.

When he came back, he was carrying the assassin's two hand weapons. They were heavy brass tubes, each with a wooden grip like a crossbow's and a large lever in the rear. Thargor stared down at them and reached out to take one.

"Don't touch that one, captain! It's still loaded. The dart it carries is tipped with *fon*-fish poison." Thargor jerked his hand back as if he had touched a snake.

"Who—or what—was that?" He shuddered.

"A Chongan *Mungan*, or Death-Bringer." That was Nond, speaking in a deliberately slow and judicious voice, as if he were trying to calm both himself and them. "Death-Sworn, or he would not have been equipped for the Embrace of Fire. And perhaps not of the first rank, or he would have had other weapons to use after his spring tubes failed. Perhaps the Chongans did not wish to use a first-rank *Mungan* for their purposes."

Arlor turned to look at the king. In the moonlight the pallor of Nond's face was unmistakable. "Your Majesty! Are you all right?"

The count did not need the king's answering growl to realize that he had just asked a silly question. *Fon*-fish poison killed or tortured horribly within seconds after entry into the body. "Of course I'm all right, oh young man of swift limbs and slow mind! With *fon* poison, one is either healthy or dead." The king's voice had recovered most of its normal bite. Arlor felt a great urge to sit down quietly somewhere for a few minutes.

Captain Thargor moved briskly into the silence. "Your Majesty, my lord count; I have a great feeling we'd best be under way before more of these wretches spring at us out of nowhere." He motioned toward the gangplank. "If it'd please you noble sirs—"

Nond looked up at the castle one last time. The gangplank

creaked under his weight. A moment after that Arlor sprang down on to the *Red Pearl*'s deck. Then Thargor's voice rose in a bellow, and after it rose the sound of running feet and scraping wood and the rattle of the sweeps running out.

Out in the middle of the Avar, half a mile from either bank, there was at last peace, a feeling of security, and silence except for the slow steady *bunk-whum, bunk-whum* of the twelve sweeps. None of the *Red Pearl*'s crew moved, except for the men at the sweeps and the tiller.

Silence, peace, and security, but no darkness. The moon rode high and full, pouring down a silvery light so brilliant that Arlor half-expected to feel heat from it as well. He would have welcomed that. The release of long pent-up tension had left him feeling weak and chilled, although even out on the river the night was no cooler than summer nights around Benzos usually were.

Along the bank red and yellow flames flickered and glowed. The blight was spreading downriver. What would happen when it reached Avarmouth? Cragor would have a fight on his hands trying to beat the port's merchants and sailors into submission. They would show great loyalty to King Nond—and pay a great price.

Arlor suddenly realized that he was thirsty. The scuttlebutt stood aft, by the tiller. He rose and walked aft, eyes on the deck to avoid stumbling over the coiled ropes and rolled hammocks littering it.

He had just passed the mainmast when he heard a voice say a single word, clear and crisp, but hushed.

"Gods!"

Arlor looked up and saw the western sky.

Over Benzos the sky was no longer black and star-filled, but scarred with a pulsing, incandescent blue. Like a fire spreading across a field of dry grass, the blue glow expanded. Each pulse sent writhing tendrils of color farther and farther out until half the horizon poured out raw blinding light. Manga Castle stood out black and massive. Then it seemed to shrink and cringe away from the light in the sky.

The light rose and spread still farther. Now there was no more blackness anywhere to the west, and the glowing tendrils were reaching up toward the zenith. The light brought everything on the *Red Pearl*'s deck out in harsh relief. It tinted blue the set and staring faces of the men, seemed to drip from the rigging and spark from every piece of metal.

The crew had abandoned the sweeps and stood or knelt on deck, staring west. The helmsmen were both on their knees, one gabbling prayers, the other vomiting into the scuppers as terror churned up his stomach. If there had been anything left in Arlor's stomach, he would have done the same. He had seen that same color before. Others aboard had heard him describe it, but he was the only one whose eyes and brain held a living memory of it.

The reaching tendrils were fading now, drawing back into the pulsing core of blue fire. The core took on a life of its own, jerking and twisting like a great snake squeezing the life out of its prey. Two red spots began to glow in the blueness.

Then in seconds it coalesced out of the blue fire—a fanged head with eyes as large and bright as suns pouring out red fire to mix with the blue. The needle-pointed fangs shimmered silver, and black vapor writhed in clouds out from between them. There was no neck or body, only the head, bobbing and swaying as though winds from an outer darkness swept past it and tossed it about.

Arlor stared in silence. He would not have spoken even if his dry throat and paralyzed tongue had let him.

The head hung in the sky over Benzos—if one could say that it had a place at all—as the minutes crawled by, and the *Red Pearl* drifted aimlessly. Then slowly its outlines blurred, its colors lost their glare, and it faded back into a blueness that was itself slowly fading. As the blue faded, a wind began to blow from the west until the surface of the river danced in the moonlight. By the time the western sky was black again, a cursing and shouting Thargor had driven his numbed crew up the rigging. The sails were spilling down off the yards to catch the wind and drive the ship downriver toward the Ocean.

Arlor wished he could feel joy at the wind. But after what this night had brought, it seemed too much like a contemptuous token from mocking gods, like a brass penny thrown to a beggar by a lord riding to a feast. Would the gods care to send anything that would carry men safely beyond the reach of whatever had just been released into the world? Could they, even if they cared? Arlor wondered.

CHAPTER 7

Gwynna's screams jerked Wandor awake. He sat up in the great bed, reaching for the knife he wore strapped to his thigh. He thrust out a hand in the darkness and found Gwynna's place empty. Head fuzzy from the deep sleep that had followed a long bout of love, he pushed open the curtains and crawled out of the bed.

Gwynna knelt by the window, the moonlight pouring in through the open curtains to tint her hair and silver her bare skin. Her head was thrown back, eyes showing only the whites. Great shudders racked her body. Each time they did, her head jerked back farther, and her mouth opened wider as she screamed. Each scream died away in a choked gurgle. Wandor sensed mortal agony in those screams.

Where it came from he didn't know. For the moment he preferred not to think about that. He darted toward Gwynna, reaching out to hold her by the shoulders and turn her around. As he touched her, she collapsed backward on to the thick rug, writhing and heaving in an obscene parody of passion, eyes still rolled up, mouth still open. She no longer screamed, because her raw throat had given up the struggle. Instead she moaned each time her body shook and went rigid, a high keening moan like a maimed animal.

Fists thundered on the chamber door.

"Master Wandor, Master Wandor, what is it?" It was the voice of the night captain of the guards. Behind him Wandor could hear the murmurs and shuffling feet of his men.

"Stay out!" Wandor shouted. "There's nothing you can do. The

Lady Gwynna is sick. Send for the surgeon!" He hoped his voice did not show the terror clawing at his own mind. Feet pounded away down the corridor, and the buzz of voices suddenly ceased. He turned back to Gwynna.

Her fists were clenched now until the knuckles stood out the bleached white of bone. Her teeth had bitten so deeply into her lower lip that a trickle of blood oozed down her chin. Wandor bent down to wipe it off, realized that he had nothing to use, stood up to go in search of a cloth.

As he rose, Gwynna went totally rigid and found voice for one more scream, one that sounded as though she were being impaled on a red hot stake. She heaved once more, then rolled over on to her stomach and lay still.

Wandor knelt beside her, clutching one of the pillowcases from the bed. His stomach was as tight as the fist that clutched the pillowcase. He bent lower, lifted Gwynna gently, rolled her over on her back. Her eyes were wide and staring, with no human intelligence behind them. But the perfect breasts that he had so often caressed rose and fell gently. And when he bent over to wipe her face, he felt a faint pulsing of warm air from between her lips.

Gradually the knot in Wandor's stomach untied itself. Gradually life and sense returned to Gwynna's eyes, though she still lay limp and quiet as a dying woman. Her tongue crept out between her blood-caked lips and licked them.

"Water," she said in a faint voice. Wandor sprang up, dashed to the pitcher beside the bed, and filled a cup. He managed to keep a hand that wanted to shake like a drunkard's steady enough to get some of the water into her.

It seemed to bring Gwynna's voice back, if not her strength. Her face might still have been that of a stone goddess, Kruga Hearthmistress preparing to set a curse on some violator of her laws. She licked her lips again.

As she did so, there came more pounding on the door. "The surgeon is here," somebody shouted from outside.

Gwynna stiffened again. "No," she said, then louder, "Don't. I don't—need him." Wandor stared. "Nothing—of the body." The expression in her eyes was so urgent that he had to believe her.

Without moving, he shouted:

"The Lady Gwynna doesn't need the surgeon now."

More confused voices outside, one recognizably the surgeon's saying something very like "Nonsense!" Someone put a hand on the latch of the door. Wandor sprang to his feet. "Stay out, I said. All of you!" His voice would have carried to the rear rank of an army of forty thousand.

Apparently it also carried conviction. As feet shuffled away, and silence fell outside, Gwynna lifted a shaking hand and gently drew Wandor back down to his knees.

"Thank you. It's nothing the surgeon can help. I'll be all right in the morning. But—gods, gods, gods!" Her voice was stronger again. She looked up at him. For a moment he thought he saw a pulse of fire glow in the red hair that formed a matted and tangled fringe to her pale face.

"Nem of Toshak has risen," she said, and fell asleep.

The sleep seemed to ease and heal her. It certainly eased Wandor. But his nerves had been stretched tight almost to the breaking point, then released like a bowstring. They would not let him sleep at all. He spent the brief two hours, until dawn trickled in through the window, trying to recall what he knew about Toshak and the High Master Nem of that long and mercifully lost city of dark sorcerers.

That was not much. He was not a good pupil for Gwynna when she tried to teach him even the basic history of sorcery. He had been too long a Duelist—eighteen of his twenty-nine years. The Duelists abhorred sorcery above all the other Orders. And Wandor did not really want to let go of the beliefs drummed into him during those eighteen years. It seemed that doing so would fling him inevitably outward toward darkness, the darkness that had crept too close tonight.

Dawn came, and Wandor splashed cold water on his face and into his burning eyes. By the time he had finished this, Gwynna was awake. Not only awake, but sitting up in bed with the blankets wrapped around her. She looked so vital and alive that for a moment Wandor's mind balked at the memories of the night. Had it been simply a particularly hideous nightmare?

Her first words knocked that fragile hope into splinters. She shook her head slowly and said, "Thank you for keeping your head last night. Gods know what sort of rumors the surgeon would be spreading if he had examined me."

"None at all, if he wanted to keep his place," said Wandor shortly. "And I'm not sure that the rumors aren't running wild, anyway. You were making a good deal of noise. And only you will ever know how close I came to not keeping my head."

She smiled. With her, he never had any cause to show the iron face he usually needed with the men who followed him. Then her expression sobered. "It caught me asleep. All my barriers were down before I was even fully awake." For a moment she could not quite keep the lightness in her voice or on her face. Wandor saw her teeth clamp down on her ragged and bitten lower lip.

Then she smiled again. "At any rate, we're both alive." She let the blanket fall and leaned back against the high-piled pillows. She did not need to beckon.

Afterward they lay in each other's arms under the tumble of blankets until they caught their breath. Then Gwynna said, "I think we should ride out after breakfast and see Jos-Pran and Zakonta." The Plainsmen leaders and their band were now camped on the eastern fringe of the Delvor farm lands as an extra protection against the Khindi.

"You want to speak of this with Zakonta?"

"I want to see if she's alive," said Gwynna shortly.

Zakonta was not only alive, she came out of her tent to greet them as they rode up. But her face was as pale as the brown-gold complexion of a Plainsman could be, and the hands she held out to Gwynna shook for a moment. The two women stared at each other in silence for a long time, as though each was afraid the other would prove to be a mute ghost if asked a question. Jos-Pran and Wandor stood in a similar silence to one side. This was not a matter in which warriors had much skill, or wished it. But both felt the tension in the air.

Gwynna found her voice first. "How was it with you?"

56

"Bad. But I was awake when it struck. I could raise my barriers fast enough to keep some control. Even so I felt as if I were being held out over a slow fire, like the *Red Seers* the slavers took. What about you?"

"I was asleep when it struck," said Gwynna flatly. "I don't even want to talk about it. You can ask Bertan if you want the details."

Zakonta shook her head. "That can wait. Nem of Toshak cannot."

"But how is it that Nem has risen?" asked Gwynna. There was a plaintive note in her voice, a note of rebellion against a monstrous injustice. "The only sorcerer who might take the risk is Cragor's ally, Kaldmor the Dark. And he never struck me as being powerful enough to wrench Nem back from the House of Shadows."

"He is not, if Nem did not wish it. There is no sorcerer alive today who could do that to Nem." Zakonta grimaced. "No, that is assuming too much. There probably is no sorcerer alive today who could revive Nem against his will. And if there is, it is certainly not Kaldmor the Dark. He is barely among the first rank. But there are ways and means of speaking to Nem that Kaldmor could use. Not easily, but they exist. If he could get the message to Nem of what was at stake, or what might be at stake, so that Nem sent forth his *powers* of his own free will..." Zakonta's voice trailed off. "We hardly have enough different impressions of last night to conclude anything. I will have Mind Speech with all the *Red Seers* later today. Each can say how it seemed to her."

"You do that," said Jos-Pran. "I do not like fighting an enemy I do not know, even if he is a long dead magician. But there is another enemy we do know. What about Duke Cragor?"

Wander nodded and began to pace back and forth. "We've been saying for months that Cragor was getting ready to strike. I think—last night—must mean that he's either struck his blow against Nond or is going to do so within a day or two. Cragor doesn't care much for sorcerers, and he'd never give Kaldmor his lead this way for anything but the biggest stakes." He looked at Zakonta, smiled thinly, then amended his last sentence. "No, I won't say 'never.' But it doesn't seem likely. An alliance with a sorcerer like Nem is rather like an alliance with a snow tiger. There's not much you can do if it decides it doesn't like the way the alliance is working.

"So Cragor moves against Nond. If Cragor fails, then Nond has done all that's needed. We can sit and wait for Nond's orders. But if Cragor pushes Nond off the throne, he'll have the Royal Treasury to use. He can hire an army of mercenaries and lead them on a fleet of merchant ships. Merchants and mercenaries are much alike—if you can pay them, they'll serve you. By autumn he could have an army bigger than the one at Delkum Pass marching against us."

"The Yhangi will not abandon the fight against the Black Duke," said Jos-Pran. "You need not fear that."

Wandor clasped the War Chief's hand. "I know that. But we can't match a balanced army such as Cragor will have with nothing but your horsemen and the March levies. At Delkum Pass we had surprise on our side. And we had five times more Plainsmen than we could ever support in a long campaign."

"So it all comes back to the Khindi?"

"It all comes back to the Khindi." He turned to the two women. "You said that the Kbindi would follow whoever found and wore the Helm of—Jagnar?" They nodded. "Then we must go into the Blue Forest and find the Helm."

Jos-Pran stared at Wander with a mixture of amazement and curiosity carved on his normally impassive face. "Have you ever been into the Blue Forest. Deep into it?"

"I hunted with your—"

Jos-Pran shook his head sharply. "Our hunters do not go into the forest south beyond a day's march. At one time they did, but many did not return. So we seek deer and boar where we can hunt and live. Even on the northern edge the forest has a—*luor* of evil. And it becomes worse as one goes farther south. The Empire of the Blue Forest left more behind it than ruins, Bertan."

Luor was the Yhang word for "aura." Wandor nodded. "I know. I've felt it, too. But do you truly think there's any other way of winning the Khindi to our side? And without the Khindi, do you think we can win? You can speak your true mind to me, Jos-Pran." The last words were intoned as a formal request. .

Slowly Jos-Pran nodded. "I think you are right in all of what you say. But being right may not keep you alive in the Blue Forest." A pause. "When shall we start?"

"Not for several days yet. I want to look over the maps in the castle, talk to Gwynna, have Zakonta Mind Speak to the *Red Seers*. Can you do this?" to Zakonta. She nodded. "Who knows," Wandor continued, forcing a light tone into his voice, "Cheloth of the Woods is supposed to be watching over the Helm. If we find the Helm, perhaps we can persuade him to come out of the woods and help us do something about Nem of Toshak."

Jos-Pran tried to laugh at that, but his attempt at a belly laugh came out more like the squeal of a snared rabbit. Gwynna and Zakonta did not even smile. "But you can start picking reliable men," Wandor went on, to Jos-Pran. "You know what will be needed in equipment better than I do. Arm them to the teeth."

Jos-Pran's white teeth flashed as he grinned. "That I certainly will do." He reached for Zakonta's hand and led her back into their tent.

Wandor and Gwynna stared at each other in a fragile silence for a moment. Then Gwynna said slowly, "Don't you believe in Cheloth, or Nem, or—"

"Stop talking nonsense," said Wander. "You know me better than that." His voice dropped, losing all of its anger but only part of its harshness. "I saw the Guardian of the Mountain in the fires under Mount Pendwyr. I saw Kaldmor the Dark invoke Na-Kaloga at Delkum Pass. I might have seen an army of sixty thousand men destroyed there if it hadn't been for you and Zakonta and the other *Red Seers*. And I saw you last night. I believe, Gwynna. I believe in all of these things that are crawling at us out of the night, for what reason the gods themselves don't even know. But sometimes I have to put that belief off from me because I can't live with it all the time without going mad. I can't even ask the question, 'Who am I?' without sometimes wanting to run screaming from all the answers that come at me. I believe, Gwynna," he repeated. "But not because I want to. I have no choice."

CHAPTER 8

Duke Cragor was happy. He would have been exalted if he could have savored his victory more fully. But his eyes were as red as the lining of his cloak from fatigue and the smoke that still hazed the air over Benzos. Sores in awkward places told of hours in the saddle, leading his men against the stubborn resistance of Nond's remaining partisans. A sullen and lumpish stomach told of too many underdone sausages washed down with the first thin, sour beer that came to hand. And he could not even go out on to the balcony to gaze in triumph over Benzos. At least not until he could be sure no hostile archer lurked behind a chimney pot, eyes watching, bow strung and ready.

So he sat in the whitewashed chamber on the top floor of his town house, behind the great desk placed so that he could see out the open windows but none could see in. A rising breeze blew through the chamber, riffling the stacks of reports and the great map of Benzos spread out on the floor. A thousand little details recorded in those reports and on that map niggled and worried away at Cragor's joy.

But joy was there, victory was his, and none could easily take it from him. Benzos itself was his, and the soldiers of the Royal Army there not yet slain or imprisoned had mostly fled, some north, some into Manga Castle. An army of his own mercenaries, reinforced by the households of great nobles who wavered no longer, was marching north. He hoped the royal troops facing the Ponans would surrender peacefully on his promise of good treatment. He had no need to keep such a promise once the last royal force was disbanded, of course. But for the moment it would give him a reputation for moderation, weaken last-ditch resistance, and save him paying the greedy Ponans still more in gold and territory to smash the northern army.

Another army of his was forming to besiege Manga Castle. Cut off though they were, its garrison had food for at least six months. Yet another promise of good treatment might save him a prolonged siege. He could afford that hardly more than a pitched battle, for Avarmouth had risen for King Nond. By rallying sailors and stubborn nobles and fragments of the Royal Army behind the city's walls, the old king might still raise an army of formidable size.

Where was Nond? The Chongan assassin had struck on his own and vanished. If he had succeeded, he had either died in so doing or reported only to his own Chongan masters. Days of doubt about Nond's fate would be days for Benzos to take heart, organize, prepare to dispute Cragor's victory.

If Nond were still alive, where might he be? The surest way to safety lay by water, along the Avar and then—where? To Avarmouth, to barricade himself behind its walls and rally an army there? Across the Ocean? Small safety there. The Royal Army in the Viceroyalty was scattered, the Marcher lords a contemptible handful in spite of their alliance with the Plainsmen. Sorcery had won them a victory at Delkum Pass, to be sure. But Na-Kaloga's image looming in the sky over Benzos proved who had the greater sorceries at their command now.

Cragor sobered. For all that he seemed to have done, Kaldmor the Dark had not returned from the Hills. Not until he did would Cragor know exactly what hideous wizardries of dead Toshak Kaldmor had drawn into his hands, ready to hurl against Cragor's enemies. In the meantime, the battles of the material world remained to be fought or finished. He rang the bell for his scribes.

Two scribes wrote busily on wax tablets all the morning and far on into the afternoon. Two more transferred the words from wax to parchment. Out from the chamber went a steady stream of messengers bearing the parchments to their destinations.

—To the commander of the army around Manga Castle: Thoroughly question all captured villagers to see if they have knowledge of Nond s whereabouts.

—To the commander of the force scouting downriver toward Avarmouth: Take hostages from each town and village. Threaten to burn them alive if any knowing Nond's whereabouts do not at once come forward.

—To the captain of Princess (or should he now call her Queen?) Anya's Guards: Keep the lady closely confined and her household staff from her until I come. I hope to come before nightfall. (A moment of savoring the anticipated pleasure of telling Anya the details of her new kingdom and how it came to be hers.) And so on and so on, with great matters and petty, until a tinge of red began to show in the sunlight pouring in through the windows.

Cragor stood up and stretched his cramped limbs. As he did so, he heard a diffident knock on the door. "Who is it?"

"S-s sire, it is Kaldmor the D-d-dark and—"

"Speak up and stop stuttering, you fool, or I'll have you flogged! Who else is there?"

A choked gurgling sound came from outside the door as the servant's powers of speech entirely left him. Then came the sound of two sets of footsteps approaching the door. One was the ordinary clumping of a pair of heavy boots. The other sounded like sandals— perhaps the sandals of the *Mungan?* Cragor took two steps backward until he had a solid wall behind him. Then he called out, "Very well, Lord Kaldmor. Enter and be welcome."

A moment later the Black Duke regretted saying that. The door swung open and Kaldmor the Dark entered. There was dust and sweat on his clothes and on his boots, and a shaggy beard of many weeks' growth on his face. He was so exhausted that he moved like a man drugged. But Cragor's attention was not for his well-worn master sorcerer. It was for the—the *thing* with him.

It had the shape and semblance of a man down to the last visible degree. In fact, it could almost be called handsome. Lean and wiry in contrast to the thick-set Kaldmor, its fine-drawn face showed high cheekbones and a massive beaked nose swooping downward toward a thin-lipped mouth. It stood more than six feet tall, a head taller than Kaldmor. Its wideset eyes could look straight into Cragor's.

Its eyes... If it hadn't been for the eyes, Cragor would not have been willing to pardon the servant's terror. He would not have had to fight so hard to keep from showing his own, either. Only the need to preserve his dignity in front of the four scribes kept him from trembling. He forced himself to look straight into those eyes, then had to force himself to look away again.

The thing's eyes were jet black, not like an ordinary man's, but solid black pools, lightless, featureless, reflecting nothing, apparently seeing nothing. Looking into the thing's eyes was like looking into a bottomless pit, or perhaps into a starless night sky, out beyond the world into whatever lay still farther beyond it.

Cragor swallowed several times before he could trust himself to let out something besides a wheeze or a croak. "Welcome, Lord Kaldmor and...?" He could not quite bring himself to give a name or even a label to Kaldmor's companion.

Kaldmor licked dry lips and broke the tension. He looked sharply at the scribes, then jerked a black-nailed thumb toward the door. "Out!"

If the four scribes had been fired from siege engines they would not have gone through the door much faster. It slammed echoingly shut behind them. Then Kaldmor's legs folded under him, and he sat down cross-legged on the floor. His companion remained standing as rigid as a statue, its face as expressionless as its eyes.

The silence went on for a long time until Cragor mustered up his voice for another attempt. "Who is your companion, Lord Kaldmor?" He almost said, "What?" instead of, "Who?"

Kaldmor took a deep breath. "I have found the tomb of Nem of Toshak. I have spoken with as much of him as lies in the House of Shadows. I have taken his help, to make an image of him. A *limar*, in the speech of Toshak. Through that *limar* Nem's powers come to me, become mine as far as I can use them. You have seen in the sky what I can do now, with Nem's aid. It has given you victory."

Until now Cragor would have snapped in reply, "It has helped me gain a victory, Kaldmor." Until now he had been very free in ridiculing and browbeating the sorcerer for the man's failures and limitations. But in the presence of Kaldmor's new—ally?—Cragor found his tongue curling up like an earthworm in the summer sun at the mere thought of contradicting the sorcerer.

Kaldmor's voice took on a more normal tone as he

embroidered his explanation. "Nem of Toshak brought down the Five-Crowned Kings. He was the greatest sorcerer in a city of the greatest sorcerers ever to walk the earth. To bring his powers from the House of Shadows to the earth and bring them to bear one must have an image of Nem himself. Preferably a perfect image, otherwise what comes through may be flawed, distorted, like something seen through the bottom of a bottle. Then I could not control or use what might come through. And Nem's powers are terrible enough even when I can control them. What you saw in the sky is only part of what I can bring from Nem into the world now." That thought seemed to subdue even Kaldmor for a moment.

Seeing Cragor's eyes wandering toward the image again, Kaldmor shook his head. "The *limar* is not human. It does not even live. It is an instrument. Nothing more. It can be nothing more." To Cragor's nerve-sharpened ears, that last sentence seemed to come out with unnatural force.

Kaldmor's head sagged downward on to his chest for a moment. Then, neck muscles quivering as though his head were made of stone, he raised it again. He even managed a thin smile as he looked at Cragor. "What I have done has never been done before. It could have been done, for the art was not lacking. I am only the latest of many sorcerers who have had knowledge of the art. But none has ever dared use it before me. I stand before you, not the greatest, but perhaps the bravest of all sorcerers since the days when Toshak stood high."

Kaldmor's resuming something of his old boasting and blustering tone restored a little sanity to the room and a little courage to Duke Cragor. He rose.

"Lord Kaldmor, you look tired and ill. You have wrought well for me. I think it is time you had a long rest. Go to the grand guest chamber, and I will have food and drink and a hot bath sent to you at once."

Kaldmor's smile broadened. "Thank you, my lord duke. At this moment, I could not cast another spell to save my life or spirit. You are gracious." He inclined his head with as much formal courtesy as he had ever shown Cragor and stumbled out. The *limar* followed him, as silent and expressionless as ever. Gasps of horror marked their passage down the hallway toward the stairs.

Cragor ignored these. The servants and soldiers were simply going to have to get used to Kaldmor's new companion. Those who couldn't—well, he could dispense with their services far more easily than he could with Kaldmor's. When the hallway was silent, Cragor rang the bell. He snapped at the white-faced servant who answered it, "Chilled wine! At once!" The man stumbled off, his face like a marble mask.

When be returned with the wine, he was accompanied by a mercenary officer, almost as dusty and sweaty as Kaldmor had been. Cragor recognized him as one of the captains sent to scout toward Avarmouth.

"Greetings and honor, captain. What news do you bring?"

"Honor and greetings, my lord duke. Bad news, I fear, King Nond has fled overseas."

"What?" Cragor's taut nerves forced the word out in a parade-ground bark. The captain flinched, but held his ground.

"We found a sailor trying to hide in a river village twelve miles west of Avarmouth. The villagers were trying to conceal him. I threatened to take a dozen of their women and turn them over to my troops if they didn't give him up. They cooperated. The sailor didn't want to talk, but we persuaded him." The captain's dust-caked face creased in a brief smile. "It seems he swam ashore from a ship going down the Avar toward the ocean. The *Red Pearl*, a royal-charter ship under Captain Bendo Thargor. Aboard it he saw a man much like King Nond."

Cragor swallowed. "Is he sure they were going out into the Ocean? Not stopping at Avarmouth?"

"Quite sure."

"Damn!" said Cragor. He kicked savagely at the desk, then swore again as he nearly broke a toe on the tough wood. "Well, bring him up to Benzos and question him again. I want to hear him myself."

The captain's face fell. "We—ah—had some trouble persuading him to talk. He died during our questioning."

This time Cragor was past swearing. His shoulders drooped for a moment. Then he remembered enough of his dignity to pull himself straight. "Very well, captain. Thank you for—what you have learned." The captain bowed and backed out, obviously relieved to have escaped any penalty for being the bearer of bad news.

Alone, Cragor collapsed into the chair behind him and let his dignity also collapse for a moment. All the fiends take Nond! Nond was still one move ahead of him, and this move threatened to keep the king alive for at least several more weeks. Pray to the sea spirits for a storm or a Sea Folk-raiding squadron!

Again his shoulders straightened. Don't rely on luck and prayers. Send word to the Sea Folk as fast as possible. And there were other things to be done. Start the rumor that Nond was dead. Don't proclaim it from the housetops—then people will know where it began. They may doubt it. But a rumor from the gods? How will they know who started it? They might even believe it.

That village—had the sailor talked to any of its people? Never mind—declare the whole village guilty of harboring rebels to Queen Anya and have them all executed. Publicly. In Benzos. And as unpleasantly as possible, with Her Majesty looking on.

Send Kaldmor and the *limar* out to the Viceroyalty by the fastest ship with a message to Baron Galkor to watch for Nond, find him, capture him if possible, and send him back to Benzos alive—also if possible. If not—well, dead kings inspire less resistance. Cragor had cherished dreams of having Nond put to death over many days while his daughter watched. But the duke would not risk his gains to pander to his pleasures. And there would be pleasure enough in telling Anya at length how her father had died. A lesser pleasure, but one he could still anticipate savoring like the wine in the cup on his desk. He raised the cup and sipped slowly.

CHAPTER 9

The horsemen drew rein outside ruined Majoldyr. For the moment, Wandor saw no need to push on. At least no need great enough to overcome his own reluctance to plunge, irrevocably in the Blue Forest. And contemplating his own work might give Jos-Pran more confidence.

Once Majoldyr had taken Cragor's gold and provided a base for the slaver raids against the Plainsmen. Those raids had taken Jos-Pran's wife and children. Then Jos-Pran had come down upon Majoldyr with all the fighting men of the Gray Mares, and the Seven Towns had suddenly become six.

It had been a year since Wandor came this way, riding to the Council of the Yhangi to ask their aid and undergo strange ordeals. More grass sprouted from cracks, more moss covered the fallen stones, more birds nested in the crumbling, leaf-clogged chimney so Majoldyr was as dead as the Empire of the Blue Forest, without even the Empire's lingering traces of sorcery. When two thousand years had passed for it also, children playing in the grass might find odd bits of stone lying about. No more.

Wandor knew enough about the Empire that had once ruled the lands they were about to enter to appreciate and share Jos-Pran's uncertainties. Gwynna had told him much, the last nights before he left. She did not weep and lament to see him departing, for they were both warriors alike, and only the gods could predict which one might be marching off and which one staying behind.

But still she had clung to him with a terrible strength during their lovemaking. And afterward, as she lay in his arms, she told him what she knew of the Empire of the Blue Forest—not much, but nearly all that anyone knew. The history of the Empire was nearly as shadowy as the forest where its ruins now lay.

The Empire had risen, ruled, expanded, and vanished within the space of a century. Yet this was a long life among all the ephemeral states and empires that had followed in the wake of the collapse of the rule of the Five-Crowned Kings.

"I think that must have been more than accident," Gwynna had said. "They had at their command more than the ordinary sorceries!"

"A revival of Toshak?" A chill, ugly thought. Considerably worse than any possible links between the Empire and even the obscene Beast-Worshipers of Yand Island.

"No. The battle against the Five-Crowned Kings took all of its powers. Toshak went down into the dust along with its enemies, and no one in those days could have revived it even if he had dared. No, the Empire's arts were its own. They had great and terrible skill in beast magic, to shape animals according to their own needs the way a sculptor shapes marble. The Plains elk and the horses of the Yhangi are descended from breeds the Empire created. And the blood of the Empire's beast wizards is in many people in this land. I think I must have some of it myself, through my mother." Another disquieting thought for Wandor.

The Empire had first spread south and east, ruling lands no civilized man had entered since its fall. Then it turned north, to finally push west across the Silver Mountains. There it had met the Khindi, or at least those the Khindi of today claimed as ancestors. With Jagnar the Forest King wielding the sword and Cheloth of the Woods the sorcery, the Khindi had defended themselves. Defended themselves, then carried the war back across the mountains, into the Blue Forest, to the capital city of the Empire. In a day and a night the city had fallen, and within a year the Empire had vanished.

But a century of powerful beast magic had left its mark on the Blue Forest and on its animals. Some of the Empire's monstrous creations had bred true; their descendants still prowled in the shadows. Few of the beasts of the Forest behaved as creatures blessed by the

Five Gods or even the Earth Voices should. It was not men or even magic that Wandor would be marching against now. It would be a twisting of nature itself, a twisting not undone by the passage of twenty centuries.

Wandor realized as he thought about Gwynna's warnings that too much such thinking and he would balk at the inevitable plunge into the forest. Silently he turned to Jos-Pran and silently he pointed southward. Across the southern horizon the blue-green mass of the forest squatted like a sullen endless wall. The War Chief nodded slowly and urged his horse forward.

The forest seemed to leap up about them as they rode into it. In one moment the trees stood wide spaced, and the sun shone warm on the back of Wandor's neck. In the next there was barely enough room between the trees to get a horse through. Overhead the interlaced branches twisted into a canopy that shut out the sun and kept the forest in blue-tinged gloom. Save for the blue ferns that gave the forest its name, the forest floor was bare. And so it was all through the first day's travel, and around the small clearing where they made an uneasy and half-sleepless camp that night.

The next day found the forest soon growing so thick in their path that they had to dismount and lead their horses. In some places those chosen to blaze the trail had to draw their knives, to hack away creepers and slice through ferns grown to the size of saplings.

After more hours of that, they came to a solid mass of young timber still more thickly grown, yet too wide to go around. By the time they had chopped their way through it, the daylight was visibly fading.

On the other side of the stand, they came out on a long, straight path running away into the distance, thirty feet wide at least. Nothing more than low ferns grew on it. Above it the branches wove themselves together less tightly, so that more of the fading light crept through.

Path? Wandor knelt down and dug into the soil around the ferns with his knife. Under a thin layer of mold and soil he felt the point strike something solid. He scraped away until a patch of dressed stone gleamed bare in the twilight.

Jos-Pran came over to him and stared down over his shoulder. "A road. I did not expect one." He looked at it more closely. "The

Empire's masons had wonderful cunning in joining stones. They took much wisdom from the Ancient Days."

The Ancient Days—days of the Five-Crowned Kings. The thought that some of that era had gone into the creations of the Empire made Wandor feel a little better. Perhaps all the shadows of the past in this forest did not reek wholly of evil.

The feeling of new confidence lasted until they stopped for the night two hours farther down the road. It continued as they made camp, piling up branches into three fires large enough to roast meat for a regiment. Perhaps this road did not lead directly to the capital city of the Empire. But if it did not, then surely it must sooner or later meet a road that did. The gods had contrived for them the best possible guide through this endless leafy blue-greenness.

A dozen arrows brought down enough game to feed them all. Bellies full of hot roast meat took away still more of the terrors of the forest. Wandor himself found it difficult to remember to even post a guard.

He was wiping his greasy hands on a bunch of fem leaves when a harsh squealing cry sounded from high above the camp. A moment later it was echoed by another, then the first two by a dozen more, and they by still more. The chorus made the night hideous and brought even the most sluggish of the party alert in an instant.

Wandor's sword was out of its scabbard before the second cry sounded. "Arm!" he shouted. "Archers—fire flame arrows up there." He jerked a thumb toward the tree tops, staring upward. Was it imagination, or did he see the firelight reflected from dozens of red discs dimly visible among the leaves?

An archer lit a tar-headed arrow in one of the fires. Then he nocked the flaming arrow to his bow, drew, and fired. The arrow soared upward, vanishing into the leaves with a swish and a crackle. The cries sounded again.

Then something huge, black, and winged crashed through the canopy of leaves and plunged downward. It came straight at Wandor, who stood his ground and drew his dagger. As it swooped at his head, he slashed with his sword and thrust hard with the dagger. Both struck

70

something solid, living. He felt the sword blade shear through bone and tendon. Another cry tore at his ears more savagely than before. The thing flopped to the ground almost at his feet, writhing and kicking and shrieking.

Calling it a bird made it seem familiar, almost innocent. Its black feathered wings spread more than ten feet from tip to tip, and the glaring red eyes were as large as small plates. Wandor's sword had chopped clean through a wing that was now pumping blood on to the ground. Wandor stepped forward to deliver a killing stroke.

As he did so, the whole canopy of the forest seemed to fall down on the camp. With ear-splitting screams and howls, the giant birds plunged down through the leaves, swooping and darting at the men. One dropped on to the shoulders of a man in front of Wandor. Before the man could turn, a sharp—pointed foot-long beak jabbed into the side of his neck. Blood spurted, then stopped.

With a sudden inner spasm, Wandor realized that the birds were vampires. He sprang forward, sword flashing down. The bird's head leaped free. Head and body fell to the ground separately. The beak opened in a final jerk, revealing a hollow tongue still jerking and writhing and dribbling the Plainsman's blood. Then Wandor was too busy to study his victim further. He ducked under the swoop of another bird; batted aside the beak of still another with his sword.

All around him the Plainsmen were swinging their heavy curved swords, not easily wielded on foot but deadly when they struck. Jos-Pran and half a dozen men stood amid the screaming, bucking horses, slashing birds off their backs as fast as the monsters landed. Wandor saw Jos-Pran chop one almost in two with a sword stroke and in the next instant reach up to snatch a second off a horse's back with his bare hand. His fist clenched around its throat, the bird's cry came out half strangled, and it fell to the ground. Jos-Pran leaped high, one foot smashing down on the bird's rib cage, splintering and crushing fragile bones.

If the birds had been able to retreat and strike again, retreat and strike again, they might have won. But under the trees they could not recover for a second pass if their first one missed a victim. Even if they drove their beaks into living flesh, swords or knives or bare hands tore them from their perches within seconds. After a few minutes they abandoned the men in favor of the horses. The men formed a double circle around the horses and kept up a barrier of leaping steel. Some unlimbered bows and began picking birds out of the tree tops or the air.

Finally there were no more birds willing to come down and attack this well-defended prey. The men were able to drink from their water bottles, wipe drying blood off their swords, refill their quivers, and count their casualties.

The Plainsman Wandor had seen go down first was dead, a wound in his neck large enough to hold a child's fist. Another Plainsman had deflected a lunging beak, but his right eye was gone and his, right cheek gaping open all the way down to his chin. Half a dozen others had gashes from claws or purpling bruises from wing buffets. One horse was dead, another so weakened that Jos-Pran drew his sacred Horse Knife and cut its throat as it lay on the blood-soaked ground. Four other horses were more or less gashed, but not beyond Plainsman skill with herbs and dressings. Luck and fighting skill had brought them through.

Wandor's mood was sober now. The Blue Forest had thrown off the mask, thrown down the gauntlet. The journey into its heart was going to be a battle every mile of the way. They could bury their hopes of anything else along with their dead.

CHAPTER 10

Count Arlor clung to the railing of the *Red Pearl* with both hands, braced both feet in the scuppers, and listened with both ears to the chorus of ship's noises. Creak of timbers as she lifted to the swell, rattle of the chains on the tiller, a clatter of blocks from aloft as, the topmen shook out reefs from the mainsail. The wind had died to a gentle murmur in the rigging, instead of the howl that had battered at Arlor's ears until just a few hours ago. Now they were in the lee of the Cape of the Seven Fires, and safe for the moment—at least safe from what the sea could do to them.

Restless, Arlor turned away from the railing. For a solid month his whole world had been the *Red Pearl*'s decks and cabins, a world a little more than a hundred feet long and perhaps thirty feet wide at its widest point. Beyond that was only the limitless sea, sometimes blue, sometimes green, sometimes sullen gray, at times heaved up by the winds into looming black mountains that lifted and dropped the *Red Pearl* until her timbers groaned and her seams gaped and every man aboard except King Nond had to man the pumps to keep her afloat.

Those waves had nearly sent them to a fate even worse than drowning—slower and uglier by far. For two days they had been in danger of driving ashore on Yand Island and into the hands of the Beast Worshipers there. Drowning was a clean death compared to being sacrificed to the teeth and claws of the Beasts.

Now they were at last coming to land, land that offered room to move, run, fight. Arlor had crossed the Ocean six times in his thirty-five years, but he always rejoiced in coming to land. He rejoiced even now, when that land would be swarming with enemies, and he was coming to it in defeat.

Now, recall that only defeat for the moment. Cragor might by now rule in Benzos itself. But King Nond still lived, sound of mind and body, in possession of all his skills and wisdom, though no longer of quite such a gigantic paunch. Even a well-stocked ship's pantry did not permit the kind of gorging Nond had done on land. Now—to get Nond safely across the coastal lands where Cragor's party ruled, through the Khindi—who might be little inclined to show mercy to their conqueror—and into the Marches.

Not an easy journey at best and now even less easy than Arlor had planned. Their intended landfall had been some thirty or so miles north of Yost, less than a week's easy traveling from the Marches. But storms and winds had done their best or their worst. Now they were here in the lee of the Cape of the Seven Fires, better than three hundred miles north of Yost and within fifty miles of Fors itself, capital of the Viceroyalty. It would now be two weeks and more to the Marches.

Could they sail down the coast to their original landfall? Arlor knew enough to not even spend breath putting that question to Captain Thargor. With three foot of water in her hold in spite of the monotonously banging pumps, the *Red Pearl* was going nowhere except straight to the bottom if she put out into the storm.

Wait until the storm died down and then make the run? Not if they wanted to preserve secrecy. Wanted to preserve secrecy? Did they have any choice? Unless Nond could be well inland before the alarm was raised, he would be caught in short order. He would be riding with less than a dozen men, not enough to fight a way through the smallest cavalry picket. And if the *Red Pearl* sailed south along the coast as the fishermen and coasting vessels put out to sea after the storm, the alarm would certainly be raised. The *Red Pearl* was too well known along this coast and too well known everywhere as a royal charter ship. Among the men who would recognize her as she headed south, sooner or later there would be one who would let visions of gold lead him to Baron Galkor.

So this would be their landing place, with a long trek to the Marches. Now—what would be the best place to look for horses? Arlor

74

remembered that all the maps were below, in Nond's cabin, and headed aft, holding himself straight with an effort. The relief and release at reaching land had drained out of him now, and he felt very tired.

Baron Galkor's grandfather had been a freedman of Cragor's grandfather. His own rise to the rank of baron and the position of Cragor's principal agent in the Viceroyalty of the East was thus the story of a driving and driven man. He had served the Black Duke since his youth with an equal lack of both nerves and scruples. So he stared little and said less when Kaldmor and his companion walked into his chamber in the seaward tower of Fors Castle. However, the toughness of Galkor's fiber could not keep him from swallowing hard several times before he spoke. And when he did speak, it was without the sarcasm and sneers he usually directed at sorcerers in general and Kaldmor the Dark in particular. In fact, a rare, fleeting whimsy darted across Galkor's mind. Was Kaldmor going around with that—with his grandfather's ghost—simply to scare people into better manners?

"Welcome to the Viceroyalty, Lord Kaldmor," he said briskly. "Do you bring word of our lord duke's victory?"

"I do," said Kaldmor. "When we sailed, Benzos was in his hands, except for scattered pockets of resistance in Avarmouth and Manga Castle. The Royal Army was broken or scattered, and Prin— Queen Anya a close prisoner."

Galkor noted the slip, promised himself, also to ask some of the courier ship's officers about the real situation. Avarmouth and Manga Castle were "pockets" easily large enough to hold some very nasty surprises.

"What about King Nond?"

Kaldmor's normally dour face darkened even further at that question. He gave a brief summary of what had been known in Benzos when the courier ship sailed, as well as a few speculations of his own. Galkor briskly cut those off.

"If King Nond reaches the Viceroyalty, then we shall have to track him down at once and kill or capture—"

"Preferably capture, my lord baron."

"I know," said Galkor, testy at the interruption. "I assume the duke has plans for Nond's death." A faint element of distaste and weariness sounded in Galkor's voice. He had long felt that Cragor indulged himself in the infliction of pain far beyond reason, necessity, or even prudence. Nond, kept alive until he could be properly tortured, might contrive to escape. Killed at once, he could do nothing—at least not in this world—and Galkor was disposed to let other worlds take care of themselves and meddle with them as little as possible.

Kaldmor nodded. "I will require a private chamber, by preference high in a tower, for myself and my assistant. I will require no servants, but my meals must be ample and on time. The sorcerer's art draws heavily on the body, and I must work some potent spells if I am to seek out Nond for us."

Galkor nodded. "Everything will be as you ask. No doubt you will want complete privacy while you are casting your searching spells? Like the time you cast them in search of Bertan Wandor?"

The baron was gratified to see Kaldmor's mouth harden into a thin line at that thrust. As with Duke Cragor, so it was with sorcerers. Galkor disliked foreswearing direct, practical solutions in favor of those that catered only to someone's exotic tastes or skills. Then he looked at Kaldmor's "assistant" again. He had to admit that perhaps this time Kaldmor's abilities would be different, if not necessarily greater.

Galkor stood up and rang for the servants. "My seneschal will show you to a suitable room. Will you dine with me tonight?" He was going to be gracious with a straight face if it killed him.

Kaldmor shook his head. "We will not burden you or the servants. We know you have much to do." He turned and strode out, the assistant following as though on a leash.

Left alone, Galkor sat back down, pulled out a knife, and began sharpening a new quill pen. Let Kaldmor immure himself in a tower and spray the whole damned Viceroyalty with spells! If he had no better luck with them than last time, he would accomplish nothing useful. And Nond would be taken by men on horseback and on foot, watching for him with their own eyes and striking him down with their own hands. The sooner those men were on the move, the better.

CHAPTER 11

A high summer evening, purple clouds marching across the western sky and the tops of the Silver Mountains turning red. Gwynna slapped more savagely than usual at a mosquito whining around her ear. Another day gone, wasted chasing wild geese—or as today, wild peasant rumors of a large force of hostile cavalry. She and Sir Gilas Lanor had ridden out before dawn with a dozen men to track down the rumor—or, failing that, the rumor spreaders.

Now sunset was close on them. They were thirty miles west of Castle Delvor and at least an hour's ride from the nearest village. Fourteen hours in the saddle had produced nothing but weariness, sweat, and dry throats in both men and horses. Even the five Plainsmen in the patrol were drooping in their saddles.

Gwynna raised her hand in signal and drew rein. Behind her the sound of hooves on the narrow forest road died away. Only the sound of long-ridden horses breathing cut into the evening's stillness. For the twentieth time she lifted a cramped hand to adjust the sweat band around her head. Then she swung herself out of the saddle on to the ground.

Sir Gilas dismounted to join her. The young knight's face showed nothing but weariness and boredom. There was a touch of mocking bitterness in his usually bantering voice as he spoke.

"Well, my lady. Do we go on looking for these nary horsemen? Or do we ride back to the villages and find out who started the tale?" He slapped his thigh with his riding crop. "If we can't catch ghosts, at least we can teach those damned peasants not to tell ghost stories! Every horse we wear out chasing rumors all across the Marches is one less ready for when we have to fight real enemies. Those louts don't seem to realize that! It's time we taught them a lesson."

Gwynna nodded. She half agreed with Sir Gilas, and in any case she was too weary to argue with him. If Bertan were here, he would no doubt have things to say to Sir Gilas about his view of the peasants. But Bertan was a week's ride into the Blue Forest, and the *luor* of long-dead magic hanging over that forest made Mind Speech between them an ordeal. She knew he was alive and still moving south, as was Jos-Pran. But five of their men were dead, and two more dying as they rode,

She saw Sir Gilas beginning to fidget and realized that she must have been staring at him while her mind was off following Bertan through the Blue Forest. That would never do. Sir Gilas no doubt felt awkward enough on these patrols with her as it was. He had once loved her—hopelessly, from a great distance—and in the end, to be dismissed by her father. And after that? No doubt it had seemed to him that a mere Master Duelist came riding out of nowhere, to sweep her away for no more apparent reason than that she was a part of some god-wrought mysterious destiny he was pursuing.

Gwynna smiled. If she was to be sucked into some man's destiny and quest like a chip of wood drawn into a whirlpool, the gods had sent as good and worthy a man as she could reasonably ask. She rested one hand on her saddle for extra support and began reciting the *Kwor* Banishment. The light spell could not drive out fatigue, but it could drive it back until it no longer nibbled at one's mind and body like rats at a carcass. *"Kwor, n'luk poh—kwor, n'luk poh—kwor, n'luk poh—"*

Then, in one moment the spell, the silence, and the evening all fell apart as men swarmed out of the bushes on either side of the road. They came forth with a terrible crashing and cracking of bushes and branches, giving the patrol in the road a few seconds' warning.

That was all most of the riders needed. Gwynna was in her saddle in a single bound, Sir Gilas in his a second later, and both were wheeling their horses before the first enemy had actually reached the road. The men who had remained mounted were already moving by then. Not fast enough, though, to drive by sheer impact through the men swarming around their horses. Swords flashed upward as well as down, and the screams of dying horses tore at Gwynna's ears.

Her own sword was out, red in the light of the dying day even before it found its first victim. A man dashed toward her horse's head, knife uplifted to stab, his other hand reaching for the bridle. Her blade flicked downward, and the knife went flying. Her wrist twisted again, and the point drove into a brown-bearded face. The man howled, clapped a hand to his cheek, and reeled aside. Gwynna dug her spurs in with a savage lunge of both legs. The horse leaped forward, straight on to a dying Plainsman.

The man screamed. The horse reared, twisting frantically to avoid the shrieking thing on the ground. Gwynna locked her legs around the horse and pulled hard on the reins with both hands, letting her sword dangle from its wrist thong.

In that unarmed moment, some hardy enemy plunged in under the horse's flailing hooves, stabbing with a short sword. The sword drove deep into the horse's belly as the hooves came down. The crunch of bone was swept aside by the horse's screams. It came down with a jarring thud, reared again, then collapsed sideways. Gwynna had barely time to kick her feet free of the stirrups and jump clear before the horse smashed down on the road.

So many enemies crowded around her now that they got in each other's way and interfered with each other's defenses. Through the confusion Gwynna lunged, clearing a path to either side of her with quick thrusts, then setting her back hard against a tree. A dozen attackers quickly formed a ring around her.

Sir Gilas came down on that ring, bellowing curses and threats impartially at the enemy and at his own horse. The ring split and broke as he forced his mount through, slashing down on both sides of him with his sword. Gwynna parried a thrust at her, took two steps forward, saw Sir Gilas reach down to pull her up beside him. She felt his hand close on her arm, felt him pull, felt her feet leave the ground, let a moment's hope flare up.

Then the circle collapsed in on them. Sir Gilas's mount reared; its front hooves lashed out like maces at the men charging it. But the jerk as it reared broke Sir Gilas's grip on Gwynna's arm. She heard the cloth of her riding tunic tear, felt his fingernails slash the back of her hand as it flashed through his, then the ground smashed up at her. Pebbles drove into her cheek with sharp little pains, and she heard herself scream, "Get out of here, you fool!" at Sir Gilas. Then half a dozen massive bodies fell on her. More cloth ripped, the pebbles stabbed again, her sword thong went tight and broke with a jerk that nearly snapped her wrist as well. A fog of acrid human smells surrounded her, flowed over her. Then everything flattened out into a featureless gray wall that seemed to surround her, cutting her off from the world.

When the gray wall faded away, Gwynna thought at first night must have come. She could make out nothing around her except moving blurs and stationary shadows. Then, as her eyes slowly adjusted, she realized that she was deep in the forest. Raising her head as far as she could, she saw the sky still glowing red far above. The movement sent a violent pain shooting through her aching head. For a moment sky and trees faded back into grayness and she had to bite her lip to hold in a gasp.

When the pain in her head began to fade, she became aware of other pains. Bruises and grazes ached or smarted in half a dozen places, and from the dull ache in her stomach someone must have kicked her there. Other pains at wrists and ankles told her clearly that she had been tightly and competently bound.

Her boots had been pulled off, and she felt pine needles under her bare feet. Otherwise, her clothes were still on, intact except for a good many ripped seams. That was little consolation. It only proved that this particular band of raiders didn't care to rape unconscious and fully clothed women.

Her signs of life brought half a dozen men out of the gloom to stand in a circle around her. The dim light smoothed out any individual differences among them and left them all looking much the same—so many variations on the basic bravo. But their leather was as polished as their weapons, their beards more neatly trimmed, if no cleaner than usual. Their shields, badges, and scarfs were boldly marked in silver and orange. That should mean something to her, those colors, but for the moment her head was too fuzzy to dredge it up.

But there were also half a dozen sets of eyes, all looking at Gwynna with the same unmistakable expression. There are no variations in animal lust. At least if there are, they are too subtle to be visible to a woman seeing it written on the faces of half a dozen men.

"You're awake, witch," said one of them. Gwynna said nothing. Any sign of fear would make matters worse. Men like these fed on a woman's cringing as much as they did on her flesh. But fear was there, with the men almost radiating pictures of what they imagined themselves doing with her, to her. She began to recite the *Red Seers' Dreil* Banishment, another light spell to control fear.

One of the men must have noticed the soundless movement of her lips. He sprang forward and slammed the copper-shod toe of his boot into her ribs. Then he drew his sword and waved its point six inches in front of her nose. Gwynna continued reciting the spell in her mind. Gradually, she felt calm descend on her.

She looked up at the six men, to commit each face to memory. They must have read her stare as further defiance because the one who had kicked her stepped forward again, dagger slipping from its sheath. He lowered the point until it was aiming straight at her left eye. It moved in closer—closer. She fought an impulse to close the eye, slammed down her mind on an image of a bloody gaping socket, but could not help holding her breath.

Then the knife suddenly flashed across her field of view and disappeared. The men around her shuffled backward as a seventh man strode into view. By the most unmistakable sign he was in command here. He was giving orders, and the others were obeying. Other than that, there was nothing to greatly distinguish him from his men. His skin was considerably darker, his brown beard definitely sparser and perhaps more neatly curled, and he wore a silver and bright orange medallion on a gold chain around his neck, but—

"Get back and stay back," he said to the men. "The witch is Duke Cragor's prize." He drew his sword and with no expression showing on his face flicked the dagger out of the first man's hand. "Pick that up and don't let me see it out of its sheath until we reach Fors." The leader's voice was as blank as his face. Definitely, its

81

brownness was more than a tan. The men backed away.

In that moment Gwynna's memory finally dragged up a name for the man standing over her. Master Besz, the half-Chongan adventurer who had risen to rule with a rock-steady hand the best-disciplined of all the large mercenary bands. Master Besz, known only by that name, his life story a mystery, his terrifying calm in every possible and impossible situation a legend. She wasn't sure whether the knowledge of being in this man's hands made her feel more frightened or less.

Besz shoved his sword back into its scabbard with a single swift motion and stood looking down at Gwynna. She found his gaze harder to meet than those of the six soldiers. They at least had seen a woman. Their eyes had showed it clearly. Besz saw nothing but an object, valuable only because of Duke Cragor's regard for it. The man was an emotional eunuch.

"As I said, Duke Cragor wants you. He has his usual plans for you. I assume you know his tastes. You would have been much better off forcing my men to kill you." He might have been discussing the qualities of different marks of Chongan leather goods. "But I had my orders, and they had theirs." Subtle notes in his voice told Gwynna he regarded that as a sufficient explanation for anything.

"Are you hungry? Thirsty?" Gwynna was silent. If he was going to see her as an object, he gave her no reason to respond like a human being and make his job easier. And she was curious to see if defiance could break that inhuman calm.

Neither shrug nor sigh nor any change of expression indicated any reaction. A brown hand reached up to flick some dust from his tunic. "We will go to Fors," he said. "We will start as soon as it is fully dark." He turned with an almost mincing grace on one heel and strode away into the twilight.

CHAPTER 12

Wandor awoke when Jos-Pran shook him. He took a deep breath as he stood up, then gagged at the smell of mold and decay hanging in the damp air. The smell had been getting stronger for two days, but only last night had they seen what caused it.

Across their path lay a wide marsh stretching four miles from the base of the hill where they had camped to the first dry land visible on the other side. At least there was another side. Wandor had checked that carefully from the top of a tree while the others made camp.

Once there must have been land here, for the road plunged down the hill and arrowed straight out into the marsh. But now green-scummed brown water eddied and flowed sluggishly around the base of a milestone, around the rotting fungus-grown trunks of long-dead trees. The next milestone would be out there somewhere in the sullen expanse of water and mud.

Jos-Pran was standing by the fire pruning a branch with an axe. A pile of other branches, already pruned into six foot staves, lay at his feet. All around the fire the other eleven able-bodied members of the party had their weapons and gear spread out on the ground, preparing for the swamp crossing. They smeared rendered animal fat on their swords, knives, and lance and arrowheads to protect them from the water. This done, they mixed more fat with soot and smeared it on their faces and hands as a protection against the insects that whined in maddening clouds along the edges of the swamp.

Wandor looked at all the busy preparations, then walked over to the two sick men. One, a Delvor forester, was still pale and weak from his loss of blood in the last vampire-bird attack two nights before. The other, a Plainsman, could not walk on a leg swollen to half again its normal size from the stings of a bed of nettles. But he could ride, swing his sword, pull his bow, and wonder aloud at the foul temper of the gods that had allowed the creation of such a place as the Blue Forest.

The farther they got into the forest, the more Wandor saw justice in such a complaint. The canopy of leaves that cut them off from the sun. The maziness of ancient spells that cut him off from Mind Speech with Gwynna except at the price of sweating strain and agonizing headaches afterward. The road, carrying them deeper and deeper into the forest, farther and farther from the human world. Two men dead from the vampire birds, one from snakebite, one stung to death along with his horse by wild bees, a fifth crushed beneath a falling tree. Two more men maimed, all the rest of the men and the greater part of the horses bearing lesser wounds. All the horses slowed in pace and thinned in flank by hunger; ferns and moss were not their choice of food. But they still lived and moved. No need yet to give a crippled man a quick death and leave his body to the scavengers.

They had cast both east and west along the banks of the marsh and found no end to it. It might well stretch a hundred miles in either direction. They could lose weeks blundering about in search of an easier crossing, then more weeks returning to the road or seeking out another. If the marsh was shallow enough to ford, they would cross those four miles today. If it was not, they would camp here, break out the axes, and build a raft large enough to take a horse and rider. Wandor was not completely sure whether he was being cautious in this decision—or merely stubborn.

But four miles of open sky was definitely a standing temptation to the vampire birds, as much as Wandor hoped they might now be south of the creatures' range. Everyone would ride with a bow strung. And there were bound to be other things in the swamp itself. "Things," not animals. The living creatures in the Blue Forest still seemed set apart. In all their days in the forest, Wandor had seen nothing as wholesome as a bear, a wildcat, or even a mouse.

Breakfast was cold roast meat from the night before, eaten in slow, careful bites. Wandor strode up and down through the camp, forcing himself to put food in a stomach that was tying itself into a tighter and tighter knot.

Finally the meat was gone, the last of the gear packed into the saddle bags, and no possible excuse left for delaying their departure a moment longer. In fact, the sooner they started, the better. The sun was well up now, and the one unspoken (because unspeakable) fear in everyone's mind was being caught by darkness out in the marsh.

They led their horses down the hill in a single line, Wandor in the lead. The water of the marsh was chilly, and a thin layer of viscid mud covered the stones of the submerged road. But under the mud the stones were reassuringly solid. Wandor moved forward at a good pace, probing ahead with his staff for potholes and soft spots. Gradually, the water rose up his boots, washed around their, tops, and began to creep up his trousers. The green scum clung to the wool, and as he waded farther out, his legs began to look like the fungus-grown trunks on either side. Ugly as those trunks were, he was grateful for them. They marked the path of the road with useful precision. As he probed immediately ahead of him, Wandor's eyes kept lifting to trees far ahead. By the height of the water on their trunks, he had hopes of judging the depth of the water a long way ahead. So far it was only knee-deep, but an altogether abominable smell of too many things far too long dead rose about him as he disturbed the scum on the surface and the ooze on the bottom. A brief look behind him showed that the whole party was now in the water. All except the two injured men walked ahead of their horses, leading them, probing ahead with their own staves.

Half an hour went by. The road curved gently from side to side. Once Wandor almost held his breath as he felt it slipping downward under his feet. He kept on, feeling the water rise above his knees, up his thighs, up to his waist. But ahead the trees seemed no more deeply submerged than before, and somehow he trusted them more than anything else he had encountered in this land. Perhaps it was because they were dead. Everything living here seemed to have its hand raised against men.

Uneasy mutterings were rising behind him by the time the water began to shrink away down his legs. Wandor took a deep breath for the first time in many minutes. Another half hour went by. Slow as their plodding, step-by-step pace was, it had now taken them better than a mile out into the marsh. The mud lay deeper underfoot, sucking harder at Wandor's boots and the hooves of his horse, but the water rose no higher.

The sun did rise higher and higher into the sky, seeming to wobble and waver upward through the vapors rising from the marsh. But for the first time in a week they saw it clearly above them. The spirits of the Plainsmen, children of an open land with an open sky above it, began to rise. One even began to sing a hunting song until a searing look from Jos-Pran cut him off. Wandor and Jos-Pran exchanged looks that told each the other shared his thoughts. Both felt that safety in this marsh lay in silence and stealth, slipping across it like marauders.

They were approaching the halfway mark now. Off to the left a low spit broke the surface, chunks of masonry rising above black steaming mud. Black and green frogs the size of rabbits hopped lumpishly about among the stones, croaking and belching.

Beyond the ruins the road began unmistakably to rise again. Wandor looked ahead to his guides, the trees. A hundred feet ahead the trees on both sides came to an end, as though the ground beneath them had suddenly dropped away. Another hundred feet farther on, they began again, just as abruptly. Wandor moved on, his staff probing the water with extra care, climbing one step at a time until the water was below the tops of his riding boots for the first time in nearly two hours. Green-coated lumps of stone stood out of the water on either side of him now.

Then suddenly the thrust of his staff met no resistance, plunging down into an unknown depth. Wandor nearly overbalanced and toppled forward into the water. He recovered and probed to the right and left. All across their path the road dropped away into a broken-edged gulf. An unmistakable current ran through the gulf, carrying along bits of scum, turf, and twigs. Here was the river that had made the marsh, here had been the bridge that had carried the road across the river when it ran docilely in its old channel.

Wandor turned back toward the rest of the party, which had stopped. He splashed back down the approach to the bridge until he was within earshot of the whole line. He briefly explained the situation, then went on.

"We'll have to try swimming it. Those of you who can't swim, hold on to your horses. Jos-Pran will lead across. I will stay with the rear and help the wounded." The War Chief nodded, although Wandor noted his lips moving in a brief prayer as he turned and faced the water.

Jos-Pran urged his horse forward. As it dropped over the edge with a splash and a squeal of momentary panic, he clung to the bridle with one hand, to the saddle with the other. For a moment Wandor stared, expecting to see both heads sinking out of sight. But both rose dripping and began to move out across the river. Wandor thanked the gods that horses swim, even if reluctantly at times.

Wandor did not clearly remember breathing during all the time Jos-Pran took to get himself and his horse across the river. But he gave a long sigh of relief as the War Chief's mount staggered up on its feet. Jos-Pran let go of the saddle and waved to the waiting men. They filed forward toward the channel, eager now to complete the crossing. One by one they slipped into the water with great splashes. Then they rose again in churning flurries and slid across the channel. One by one they and their mounts rose into full view again. Two men were carried out of the line of the bridge and road by the current. But their horses managed to wallow through the mud and up on to the firmer footing of the road.

In time there was only Wandor left, with two able-bodied men and the two wounded. The first two swam their horses across, left them with their comrades, then swam back. Each took the bridle of a wounded man's horse. Wandor looked at all four men, then turned and urged his own horse forward over the edge of the broken bridge.

Wandor's heavy boots pulled him down until his head slipped under. But the horse swam strongly and pulled him up and forward. He kicked furiously with his feet and thrashed with his free arm, constantly looking back to the men behind him. All four were in the water now, moving slowly but steadily forward. Ahead the men and horses standing on the far side were getting closer. But below him there was still no bottom, nothing but the chill dank waters.

Behind Wandor sounded a splash that was not a horse's or a

man's. He saw men on the far bank start, point, and open their mouths to shout. He turned his head again, to see something long and gray and shiny break surface between him and the other four men. A plate-sized green eye glared at him as the thing's head lifted into the air. Then powerful jaws snapped shut with a *clak*, and a bubbling scream rose as they closed on the neck of the first horse. The scream was echoed by cries from the two men with the horse. Then all the cries died in a burst of splashing as the creature sounded, jaws still tight around the horse's neck, plucking horse and men below like a ripe fruit from the branch of a tree. Within a minute from the first splash, nothing marked where the beast or its victims had been except a patch of water discolored by bubbles and blood.

The suddenness of the attack let Wandor keep calm until he had landed himself and the two surviving men on the far bank. Then he clutched hard at his saddle while he gulped air into lungs that suddenly seemed to have shrunk and fought a battle with his stomach over keeping his breakfast down. He won—barely. Then he turned to Jos-Pran and said, "Let's get out of here."

A popular suggestion. Compared with their ponderous approach to the channel, the march toward the farther edge of the marsh was almost a scramble. Fear of being benighted in the marsh had given way to a new, equally unspeakable fear. Was there more deep water between them and the far shore? And if there was, would there be more of those swift gray shapes lurking in it?

They found no deep water, no signs that anything larger than frogs and insects lived in the marsh, in the hour it took them to reach the far bank. On dry land once more, they kept going, squelching along in their wet boots and sodden clothing, until the trees shut out the view of the marsh.

After two miles, Wandor finally led his men off the road and under the trees. Fire kits came out of oiled-leather pouches, axes hacked into dry branches, and soon two large fires were blazing. Horses and thirteen naked men stood around the fires. The men watched their clothing hang from branches thrust into the ground and slowly steam dry.

Finally, Jos-Pran found his voice.

"What *was* that thing in the marsh?"

Wandor shook his head. "The Empire of the Blue Forest created strange servants with their beast magic. That must have been one of the ones that bred true. Something like that would make a good guardian for a castle moat or a river. Imagine an army trying to ford a river swarming with those things."

The clothes dried; the hunters went out and came back with dinner. Other men brushed down the horses and gathered for them what fodder the forest provided. The hunters' victims were dressed, spitted, and roasted over the fires. The comforting odor of roasting meat rose into the twilight.

Wandor sat cross-legged in his breechclout on the ground, slowly scraping the dried mud and slime off his boots with a stick. He stared into the fire, watching its brightness seem to grow as twilight settled down more heavily on the forest. Then the light of the fire vanished in a sudden rainbow-colored blaze, as Gwynna's mind drove in one convulsive spasm across the miles separating them. No words came from her, only a voiceless pain and distress, and a vision. Mounted men, mounted men all around her, riding along a forest road. The hard briskness of trained soldiers in their movements and the look of experienced and well-disciplined mercenaries in their arms and gear. The view of them was distorted and for a moment unrecognizable, then Wandor realized that Gwynna was riding—or being carried—flung over a horse's back. He did not need to see silver and orange colors on the mercenaries to realize what had happened to Gwynna. He sent a pulse of pure emotion back across the miles—love, concern, determination, wrapped up in a single wordless, "Hold on." Then at both ends the link dissolved.

After a minute Wandor found himself lying on his back on the soft ground. Jos-Pran was sponging the grease and soot off his face with a handful of damp leaves. Wandor pushed the War Chief's hand away and sat up.

"Gwynna has been captured." he said. His voice was low, for he did not want the news to get around among the rest of the men. With all the troubles of the journey, they were already under enough strain.

Jos-Pran kept his face straight, but his eyes dropped for a moment, and his hand clasped Wandor's until both sets of knuckles stood out white.

"Where is she?"

"Going north, I think. Baron Galkor is in Fors, so she'll probably be taken there."

"A long journey."

"I know."

"Have they—abused her?" The Plainsmen were normally blunt spoken to a degree. Wandor understood and appreciated Jos-Pran's somewhat awkward delicacy.

"It doesn't seem so. The men around her look like the best kind of mercenary."

"If there is such a thing."

"I recognized silver and orange colors. That means Master Besz."

"Then Gwynna's safe for the moment."

Wandor shook his head. "Not safe. Alive."

CHAPTER 13

For the first time in the long journey north, Master Besz was allowing Gwynna to sit in the saddle instead of being slung over it like a feed sack or a corpse. Her hands were still tied behind her back with skin-gouging tightness, her feet tied to the stirrups.

But even sitting upright again helped Gwynna's sagging spirits. Following the example of their leader, Besz's mercenaries virtually ignored her during the trip north. None of them except Besz himself even spoke to her. And if someone touched her when lifting her on and off her horse or tying and untying her for meals, their touch was as impersonal as if she had been a sack of walnuts. This went on until she was not far from wondering if she was alive. Those doubts in turn had pushed her into a savage struggle for sanity, which had absorbed most of her mind's resources. There had been nothing left for Mind Speech with Bertan. He might well be dead in the Blue Forest or pushing onward in sweating doubt if she were alive or dead. An ugly thought. She knew, in no spirit of feminine egotism but as a warrior who has measured the strength of an ally, that her death would come terribly close to breaking Bertan. As close as his would come to breaking her.

She pushed that thought away and concentrated on her own immediate future. Unless Duke Cragor himself had reached Fors, Baron Galkor would take her for safekeeping. A practical man, she had heard. Left to his own devices, he would have her at once run through or burled off the castle battlements. As she would him, if chance so contrived it.

But Cragor's tastes were well known, his orders no doubt explicit, and his authority unquestioned by either Galkor or Master Besz. So she would live until Cragor came to claim her for his own amusements. For the moment, she owed her best hope of life to Cragor's lust for torture.

They were moving downhill now. The soil underfoot showed streaks of yellow sand; the pine trees on either side grew stunted and bent by fierce winds. The smell of seaweed baking in the sun and the harsh screaming of gulls came to her on a rising wind. A moment later they broke out into the open, and she saw blue ocean spreading out to the horizon on the left. They reached the level of the beach and rode along it for a mile or so to a small stone pier. Across another mile of open water rose a round-towered castle, squatting with the sea lapping at the very base of one tower, and behind it the roofs and smoke plumes of a city. Fors.

Fifty thousand people lived there, inside a full set of walls, worshiping at temples to each of the Five Gods, guarded by a castle, and boasting a history extending back beyond King Nond's conquest of the Viceroyalty. A century of trade with the Khindi had preceded their conquest, a trade centered on the little peninsula where Fors now stood. Easily defensible against an enemy with few boats, it had successively held a trading post, a castle guarding that trading post, an army garrison, a town that lived off that garrison, and finally a city. Set at the narrow mouth of a land-locked bay that offered the best harbor in the Viceroyalty, Fors lived well by its garrison, its fishing fleet, its shipbuilding ways, and its merchants' warehouses.

A ferry propelled by twelve sweeps lumbered across the channel and began loading the mercenaries aboard. Gwynna went with the first party, along with Master Besz himself. Two of his men cut the cords binding her feet to the stirrups and let her dismount. But they held her tightly all during the crossing—tightly and not impersonally. They practically dragged her across the salt-sprayed stone jetty at the castle's water gate, and they did drag her up endless flights of stairs to Baron Galkor's chamber high in the tower. Master Besz followed behind them at his usual unruffled pace.

Galkor rose as they entered, came out from behind his desk,

and clapped both hands on Master Besz's shoulders. For a moment distaste flickered across the mercenary's face—the first actual emotion Gwynna had seen him display. It was a relief to see the iron mercenary captain brought down for a moment to an almost human level.

"Master Besz," said Galkor. "When your courier arrived saying you'd captured the witch, I wasn't sure whether to give the man gold for bringing good news or flog his back raw for telling tales. And even if you had taken her, I thought it likely she would manage to escape on your way north. Forgive me for doubting your ability, but she's incredibly cunning."

"It is not important," said Besz. "My men know how to keep a prisoner, and I have had dealings with witches and sorcerers before."

"So you have, Master Besz. I had forgotten." Galkor pulled the bell cord. In a moment a dozen of his own household guards clattered up the stairs and into the chamber. "You'll have Cragor's promised reward and anything else in the castle you want and can carry away." He spread his arms wide in an expansive gesture. "My sergeant will show you and your men to your quarters." He nodded in dismissal, and one of the household men turned and led Besz out the door. Besz's men fell into their usual precise line and followed their captain.

Slowly, Galkor walked around Gwynna in a complete circle, never coming within arm's reach of her, never taking his eyes off her. Finally he completed the circle and stepped back to survey her, arms folded across his chest and eyes going over her again from head to foot. There was a repellent thoroughness in that gaze, as though his eyes were dirty hands stripping her to the skin. Then he spoke. His voice was filled with the satisfaction of a man who knows that everything is working out as well as it can.

"Delvor's witch daughter," he said. "I never thought I'd see you here, this way. I worked long towards this moment. I even prayed and sacrificed. The gods know that. And they answered. Oh, they have answered."

He began walking briskly around her again. "Cragor rules in Benzos now. The last of Nond's supporters have surrendered or fled. The Royal Army in the north has surrendered, and Avarmouth was betrayed by some of its own people. Cragor's army entered and showed what folly it was to resist him. So you are alone here in the

93

Viceroyalty. Alone, friendless, and doomed. Have you thought of surrendering, also? The duke might consider at least granting you and your friends exile in Chonga."

Gwynna spat on the rug in front of him. He shrugged. "I thought that's what you'd say. Well, don't say I didn't warn you. You and your father—yes, and that damned Duelist—are good supporters for Nond. You're all just like him—brave, stubborn, and too thickheaded to know when you're beaten and it's time to submit."

Galkor shrugged again, and this time he seemed to be shrugging off the politeness in his manner. His voice was clipped as he went on. "Very well. If I was free to follow my own judgment, I'd have you drugged and passed around the barracks. Every man in the castle would get a chance at you. Then I'd chop what they left of you into pieces and throw you to the dogs. You're dangerous, witch. I don't mind you knowing that I don't like having you around.

"But I'm sure you know Cragor's tastes. He doesn't get a chance at somebody like you very often. A woman, young, beautiful, and a dangerous enemy. He wants to get his hands on you so badly he can taste it. And he isn't going to turn you over to his experts. He'll do you himself. I've got to keep you safe for him until he comes to get you or has you sent across to Benzos. And I will.

"But don't get careless, witch. Don't try to escape or make a nuisance of yourself. Cragor likes his pleasures, but he'd rather give them up than have you lose again. One attempt to escape, and you go to the barracks. Understand me?" Gwynna was silent. "Understand?" he said more sharply, and pinched thumb and forefinger into the sides of her jaw until she felt the nails gash her skin. She set her jaw more firmly.

Galkor shrugged yet again. "All right, witch. Be the tough little girl as long as you can get any pleasure out of the act. But that mouth won't stay shut when Cragor starts pulling your teeth." He turned and snapped out a string of orders to the guards.

"Take the witch to the dark cell Strip her, chain her, lock and bar the door, and post a double guard. Food, water, and a bucket will be sent in twice a day. No one is to enter the cell without my permission in writing, and never less than four fully armed men at a time. Anyone who disobeys will find himself in the cell next to hers."

Gwynna was ragged, filthy, totally unarmed, and exhausted. She doubted if she could have either fought or cast even the smallest spell to save herself from a whole army of Cragor's torturers. But from somewhere came the strength to grin, then laugh. She went on laughing as Galkor's face grew at first perplexed, then angry. She stopped when she realized that a hysterical edge was beginning to show in her laughter.

Then she shook her head. "Oh great baron," she her voice still half choked with laughter. "One woman, weary, naked, and unarmed. And you will send four—*four* of those great clumsy stupid hairy brutes you call guards into her cell. What happens if you capture Bertan Wandor? Are you going to have enough guards in the whole castle to deal with him if you need four to deal with me?" She shook her head helplessly.

For a moment raw fury flared in Galkor's face, and his hand snapped toward his dagger hilt. Just as abruptly it snapped to a stop, inches away from the hilt. Then he managed another shrug. "If your beloved Bertan Wandor ever falls into my hands, I'm not going to bother guarding him at all. He'll need a man at his head and another at his feet to carry him down to the water gate. That's all." And to the guards: "Take her out."

Four of the guards seized Gwynna's arms and legs and hoisted her into the air. So many others crowded around, eager to feel the witch's flesh under their hands, that it took much swearing from Baron Galkor to get the ragged company on its way out the door.

As they rushed her down the stairs, Gwynna was clutching hard at three bits of knowledge. Galkor's flare of rage at her taunt. The fact that he had not mentioned Nond's death. And the fact that he hoped her capture would bring Wandor rushing into a trap.

So Galkor's self-control could be broken. Taunting Galkor until he broke loose and killed or wounded her could be one way of sowing trouble between the baron and his master. A desperate way, but things might come to that.

Nond was still alive. Or at least Galkor and Cragor did not know if he was dead. If they didn't know, others might be equally ignorant. Start rumors that Nond was alive and spread them to give hope and strength to the loyalists? Cynical, but things might come to that. And if Nond were really still alive...

And Galkor did not know about Wandor's journey into the Blue Forest. Nor about the Helm of Jagnar, nor about what it might do to bind the Khindi to Nond's party. Above all, Galkor did not know about Cheloth of the Woods. Kaldmor might, of course. But Kaldmor would hardly volunteer information on such a topic.

The whole scrambling pack of guards was just reaching the next level below when raw pain slashed and tore at Gwynna. Again the attack was so sudden that her barriers went down as though they did not exist. The pain flooded in. Beyond shame or self-control, she screamed and writhed in the tightening hands of the guards. Then with her last scraps of will, she pushed herself over into unconsciousness. Before blackness swallowed her, she felt an inner chill, knowing what was at work again.

Somewhere terribly close, someone was casting a spell of ancient Toshak.

Gwynna's screams echoed up the stairway and through the heavy oak door of Galkor's chamber. He rose and went to the door, ready to order the guards to stun Gwynna. He did not want an uproar in the castle. People might hear, and what they heard they might tell. His party had a less firm hold on the Viceroyalty than he had admitted to Gwynna. The fewer rumors to run through the streets and taverns of Fors, the better.

But the screams died away as his hand touched the door latch. Satisfied, he turned back into the room, hesitated for a moment, then turned further and stepped out on to the balcony.

It jutted out over the central courtyard of the castle, giving him a fine view of the whole castle and, beyond its towers, the roofs of Fors, red tile and bleached gray stone. But Galkor's eyes were fixed on a small round window in the uppermost level of the castle's landward tower. The window was barred on the outside and heavily curtained within.

Not heavily curtained enough, perhaps. Vagrant flickers of blue light kept striking into Galkor's eyes. Send a servant up there to close the curtain or ask the sorcerers there to do it? To be sure—and condemn the servant to death or madness, making rumors fly about like bees from a broken hive.

Galkor had led Kaldmor and his assistant to that tower room personally and with his own hands helped them sweat their trunks of magical apparatus up the cobwebbed stairs. That was as it should be. He did want people getting into a panic, and many of them would. Nor did he want others getting their hopes up, and some people would. Kaldmor had promised a great deal, but Galkor knew that he would still be agreeably surprised if the little man in the purple robes produced anything.

It was time to start looking for a campsite, Count Arlor realized. There were several more hours of daylight but they would need most of that to find a safe campsite and conceal it thoroughly. There were traveling villagers to avoid, and now that they were five days in from the coast they might also expect Khindi.

But the worst problem wasn't villagers, and it wasn't Khindi. The word must have reached Galkor that Nond might be in the Viceroyalty. That efficient servant had promptly sent out every man he could spare. So Nond's party had managed to take to the bush or the deep forest in time to avoid the mounted patrols as they trotted past.

Their disguises helped. Arlor had applied his skill to an eight of the party and done well by them. Even Nond admitted this after the proper amount of grumbling. They might have been any party of footloose men—mercenaries looking for a captain, settlers looking for land to claim, builders looking for work, even gamblers looking for opportunities. Their clothes were too shabby and their steel too visibly abundant to make them a tempting bait for robbers. Even the king had been marvelously altered, though his protests at having his beard trimmed might have been heard in Fors or even the foothills of the Silver Mountains. But a trimmed beard, shabby clothing, and a further reduction of his paunch gave even Nond a chance to slip past unnoticed.

Ahead, a thick stand of pepperberry bush and birch trees spread away on either side of the trail. If the half-starved horses could be kept from gorging themselves into bloat and indigestion on the spicy berries, this might be a good place to spend the night. Well inside the trees, they would be out of sight and hearing alike of any patrol that might ride past.

Arlor pointed toward the trees and looked inquiringly at the forester riding beside him. The man shrugged.

"I'm asking you for advice, damn it!" Arlor snapped.

"Can't rightly say, sir. But one thing—nobody'd believe we's in there less'n we leave a trail a blind baby could follow."

"All right, then. We won't make a trail." It took an inhuman effort for Arlor to control his voice. Two months of rising strain had been followed by day after day of still greater strain and intense physical activity on perhaps three hours of sleep a night if he was lucky. He was not often lucky. He wondered what he looked like and thanked the gods there was no mirror in his baggage. One look at himself and he'd probably fall down in a fit. The others were certainly turning into filthy, foul-smelling, red-eyed husks of men. Soon their battered appearance would be attracting more attention than it turned away.

Arlor dismounted and drew his hunting knife as he approached the fringe of bushes around the trees. The knife suddenly seemed heavier than usual. It took an enormous, sweating effort of his right arm to raise the knife from its sheath on his hip into position for a slash at the brush.

Surprised, he looked at the knife. It seemed the same as ever. Why did it suddenly seem to weigh so much? Why was it getting blurred and wavery as if he were seeing it through running water? He tried to look upward, and it seemed that his neck muscles could suddenly no longer support the weight of his head. He managed to raise his eyes to the tree tops high above him, and they, too, were wavering and dancing. But there was no wind.

A crash and a gasp behind him. He turned, with only the strength to move one step at a time. The forester had collapsed out of his saddle on to the grass. He lay full length and face down, and Arlor's straining ears caught the sound of a great rolling snore.

Arlor swore softly—he had not the strength to shout—and reeled with more than the weariness flooding his limbs and the dizziness flooding his head. Powerful sorcery had sought them out, was being focused on them, was numbing their limbs and brains.

Nond was down off his horse now, by a miracle of will, and lurching across the turf toward Arlor. The count forced himself forward one, two, three steps, arms outstretched to aid the king. Then the knees of both men gave way in the same instant. Side by side, but facing opposite ways, they slipped down on to the grass and lay on their faces. An insect whined in Arlor's ear, its shrillness softened by his fading hearing. As that and all his other senses faded out entirely, Arlor had one last fleeting thought, and the sickness that thought brought him was his last clear sensation. The sleeping spell had brought them down in the open. If someone came along...

Someone did. Arlor was not happy, but neither was he particularly surprised to awaken with a spear point at his throat. Nor was he particularly surprised to see that the man holding the spear wore Baron Galkor's colors.

CHAPTER 14

Wander had no idea what time it was when they began the day's march. So thick did the trees grow overhead now that there was no longer a morning, afternoon, or evening, only a continuous twilight sometimes brighter, sometimes darker. Even the blue tinge was gone from the twilight, for they were so far south that the blue ferns no longer grew thickly.

The sun had begun to seem like a myth, likewise sun set and sunrise and all weather except the too real, too frequent rain. Showers pattered on the leaves far above. And storms broke with dimly heard thunder and even more dimly seen lightning. But rain poured down, further drenching clothes already beginning to turn green with mold. And wind clawed at the distant branches, sending down twigs and bird's nests and sometimes great branches that could and did kill unwary man.

Only eight men rode out through the gloom that morning. Wandor did not mourn the others or feel guilty of having led them to their deaths. Such thoughts could not bring the dead back to life. Instead, he took what consolation he could from what was good in the situation of the survivors.

They were almost adequately fed, though there had been little game worth wasting arrows on for several days, and they were moving too fast to set snares and deadfalls. But the men had died faster than the horses. And roast horse meat—or even raw horse meat—could keep up the strength of a man who would eat it.

At first the Plainsmen would not. Even Jos-Pran would not urge his warriors until, he had spent a whole night apart in the forest meditating and praying. When he returned the next morning, he was drawn and pale, but firm in the belief that it was better to eat the flesh of horses than to die in these accursed woods. This notion did not pass undisputed among the warriors. But a brief flurry of blows that left one warrior holding a lame wrist and another clutching his stomach ended the dispute.

Well-fed the eight were, and also well-armed. Generous coatings of grease kept blades and points from rusting, and Wandor inspected each man's weapons every night and every morning. They had also scavenged weapons from the dead. Each man now had a sword riding in his saddlebags as well as the one on his thigh. There were axes and knives in plenty, and even a good supply of arrows. They could fight against whatever the Blue Forest might yet throw at them as well as any eight men could.

Not knowing what might be yet to come gnawed at the men as much as any physical want. It had been three days since they lost a man—vampires again, but this time hideously spotted pulpy vines instead of birds. Easy enough to avoid if one saw them in time, but the Plainsman, half-blinded by swarming insects and fatigue by the end of the day, had not. Now his drained carcass lay amid the vines, perhaps consoled by the Yhang rites performed by Jos-Pran as he stood at a safe distance outside the vines' reach.

"Perhaps," because Wandor was no longer sure *what* powers ruled over this forest. More and more it seemed like a land where gods and demons and spirits had fought each other to mutual destruction, like the Eight Chongan Kings in the half-legendary Battle of Krothus. And this land they would have to penetrate still farther, then re-cross on their way north.

Wandor did not want to think about the return trip, for then he felt the fluttering wings of panic beating at his spirit. But he was the leader, the one who could not avoid thinking about such things. Was there somewhere in the world a people whose name for "leader" meant, "He who worries for all"? It seemed to Wandor that this would be appropriate.

There were no signs of the city yet, for all their days of

101

traveling. Abundant signs, to be sure, that men had once lived and ruled and built in this forest. More bridges, some still usable, others crumbled into causeways of rubble too uncertain to offer footing to man or horse. Milestones still rising beside the road, too weathered and moss grown to be readable. Dimly seen piles of tumbled stone well back in the trees. And the road itself.

Wandor was beginning to doubt that the road was as much of a friend as it had once seemed. Could they be plunging along it, south past their goal, south into unknown lands? Certainly they must already be well beyond the southernmost point of the Viceroyalty. They would have to turn back before their numbers shrank still further, or their horses died, Cheloth or no, Helm of Jagnar or no.

Wander grimaced. It was a hard and ugly decision, but one he could not escape. If two more days' advance did not bring them to the city, he would give the order to turn back. He had set a limit to their ordeal. For the moment he found that the knowledge of having done so was strangely calming.

Wandor did not notice it at first; Jos-Pran had to point to the trees on either side of them.

"I think the road is getting wider."

Wandor's eyes followed the Plainsman's gestures. For days now the edge of the ancient road had been marked by a line where ferns and saplings gave way to full-sized trees. And for days the two edges had been thirty-odd feet apart. Now, suddenly, the distance was twice that or more.

Wandor did not want to say anything. He could not escape the feeling that the trees were held back where they were by a spell that words of his might shatter. Then he said quietly, "Spread out. Form two lines. I'll take the right-hand lead."

Now they moved on in two lines of four. The branches of the trees beside the road no longer met and intertwined in a solid canopy overhead. For the first time in days, Wandor could look upward and do more than guess at the weather and the time of day. The sky was a sullen flat gray, a single lighter patch marking the place of a sun now up toward the eleventh hour. The grayness and the heaviness in the air promised rain.

It came before they had ridden another hour. No passing thunderstorm, either, but a steady rain that turned the earth to mud and made saddle leather glass-slick. Wandor was tempted to lead the men off the road into what shelter the trees might provide. But each time he was on the edge of giving the order, he would catch sight of another pile of spilled stone beside the road, to drive him onward.

The twilight had returned with the coming of the rain, making it hard to decide what each patch of ruins had once been. Sometimes a solitary column or wall rose from amid a tangle of vines, the living green ones and the brown and rotting dead ones all twined together. None ever gave more than tantalizing hints of what had stood there. But their sheer numbers gave more than a hint of something far more important. Not far off lay—a city, perhaps?

Another hour passed. More rain, more ruins. Wander now rode with his sword drawn, as much to ease his nerves as in fear of encountering an enemy. There was nothing to see but the rain, the ruins, and the trees, nothing to hear but the rain and the squashy thudding of the horses' hooves into the mud.

Another hour, past the time when Wander would normally have called a brief halt for a bite of food. But he was no longer capable of feeling hunger and thirst. Every one of his senses was focused on the twilight ahead, as if he could somehow strip away the veil of rain and forest and expose what he knew must be there. No, that was letting his emotions plunge on ahead of the facts. The city did not *have* to be there.

A third hour passed in the drip of rain from hat brims and noses and the trickle of cold drops down inside collars and gloves. Wandor himself was beginning to think of roaring fires and dry clothing, but the gods alone knew how they were going to contrive either in this sodden wilderness.

And then, with no further warning, they were there.

On either side of the road the trees ran on ahead for another hundred yards. Then they stopped. In their place towered an immense wall stretching away on either side until it vanished into the forest and the rain. A few stones were missing here and there, and the blackened face—as high as a five-story building—supported its own private jungle of tangled vines. But two thousand years of assaults by forest and weather had done nothing more. In the center a doubled-arched gateway surrounded with flaked and moss-grown carvings carried the road through the wall. The gates themselves had long since perished, probably in the storming of the city by Jagnar's army. At the other end of the dark tunnel through the walls, Wandor could see a broad street flanked with ghost-dim buildings.

He reined in his horse and turned to look at Jos-Pran. Now that they were actually there, he found it impossible to simply ride straight on through the gateway into the city. Once again, he had the feeling that a sudden move would break a spell, the walls and gateway would vanish, and the forest would return, rolling on endlessly southward.

Jos-Pran was equally silent for a moment. Then he said quietly, "Well, my friend. Let us get inside and out of this rain." The matter-of-fact suggestion broke the tension. Wandor grinned, then motioned his party forward.

Much of the city inside the walls had been built of wood. The fires of the storming had taken much of that, the passage of time the rest. Now tall trees grew in such places, and their roots bulged and cracked the pavement upward in a thousand places, while their dead leaves covered the broken slabs with inches of brown mold.

But the men of the Empire had also built in well-wrought and solidly fitted stone, leaving behind them long streets of six-sided domed buildings. Neither Wandor nor Jos-Pran cared greatly what these might have been. At the moment they wanted only to find one whose dome was solid enough to keep out the rain, whether it had been house, shop, school, stable, temple, or prison. They turned down the first street they came to on the left and rode slowly along it until they found what they sought. Six stories tall, it had a double-height first floor, once perhaps a storeroom or stables. But for the moment all that mattered was that the floor was dry.

As if their getting under a roof for the first time in far too many days had been a signal, they were just unsaddling their horses when the rain stopped. And before they had stripped off their sodden clothes, a rising breeze began to tear away the clouds over the city. Slowly the grayness above broke apart, letting sun down on the city.

Dressed only in sword and breechclout, Wandor climbed the dusty stairs of the building to the roof and surveyed the city. In the sunlight it took on at least the semblance of life that cosmetics can give to a well-embalmed corpse. The wet leaves of the trees and the wet grass in the parks shone green, and here and there domes glowed faintly with peeling, scabby remnants of their original colors.

Far away over miles of domed and flat rooftops rose the largest dome of all. The walls that supported it rose three times as high as the wall of the city. The dome itself rose in a perfect hemisphere a hundred feet high and twice that in diameter. Once it must have been gilded, for patches still shone dull gold in the sunlight. Alone of all the buildings Wandor could see, it matched Gwynna's description of the Temple of the Dwarf God. The Temple of the Dwarf God, where Cheloth lay in his slumbering vigil over the Helm of Jagnar.

Again Wandor realized that he wanted to believe this regardless of what the facts and probabilities might be. He was too weary to even contemplate searching the whole city for the temple. Unless Cheloth of the Woods were to emerge from one of those dusty doorways and guide them to it? Wandor laughed, but not loudly and not easily. Laughter seemed out of place in this city, after this journey.

The breeze had dried him off now. He turned back to the stairs and descended into the darkness to where the other men waited.

Wandor's desire to set out at once for the Temple of the Dwarf God was not enough to overcome the terrible weariness of the other men. Even Jos-Pran would not bestir himself to urge the men out into the streets. In fact, nothing short of a direct message from the gods or the threatened collapse of the building about their ears would drive the other seven out into the streets again that day. And prowling through the streets of this city by night was something not even Wandor felt like undertaking.

So Wander held his peace, all slept, the night passed, morning came, and with it came new strength. They rose in the darkness before dawn, ate cold dried meat in its gray light, and moved out as the sky over the city turned pink and then blue. They kept their horses with them rather than split up the party to provide a horse guard. By everything Wandor's eyes could see and ears could hear, the city was dead. But he would not risk men or horses on that belief.

In places boots and hooves thudded softly on mats of dead leaves sodden from the rain. Elsewhere the clop of hooves and the lighter thump of boots echoed from a thousand faces of sterile stone. It was a sound softer than the wind piping in long-cold chimneys, yet to Wandor it sounded like a continuous roar that might cover the approach of—what? He didn't know. But once again, he would not risk much on the notion that the city was as dead as it looked.

They were at the Temple before they expected, before they could prepare themselves for the shock of seeing it looming monstrously above them. Wandor's eyes roved over it, matching features with Gwynna's description, picking up details he had not noticed from a distance.

Two of those details he found disquieting. The windows and doors of one of the flanking buildings linked to the main temple were solidly bricked up, with glazed brick that shone lighter than that of the building itself. And the double bronze doors, three times the height of a man, showed no trace of mold or tarnishing. They shone as though a crew of industrious workmen had burnished them only the week before.

With three men behind him and all four swords drawn, Wandor stalked toward the door. There was no dust or debris on the stone walk in front of it, either. But that might be just the rain. He stepped up to the doors and pushed on the left-hand one. Silently, smoothly, with no creaks or jerks, it swung open. Wandor stepped forward, into the shadows within. As he did so, a harsh barking scream sounded from above him.

Wander had his sword up by pure reflex before the thing that screamed launched itself from its perch above. His slash caught it in midair. It gave another scream as it seemed to fold itself over his sword blade. But there was still life in it as it hit the floor, and clawed hands flailed out, shredding Wandor's breeches. He thrust downward, then, as it jerked and finally relaxed, he took a good look at the thing he had

106

killed.

Man or ape? Short legs, long arms dangling on either side of a wide squat torso, thick gray fur. But the forehead rose high above large pale eyes that stared up at Wandor with a fading awareness that was, not an animal's. And clutched in one paw was a stout wooden club, in the other a circular wooden shield.

Before Wander could move farther or the other men could join him, the screams sounded again. Wandor sprang backward five feet at a single bound, so none of the leaping ape-men landed behind him. Half a dozen of the creatures hit the floor as the men behind Wandor threw open the other door.

The ape-men shrank back from the light, raising their shields—dark green, Wander saw now, with a silver triangle in the middle to protect their eyes. Behind Wandor the three men raised their swords, and one growled, "Now, lord?"

"Wait!" Wandor's voice barked with more assurance than he felt. Those ape-men were dangerous. They stood across what might well be the path to the Helm and all that meant. But as he had sensed life in the city, so he now sensed that there would be a—a *wrongness*, he could only call it—in killing these—what? And he remembered, also, Gwynna's words about approaching Cheloth of the Woods, a master of beast magic, "in the proper spirit."

Without lowering his sword, Wandor focused his mind on a mental picture, as he had done the day he had to ride the King Horse. A picture of the apes standing to either side, their clubs and shields lowered as Wandor—and Wandor only—walked down the corridor to whatever lay in the darkness at the end of it.

He had never tried Mind Speech on any animal but the King Horse. He did not know if he could do it. If Gwynna had been here... But she was a prisoner in Fors Castle. It was his problem. He gritted his teeth in a ludicrous feeling that somehow a physical gesture could increase the power of his mind, push his message more easily through whatever barriers lay between him and the minds of those creatures before him.

One of the shields wavered. Two of the clubs that had been held high sagged toward the floor. One of the creatures whined and shook its head. Then all six backed out of Wandor's path and stood against the wall. He half expected them to raise their clubs into a saluting position, like halberdiers of the Royal Army of Benzos.

He took a step forward. One of the men behind him started to follow. Without turning his head, Wandor said sharply, "No. This is for me alone." He pointed at the dead ape-man on the floor. "This was a warrior defending the Temple of the Dwarf God. Treat his body with honor and perform the rites for an honored foe."

The man choked. Wandor turned his head until he was looking at the man over his shoulder. The man looked full into Wandor's face, and Wandor saw him jerk backward as though he had been slapped. Without another word Wandor turned and strode forward into the darkness.

The corridor ran in only a few yards, then ended at the foot of a flight of stairs. Wandor began climbing the stairs. The darkness was total to him, but no doubt the ape-men could see in such darkness. The way they had flinched back when the door was opened wide suggested that their eyes were sensitive.

As he climbed, part of Wandor's mind was focused on the problem of finding the next step upward. The other and larger part was projecting the image of the guard at the door standing peacefully, cautiously watching the men he had left down below. He hoped the men also were standing peacefully.

The stairs wound upward. Sometimes the bends were so sharp Wandor had to fumble for the next step, probing at the wall with his sword. The scrapings of metal on stone floated away into the blackness. At intervals his sword point struck the wood or metal fittings of a door. Whom should he thank for the inspiration that had led him to use the Mind Speech with the ape-men? Without it he would have fought the six below and no doubt killed them. But then their comrades would have been lying in wait behind every door on this night-sunken staircase. For all he knew, they still were. The idea made him increase the effort he was putting into the Mind Speech.

He knew the Temple of the Dwarf God rose high, that the base of the dome was as far above the ground as the top of the keep of Manga Castle. But in the darkness and the stale air it seemed that he had already climbed twice that far before he suddenly found himself taking two, three, four steps forward, instead of upward. He reached out with his sword and swung it in a full circle around him. It met no solid obstacle. He stepped forward and swung it again, faster.

There was no resistance this time, either. But along the path Wandor's sword had cut in the air, green light began to glow, incandescent, pulsing. It was as if he had cut into a great black bag filled with green light. It poured out all around him, over him, past him. It rose upward. It lit up the interior of the great dome, every square inch of dome and floor enameled in shimmering green. It was like being inside a gigantic emerald.

In the center of the dome rose a stout tripod of gleaming metal rods. Perched on top of the tripod was a circular platform. On that platform lay a human figure, and at his feet stood a helmet that made a little splash of gold in all the greenness.

Wandor lowered his sword and after a moment's hesitation thrust it firmly into its scabbard. Then he moved forward again. There was a moment of tingling skin, like bathing in a fast-flowing, bubbling stream. Then the tingling faded.

As he reached the base of the tripod, the figure on the platform stirred. Its limbs moved with a painful slowness, like the wheel of a mill starting up again after a century of abandonment. It rose and turned toward Wandor. As it turned, Wandor saw that it was dressed almost entirely in green-tunic, trousers, cloak, and ankle-length boots. But heavy silver gloves concealed the hands. And its face was invisible behind a pointed helm with a shimmering silver finish, broken only by narrow slits for the eyes and mouth.

CHAPTER 15

There was triumph in Baron Galkor's face as he looked at Count Arlor and King Nond standing before him in his chamber in the seaward tower of Fors Castle. Triumph not merely naked, but triumph that ran around flaunting its nakedness before all who looked on.

Count Arlor would have much preferred not to be looking on. But he was standing with his hands bound painfully tight behind his back, flanked on either side by one of Galkor's guards, trying to keep the desolation he felt within from showing on his own face. For no good reason he felt that letting Galkor see his despair would break down the last barriers he was raising against it. Nor did he want to show weakness before King Nond. How much of courage in the end was what other people would say of your cowardice?

If Nond was at all aware of what went on around him, no sign showed on his face. That face might have been a stone, and the thick graying beard and hair, moss growing on it. A surprisingly neat beard and hair, too. With nothing but his fingers. Nond had done a thorough job of combing out the leaves and brambles left in them by the days in the woods. Now he stood massively in the exact center of the room, legs braced well apart, hands clasped behind his back.

Those hands were not bound. Nond had done everything but kiss the feet of his captors to persuade them to leave him unbound. He painted himself in pathetic detail as a fat old man, too weak of wind and limb to harm a child and too slow of foot to outrun a turtle. Let them leave him his dignity if they could not leave him his crown. Arlor would have been disgusted by Nond's act if he had not known that it was just that. The king was applying his wholly unslowed and unweakened wits to the situation.

Galkor finished his inspection of the captives and stepped back behind his desk. Arlor heard sounds from the stairs—several sets of ascending feet, accompanied by the clink of chains. Galkor grinned.

"Your Majesty, Count Arlor," he said. "You came here hoping to flee into the Marches, where you think your cause is strong. No more." With a conjurer's wave of his arm he pointed at the door. For a moment it stayed closed, and Arlor saw the baron's face darken as his grand gesture sagged and faltered. Then the footsteps reached the top of the stairs, and the door swung open. Four armed guards tramped in, escorting a small figure, pale, and sagging under the weight of chains and weariness.

Gwynna.

Galkor's office seemed unchanged to Gwynna. After the long darkness of her cell, even the candlelight in the chamber half dazzled her. The baron stood squatly behind his equally low-slung carved desk. The two greatswords, hung crosswise on the wall behind him, still sent blue gleams darting into the room. Several massive chests stood by the walls. The thick carpets on the floor were the same solid colors as before.

Sickness nearly gripped her and dashed her helplessly down on the floor at the sight of the king and Count Arlor. Silently, she began to recite the *Dreil* Banishment. She *had* to stay calm and alert, however much despair seemed to be rising up inside her like a tide and threatening the ragged remnants of her self-control.

The spell began to take effect, clearing the way for other ideas to move freely about in her mind. Three people together in one place might contrive something against their captors. At least they would have a better chance than one person alone. No, two people, not three. Nond was unbound, but could he be relied on for anything? Her father's stories of Nond the warrior-king were stories of a Nond gone for the better part of thirty years. But Count Arlor was known as a deadly fighter, armed or unarmed. She couldn't make the first move herself. The chains would hamper and slow her too much. But she could be alert to follow up somebody else's move.

There was a long moment when Count Arlor did have to fight off the despair Galkor was trying to create in him. His mouth went dry, and his breath came harder than it had in the middle of some deadly battles. Then he looked at Gwynna more closely, saw her more clearly. As he looked at her, he saw her change. The eyes that had been half dosed and glazed with fatigue and shock were opening now, searching the room. The slim body straightened, as though the weight of the chains had suddenly vanished. She was like a bowstring now, ready to receive the arrow. But Arlor could only shift his feet an inch at a time, until he was braced for a leap or a roll. He could do nothing with his bindings, not in plain sight of eight guards and Baron Galkor. Not without alerting Galkor. And that man was no fool. He might have already noticed the change in Gwynna. But even so, Arlor could not help shifting his eyes slightly, from Galkor to Nond.

Nond did not acknowledge Gwynna's entrance by so much as a flicker of an eyelid or a pause in his even breathing. The outside world had lost its power to affect him. He saw it from a great height, as an eagle sees a lamb on the earth below.

He knew the sensation, although he had to throw his mind back thirty years to find its twin. As he led out the heavy cavalry at the Battle of Yost that had given Benzos this same Viceroyalty, the world had looked so. The eagle's vision had lasted him all the way to the enemy lines and through them.

Now he sensed Gwynna's alertness and Arlor's eyes shifting on to him. His own eyes lifted to rest on the greatswords hanging on the wall behind Baron Galkor.

As he saw Nond's eyes come to rest on the greatswords, Arlor could not help taking a deep breath. But before Galkor could react—before he could have reacted—Nond moved.

Without any warning tensing of muscles, his arms rose to shoulder height, then straightened with a sudden snap. Huge fists, clenched rock-hard, smashed like battering rams into the heads of the guards on either side of him. The men flew in either direction as though they had been kicked by a horse. Before either man had hit the floor, Nond plunged forward toward the desk, Baron Galkor, and the greatswords.

If Galkor had been a single foot farther to the left, he would have died in that room at that moment. As it was, he managed to duck around the end of his desk as Nond came at him. Nond's right fist swung at the Baron's head like a flail, grazing his temple but not stopping him. Ignoring everything except the need to get out of the room, Galkor vanished down the stairs like a ferret plunging down a rat hole.

The desk crashed back against the wall as Nond's charging bulk drove into it. Nond heaved himself forward until both hands clutched the hilt of one of the greatswords, then jerked. With a rasp of metal the sword came free. The king whirled with terrifying speed. The six-foot sword whistled through the air as he swung it in an arc, clearing a space around himself.

There were six guards left on their feet, four around Gwynna and two around Arlor. The count was bracing himself for a backward flip and roll when the door flew open and two more guards charged into the room. Their swords were already out, and both went straight at Nond, trying to rush him and get inside his guard.

Now it was Gwynna's turn to move. She plunged forward as though she were diving into water. The top of her skull rammed hard into the back of the guard immediately ahead of her. Thrown off balance, the man staggered forward, then went down squarely in the path of the two men charging Nond. The leader tripped over the falling man and in turn sprawled on the floor with a crash. The man in the rear was delayed a few seconds in getting around this sudden obstacle. That gave Nond's sword all the time it needed to slice through the man's neck as if it had been a stalk of asparagus. Nond stepped forward, and the first man drew a dagger and thrust frantically upward at the massive figure looming over him. Then there was a crunching sound like a market basket being smashed as Nond slammed a booted foot down on the man's chest.

Meanwhile, Gwynna was following up her first move. As she pitched forward she twisted at the hips, rolling to land on her back. Her legs came up and lashed out, driving both feet at a guard rushing at her with this truncheon raised. If he had used a sword, he might have had a chance. Instead, he folded up like a sailor's clasp knife as her feet took him squarely in the groin. He crashed down without even enough breath left in him to scream. Gwynna rolled to one side to clear the falling body, then rolled back, her hands feeling for his dagger. They closed on its hilt and jerked it free.

As Arlor saw that, be saw also that his own turn had come. He had fallen back toward the opposite side of the room, to give his two guards the impression that he was determined to remain passive. Both had taken their eyes off him, drawn their swords and daggers, and were staring at Nond, waiting for a chance to rush him.

Arlor took them from behind. Pivoting on his left foot, he swung his right in a scythe stroke at the right-hand man's back. It connected, hard enough to make the man scream and crumple. As the man did so, Arlor continued pivoting until he had his back to Gwynna, then sprang backward off his left foot He landed in a sitting position with his bound hands in easy reach of Gwynna 's dagger. The dagger had a razor's edge. It slashed through the ropes in a single swift motion.

As Arlor swung his arms out and sprang to his feet, the second of his guards ran at him, sword and dagger raised. For one moment Arlor saw his death approaching. Then Nond surged out of his position, into range of the man. There was not enough head room for an overhead stroke, so once again the sword flashed in a level arc, and once again a severed head flew high in a flurry of blood.

Nond's attack also saved Gwynna. The last two guards had pinned her arms to the ground and were within a split second of driving their swords into her heart. As they saw Nond surge forward, they forgot all about Gwynna and sprang toward the door. Arlor lunged bare handed at one before he could get his sword up to block, driving him back against the wall so hard his skull cracked on the stone. Gwynna rolled sideways against the other's feet, and he went down. His panic-stricken scream of denial that any of this could be happening to him ended abruptly as Nord's sword came down again. It was not a full-strength blow, but Arlor didn't notice the man moving afterward. As the echoes of the last scream died away, Arlor straightened and stared around the chamber. The only one of the ten guards still moving was the one Gwynna had butted in the back. Arlor went over to him and kicked him smartly in the head. He stopped moving. The guards Nond had felled were still breathing, but unconscious. The other seven were as dead as a mummified High Priest. Arlor locked and barred the door, then turned to Gwynna.

She was struggling to get to her feet, but her chains and her weakness kept her writhing feebly on the floor. Arlor went over to her and applied the point of a dagger to the locks on her chains. The locks were crude, Arlor was skilled, and Gwynna's hands and feet were free within moments. It was not until Gwynna stood on her own feet, tottering slightly, that Arlor turned to Nond.

"The gods must love you, sire," he said. "That could not have gone better if we had been practicing it for weeks." It was an inane remark, but he couldn't find words matching all the mixed emotions that were bubbling inside him. He wanted to shout out loud. But as he looked at the king more closely, fear swept all the other emotions into the back of his mind.

Nond was leaning on his sword like a beggar or a wandering priest leaning on his staff, and his normally ruddy face had gone pale. A broad red patch stained his robes at waist level, and the patch broadened still further as Arlor stared.

"Don't stand there gaping, Count Arlor," said Nond. His voice had much of its old peremptory tone, but not much of its old force. For a moment Arlor felt sicker than ever. Then he took a deep breath and felt the fear ebb.

"Good," said Nond. "You and Gwynna had best take your leave now."

Arlor must have gaped again because Nond's voice boomed out with almost its old power. "Stop worrying about me, you young idiot! There's nothing you can do for me. You and Gwynna can get out the window and swim for it."

With a great effort Arlor closed his mouth, slowed his breathing, and nodded. Nond was right. It was a clear drop of no more than sixty feet to the waters of the channel—not beyond either his powers or Gwynna's. Once in the water the darkness and the fog should hide them while the flowing tide carried them across the three miles of bay to the fishing villages.

"Good," said Nond. Knowing his last command to Arlor would be obeyed seemed to calm him. Now the king turned to Gwynna. His voice had notes of tenderness and something else Arlor could not name in it, as he spoke to her.

"My lady, I thank you for all you have done. Take my thanks to your father when you see him." Arlor noted that Nond did not say "if." His last moments at hand, Nond's self-confidence was actually increasing. "Tell him that such a man as he was—is—is a blessing the gods send to few kings. And tell Master Bertan Wandor, your husband—" the strange note was strong in Nond's voice now "—tell him that I wish him well. That is all a mortal king can do for him, even a King of Benzos."

Now it was Arlor's turn again. "Once more, Count Arlor, you have done all that could be done. As you did for all the years you served me. The gods keep you and speed you to safety. And do not grieve or lament that I will not live to see Cragor's end. Do not think that I will rest until he is dead and all who follow him destroyed. Never think that."

If Nond had wanted to say anything more, the sound of feet on the stairs cut him off. His pale face hardened, and he straightened, although the effort made him gasp and the stain widen further. "Galkor has his courage back and his men on the way. Time for you to leave." He took one hand from his sword hilt to raise in a farewell blessing.

Arlor bent and began unlacing his boots. Gwynna pulled on the shirt and breeches of one of the dead guards and strapped on a belt to which she tied three sheathed daggers. Barefooted, Arlor went to the window, opened the glass, and looked down. The slit in the heavy stonework had barely room for him to push himself through it. And it was a long way down. But the lapping of the water at the base of the tower was gentle, the ripples clearly visible through the fog.

Breathing hard, skin scraped raw by the rough stone, Arlor pushed himself through the window slit until he could press his hands against the outer wall. He took a deep breath, braced himself with both arms and legs, and with one mighty jerk of all his muscles plunged out into space and darkness.

King Nond saw Gwynna silhouetted for a moment, pale against the darkness outside. Then in a flicker she was gone. Now, except for that wolfpack howling on the other side of the door, he was alone. But it would hold them back for a little while. He considered dragging Galkor's desk against the door. But that would only speed the inward bleeding, so that perhaps he would be dead even before the men outside gathered up their courage to break in. And he wanted at least one more chance at his enemies before the life of his body flickered out.

Irony. A king who had once moved fifty thousand men across three thousand miles of Ocean with a few words on parchment now unable to move a desk against a door with his own muscles. But he saw clearly now how he had brought himself to this situation. He did not regret that this clarity of vision had come too late for him to use it. Only—now he could not even give advice to those who might come after him.

He had loved a war and a woman too much. The war in the Viceroyalty had been a beautiful dream for a young king anxious to see his fame blaze high, but also a fearfully expensive one. Estates and powers and privileges laboriously accumulated by the previous Kings of the House of Nabor had gone right and left to finance that dream. He had won his dream, but brought a nightmare to life along with it—the nobles of Benzos waxing mighty and mightier, as they had not done for six generations, until they needed only a leader to move against the Leopard Throne itself.

Through Nond's love of the one woman the nobles had found that leader. Queen Elrissa had not been a woman to every man's taste. Many thought her too domineering. To Nond she seemed as close to human perfection as possible, perhaps because he could never understand her. But he could understand well enough what he felt and what he resolved when she died giving birth to Anya. Another daughter had died at the age of three, but a third daughter and a boy of six could carry on the line. He could please himself, and it pleased him to remain faithful to Elrissa's memory.

Then suddenly the other two children were gone, and there was only Anya. Though Nond did his best to make up for the years when he had scorned and rejected Anya as her mother's murderer, the damage had been done. And perhaps he had not really wanted to undo it? The gods alone knew, and at this point they were the only ones to whom it made any difference.

So Anya grew up, the physical image of her mother, but with no smallest spark of her mother's character. Duke Cragor had not cared about Anya's lack of spirit for reasons that Nond now knew far better than he needed to. Cragor had also offered a mighty sum to the Royal Treasury in return for Anya's hand. To get rid of his accursed daughter and prop up his sagging finances at one blow was an opportunity Nond could not resist. So Anya married the Black Duke, and from that day ten years to this night Cragor's power had never ceased to wax Nond's to wane.

In fact, it was almost time for Nond's to go out like a snuffed candle. His senses were beginning to blur from the loss of the blood that now dyed the whole lower front of his robe. Thumps and curses and scrabbling footsteps outside suggested the men there had brought up a ram.

So why wait? Why let them choose the time? Nond's footsteps were silent as he moved to the door. His hand gripped the sword tighter, as his left reached down for the bar of the door. In a single swift motion he lifted it free and threw it away. It clattered to the floor as he raised the latch and stepped back, lifting his sword. A moment's silence from outside, and then the door flew open with a crash and Galkor's fighting men poured into the room.

Nond allowed himself a moment of regret that Galkor was not leading them, then settled down to his final battle. A man in full armor led the rush into the room, one who must have run up the stairs of the tower in that armor. He was slow on his feet and loud in his breathing. He tried to rush Nond, but the king backed away to the extreme limit of his sword's reach and then swung. The greatsword beat aside the attacker's shield and immobilized his shield arm. The return stroke beat aside his sword and crashed into his helmet. The man staggered, took a step backward, then collapsed into the ranks of the men behind him. His falling weight swept three of them off their feet, and they in turn others. Men fell with yells and clangings of armor and weapons that sounded like a blacksmith's shop violently upended and hurled down the stairs.

But three or four swordsmen made their way into the room past the fallen man. Too many, for suddenly they were all around Nond, and these men had no scruples about striking from behind. As he cut one in two with a slash that went on to tear apart another's thigh, Nond felt a searing stab in his lower back, then a second higher up. Dimly he was aware that the second stab had reached his lungs, that blood was welling up in his throat. He coughed and felt blood spurt between his teeth, with a fading vision saw it spatter the rug. A little more blood didn't matter now. There was so much already.

The sword dropped from his hands, and he felt the floor jar against his knees. He sagged forward, seeing the floor come up toward him, the gray stone turning darker, darker. Total darkness came down on him as be felt his face strike the rugs.

"I am dead."

Far off in the darkness tiny golden lights began to glow, like broken fragments of stars. They grew brighter, more numerous, spread out toward him, bobbing and darting like leaves on the surface of a fast-flowing stream.

"I am not dead. I fear this, and the dead cannot feel fear."

"You are dead. But you need not fear." The golden lights began to dance to the rhythm of the voice as it came out of the blackness. "I welcome your joining with me, Nond."

The golden lights were moving faster now, swirling like snowflakes before a blizzard. But there was a pattern to their swirling, as one by one they joined together, building a face out of the darkness. A brown-skinned face, black-bearded, eyes dark and grave, surmounted by a small gold cap. Then a powerful neck, broad chest, a warrior's muscles standing out. Around the neck a necklace, with five small gold crowns hanging from it.

"I do not fear," said Nond. "I join with you, Guardian of the Mountain, Five-Crowned King."

Gwynna and Arlor were swimming on their backs with slow steady strokes that made no splashes to attract attention. Not that they expected to attract any in the darkness and the gently swirling fog. At least the gods had contrived the flowing tide to give them some sense of direction across the bay.

Then the darkness was no longer complete, as a faint light the color of burnished gold began to pulse where the castle's seaward tower should be. In another moment they could both see the tower standing out black in the golden blaze. The light was all around it, behind it, dancing on the water, pouring from the windows and even seemingly from the stones. Now the whole castle stood out in the night, its bulk scarred by black shadows. It seemed to shrink and expand as the golden light pulsed and flickered.

Arlor's breath stopped the way it had done when he saw the sky flaming blue over Benzos. But there was only awe in him now, not the stark fear there had been then. This also was the light of great sorcery, but not the sorcery of an enemy. Arlor felt that deep within, and a quick look at Gwynna's face made the feeling stronger.

Pinched by confinement and cold as it was, Gwynna's face showed rapture as well as awe. It did not change until the golden light began slowly to fade.

"You look as though you had seen that before," said Arlor softly. "What is it?"

Again she shook her head. "I have not seen it. Not myself. But Bertan has seen it. He knows what it is. And he will tell you." Her voice trailed off, and she swam on in silence. Arlor was not sure that he wasn't glad she had chosen not to explain what lay behind them in the fading golden light

As he set his own limbs in motion again. Arlor looked back a final time toward the castle. The golden light was dying fast now, the masses of stone slipping back into shadow. But just before the darkness came down again, Arlor saw another brief flicker of light around the tower. Not golden, this light. Rather a luminescent green, darting around the tower with a fluttering motion like a moth around a candle flame. In one moment it was there, in the next moment it was gone, and then only the darkness remained.

In the blackness of the forest camp a faint noise near him

broke Wandor's sleep. He was instantly awake and alert, hand on his knife.

Cheloth of the Woods stood over him, silver-helmeted head bent toward him and silver-gloved hands crossed. The sorcerer's voice came out more muffled, less steady than usual. If he had wanted to apply human terms to Cheloth, Wandor would have said the sorcerer was breathing hard.

"Your wife Gwynna and Count Arlor have together escaped from the castle of Fors," said Cheloth. "They have reached the landward side of Fors Bay safely. They plan to steal horses and ride south toward the Marches." Wandor was up on his feet in a single movement. "How do you know?" The question burst out before he realized that he didn't altogether want to know the answer.

"I sent my Watcher to Fors," said Cheloth. "What It saw, It told me." Wandor decided he most certainly did not want to know more. "It also saw King Nond die in battle with the fighting men of Baron Galkor while covering the escape of Arlor and Gwynna. But only his body is slain. The rest of him has for a time joined itself with the Guardian of the Mountain."

Wandor sat down again, ignoring a sharp stone that jabbed into his thigh. So the Guardian of the Mountain had reached out again, this time to receive Nond's spirit. The Guardian of the Mountain had struck into the world. Nem of Toshak—or at least his powers—were abroad. Cheloth of the Woods rode north, with a Watcher that could tell him of events a thousand miles away. On all sides things dreadful or merely awe-inspiring were pouring into the world like water through a broken dam.

Wandor would have been frightened, if he had thought it would do him any good.

CHAPTER 16

A week passed, another week toward autumn and the end of the campaigning season for all save the bold or the desperate. But this year there were enough of both in the Viceroyalty of the East to make peasant and burgher alike go about their daily business in the knowledge that war would flare even through the winter snows. Few welcomed it, except those to whom it promised a profit. Few knew all that was at stake, or cared. Most found more interest in the abundant harvest, the most abundant in the history of the Viceroyalty, and in wondering whether Duke Cragor would demand grain be sent across the Ocean to eke out the scanty harvest in Benzos itself. But those who had seen the blue fire of Toshak or the golden fire of the Guardian of the Mountain playing about Fors Castle looked toward the autumn with apprehension, even terror.

In that week Arlor and Gwynna rode south toward the Marches on a succession of stolen horses, hungry, weary, constantly looking over their shoulders for signs of pursuit. Wandor and Cheloth of the Woods rode north toward the Plains. Cheloth's magic kept the menaces of the Blue Forest at a safe distance, and Wandor rode with a song of triumph in his heart and the Helm of Jagnar in his saddlebags. Flawing his happiness was only the knowledge that Gwynna and Count Arlor were not yet safe within the Marches.

Arlor's horse began to pant as the trail steepened. He saw the trail ahead vanish upward along the gloomy slopes of still another forested hill. Gwynna pulled up alongside him as he reined in. She swayed gently in her saddle. Arlor stared at her face, even whiter than usual in the shadows under the trees. That she didn't fall from the saddle in sheer exhaustion was a miracle wrought daily since they left Fors. She had long since tapped her last resources of physical strength and such magic as she could perform without a physical drain. Now sheer will power was pushing her along. Arlor had known many women and loved or at least made love to his share, but he had never before been in awe of one. That Wandor had taken this woman to wife suggested things about him the count had never considered before.

With an obvious effort Gwynna focused her gaze on Arlor. "We don't want to stop too long. We have to reach the next village before dark. It's not safe to sleep in the woods, anymore. This is Khindi hunting territory."

Arlor nodded and jabbed his spurs into the horse's side. It barely responded. They would have to look for fresh mounts before another day's riding. Slowly the horse began to put one hoof in front of another, its head drooping toward the beaten grass of the trail.

They came upon the village, and the Khindi came upon them almost in the same moment. For a few seconds they stared at the huddle of log huts in the clearing, the smoke curling out of their chimneys, the furs and hides hung on poles—all visible in the clearing by the trail, seemingly close enough to touch. Then across their vision of the village flitted a score of dark figures, bows in their hands, feathers bobbing in their hair.

Arlor was out of the saddle with his sword in his hand before his thoughts caught up with him. When they did, he did not stop or slow down or put his sword away. He and Gwynna could not hope to flee, and he knew that he at least would not be captured again. Not alive.

The Khindi scattered like field mice caught by a hawk as Arlor plunged in among them. He knew they carried no close-combat weapons but knives and hatchets. He knew also that no man alive could survive with one of those against his swordsmanship. He would slash and hack and kill, feel bones smash and see blood spurt, until the madness within him was purged or the Khindi managed to bear him

123

down by sheer weight of numbers. All the months of frustration spewed up from him now like lava from a volcano.

The lava overflowed on to the Khindi. Arlor's sword darted out like a steel snake's tongue and licked along the arm of the nearest warrior. The man made no sound, but leaped aside as Arlor closed, raging that he had not killed the man with one stroke. It took him two more before the Khind was down, arm severed at the shoulder and neck gushing blood.

Now the Khindi were forming a circle around Arlor, slinging their bows and drawing their hatchets and knives. Arlor spat on the ground at the sight, roared curses and threats of what would happen if they dared close against him. The blood pulsed in his temples until he felt his head was going to burst open like an overripe fruit.

Then Gwynna ran up to him, mouth wide open. He realized she was screaming, not in fear or pain, but at him. But the roar of blood and fury in his ears was drowning her out. Like a figure seen in a dream, she opened and shut her mouth, but no sound came out. He started forward again.

A Khind warrior rushed to meet him, hatchet in one hand, knife in the other. Arlor's sword sliced off the hand that held the knife. But the warrior kept on coming. He swung the flat of the hatchet at Arlor's head, leaped in as Arlor ducked and missed his thrust. The warrior clamped his good hand down on Arlor's sword arm and thrust his spouting wrist in the count's face. Surprise and the hot blood gushing in his eyes left Arlor half blinded and half paralyzed. The Khind tightened his grip, and Arlor felt red-hot pain shoot up his sword arm as nerves protested. He was vaguely aware of his fingers opening and his sword falling to the ground. He was terribly aware of a knee corning up into his groin and doubling him up. He was dimly aware of collapsing on to the ground, pebbles digging into his face. And after that he was aware of nothing.

Cheloth's figure, for long minutes rigid as he stood beside the road, now showed signs of life. Slowly the silver-helmeted head turned toward Wandor. Although no more of Cheloth's expression than before came through the narrow eye slits. Wandor was instantly certain that

Cheloth had bad news.

"Bertan Wandor," said Cheloth. His voice was as subdued as an almost totally expressionless voice could be. "Gwynna and Count Arlor have been captured by the Khindi. Arlor was in a great rage and slew one Khind, wounded another. I do not know whether he will be kept alive or not."

For a moment, Wandor, too, was in a great rage. In that moment, if he could have, he would have blasted the whole Khind people from grandsires to newborn infants with a curse in this world and in all the worlds to come. But the moment passed swiftly. In large part it passed because Wandor was too near exhaustion to sustain any powerful emotion for long.

Cheloth seemed to sense the flare of rage and its passing. He stared at Wandor in silence, then said, "Do not expect the Mind Speech from Gwynna. She is almost at the end of her strength. I will keep my Watcher close about them, and in time I think I can intervene to good purpose."

"Why not now, for the love of all the gods?" exploded Wander, loud enough to make the other men tum in their saddles and stare at him.

"The time is not ripe. We must wait until Gwynna and Arlor come before a Tree Sister of the Khindi."

The Tree Sisters were the most revered priestesses of the Khindi. Wandor fell silent. Cheloth obviously had some plan of his own. Even if he had not, there would have been little use in protesting. To move Cheloth from a decision he had taken was as pointless as matching a child's spoon against a sword in a duel.

The rage still burned in Arlor when he awoke, making his throbbing head throb still more. To find himself tied upright to a stake set in the ground did not improve matters. Nor did seeing the Khindi piling brush about his feet. And least of all did his hearing what they were saying.

"Is it wise—sacrificing this one?"

"No pay for him. Black War Leader wants him killed. The woman—both sides want her. We give her to the one that pays most.

Look at her, see a thousand iron hatchet heads. Then you will stop wanting to bum her."

"Good thought."

"And this one is a stronger war spirit. The High Hunter will be more pleased."

So he was to be sacrificed to Masutl, the High Hunter of the Khindi. No doubt to ensure a safe trip home or something equally petty. If his rage had left room for any other emotion, Arlor could have felt the ignominy of his career and hopes all ended for no other purpose than to speed a Khind hunting party safely home.

Then on the far side of the small clearing, Arlor saw Gwynna sitting on the ground. Her face was still more pinched and white, as though she'd been drowned. Their eyes met, and Gwynna seemed to sense the rage sputtering in Arlor. She shook her head. His jaw tightened, and he was on the edge of blazing out at Gwynna. What in the name of all the gods was she doing? Or not doing?

Then Arlor's volley of oaths died unspoken, and his mouth was suddenly as clogged and dry as if it had been filled with feathers. Near the top of a tree on the opposite side of the clearing a green light began to glow. It brightened, then drifted away from the tree and downward with a fluttering motion. It drifted back and forth across the clearing, reminding Arlor of a hunting dog on a scent. Then suddenly it stopped in midair, tightened itself into a compact ball, and plummeted straight down at him. Even Gwynna started and jumped to her feet. As for the Khindi, some flung themselves flat on the ground and began muttering prayers. Arlor heard a flurry of snapping twigs and thudding feet as the rest scattered into the forest.

Tied to the stake, he could not have run if he had wanted to. But there was still too much anger in him for that, an anger no longer hot but icy cold. He raised his head to glare at the falling light and raised his voice in an angry bark.

"And what's your game, little green thing?" he snarled. "Or are you playing somebody else's?" As if it had heard him, the green light stopped dead in the air a few feet above his head. Then it darted around behind him. Arlor felt a pulsing coolness flowing around him and something tugging at his wrists. Then he realized that the leather thongs tying him to the stake were gone. He was free. He kicked the brushwood away from around his feet and stepped away from the stake.

But still he did not run. Half of his mind told him that no material weapon would have any effect on the light. The other half told him to snatch up a fallen hatchet and let fly. The second half won out. The hatchet arched upward, straight into the heart of the greenness. A sizzling sound like an egg dropped on a hot frying pan, a puff of acrid smoke, and a flare of green light that lit up the whole clearing and drove several more Khindi into the bushes. Then the green light soared up and vanished into the twilight above the trees. The hatchet dropped to the ground with a thump. Its handle was now a few charred splinters, the iron head blackened and half melted.

How long Arlor stood staring at the ruined hatchet he never remembered. Certainly long enough for the Khindi who had fled to overcome their fear. One by one they crept back into the clearing. They gathered around Arlor, staring at him, not trying to bind him to the stake again.

One of the warriors stepped forward until his hooked nose was almost in Arlor's face. "Fear-No-Devil," he said slowly, then looked about for a response from the other Khindi. There were nods and murmurs of agreement from all of them. "Fear-No-Devil," repeated the warrior.

Arlor realized that he had just been given a praise name, according to Khind custom. This meant also that he could no longer be sacrificed to Masutl. But it did not mean that he as safe. It merely meant that he and Gwynna would be kept alive until they could be brought before some person or persons of higher rank among the Khindi.

In any case his rage was ebbing now, and he no longer wanted to get his hands around the nearest Khind throat and squeeze. The Khindi were leading Gwynna forward now, cutting the bonds on her wrists as well. He took her hand, feeling all the bones under the thin layer of flesh, and squeezed it gently.

"The Khindi are taking Arlor and Gwynna to a Tree Sister," said Cheloth. "The Watcher has done its work. And Arlor has gained a

Khind praise name."

"What is it?"

"'Fear-No-Devil'."

"So." The monosyllable summed up the emotional emptiness in Wandor's mind. In that emptiness echoed the words of the Guardian of the Mountain:

"Go and win the faith of Strong-Axe and Fear-No- Devil."

Berek was Strong-Axe. He had sworn the Oath of the Drunk Blood to Wandor, the most potent of all oaths that one of the Sea Folk could swear. Now there was Count Arlor, and he was Fear-No-Devil. What oath would *he* swear? Wandor knew he would have to tell Arlor the whole story. The count had become part of Wandor's mist-shrouded destiny. Or was it so, anymore? Bit by bit, the mist seemed to be blowing away.

Wandor shook his head and clucked his tongue at his weary horse. They moved on through the drizzling rain.

The Khindi and their captives reached the Khind village on the evening of the fourth day. The ground was still squishy-damp underfoot, and thunder rumbled vaguely in the west, but for the moment a pale sun leaked a golden glow through breaking clouds overhead.

The village was a large one, but Gwynna's world had shrunk so that she could make out none of the details, shrunk to the ground one step ahead and the endless battle to take that one step. Then in time there was darkness overhead and a floor of beaten earth underfoot. They were inside a Khind hut. She sagged to me floor and lay there, too exhausted to use either sleep or magic to restore herself.

In the formless time that followed, she was aware once of a gaunt figure with a brown face standing over her. Wide-spaced dark eyes that seemed out of place in that face stared down at her. A sure hand pressing a wooden cup of something hot, steaming, and acrid to her lips, keeping the cup there until most of the liquid had gone down her throat, then wiping off what had dribbled down her chin. Then the hand vanished.

Gradually the world again took shape around Gwynna. The

smoke-grimed poles and slabs of bark of the roof overhead. Clay pots and woven rush baskets piled against the walls. Count Arlor, face dark as any Khind with sun and dirt, squatting in the middle of the floor. But before he could move, the gaunt figure was there again, seemingly grown from the dirt floor.

The Tree Sister looked neither powerful, mysterious, nor terrifying. The dark eyes were incongruously young in the wrinkled brown face, but otherwise the woman looked more like a cheerful old country midwife than a priestess. Gwynna felt an extra warmth, an extra restoring power from the Tree Sister's smile.

"There, daughter," she said, The Tree Sister knew no Hond—few of the Khindi of the forests did—but Gwynna's Khind was good enough that it stayed with her even now. "You were far along the road back to the Spring of Life, but you will stay with us now. You have much to explain, you and Fear-No-Devil. There is much that you have done and seen that I want to know."

Before the drink and the old woman's soothing presence did their work, Gwynna could not have said two words to save her life. But now she found herself pouring out the tale of the past few months, with all its battles, intrigues, sorceries, and quests, Her mention of Wandor's journey into the Blue Forest in search of Cheloth and the Helm of Jagnar brought the Sister up short.

"How now, this is news I had not heard."

"We wanted to—"

"Keep it a secret. Indeed, and that was fitting and proper. But I understand now that green light that sent a dozen good Khind warriors scampering into the bushes. Though I don't know," she said slowly. "I swear by the Spring itself, the thought of Cheloth again almost frightens me. So much of great sorceries these days, and so little of the small clean magics I can understand." She shook her head wearily. "Well, going backwards never brought man to his goal, unless by chance he walked in a circle. You say you have the Mind Speech with Wandor?"

"Yes, but—"

The Sister motioned Gwynna to silence, then poured another steaming cup from the jug. This time she also crumbled a handful of herbs into the liquid. "Go on, daughter. Drink. It's no drug. Just a brew that will help you find the last little bits of strength in you, wherever they're hiding."

Gwynna took the cup and drained it. After all, if they were going to poison her, they would do so sooner or later. She slapped at the shaft of despair the way she would have slapped at a buzzing insect. Then it seemed to fade away by itself as the herbs took hold.

A distant drum began to roll faint and low in her head. The pain from her bruises and blisters faded. She heard the hiss of air in and out of her lungs, the *lub-dub*, *lub-dub* of blood in and out of her heart. She lifted a hand, and it seemed to rise on the subtle currents of the air like a bit of dandelion fluff. The drum roll sounded louder for a moment, then suddenly faded. As it did, she knew that her mind was clear again, her strength somehow restored. Slowly and carefully she began the familiar pattern of focusing her mind for Speech with Bertan.

For the first time in weeks Wandor sensed one of Gwynna's Mind Speech probes at the fringes of his own awareness. He put all the effort he could into concentrating, to responding, to breaking through to her.

Then he was aware of another mental pulse, sweeping in between his mind and Gwynna's as they struggled to reach each other, completing the link. He did not dare break his concentration enough to turn and look at Cheloth. The link solidified, and meaning began to flow through it.

("Bertan. Where are you?")

("A day's north of the river. Moving fast, though. We—")

("Is Cheloth of the Woods with—is that other Che—?")

("I am.") Even Cheloth's thoughts seemed to come out cool, expressionless.

A moment of jumbled and barely controlled emotions that nearly shattered the link in spite of Cheloth's efforts to hold it again. Then:

("Have you the Helm of Jagnar?") More raw, confused emotion in that question.

("Yes.")

("Then you must show—")

("You must both have my aid,") came from Cheloth. If there had been an emotional tone in that thought, Wandor would have called it superciliousness.

Cheloth took two steps aside from the road. At the third step he seemed to freeze into a wooden rigidity. His thoughts came to Wandor.

("Take the Helm of Jagnar the Forest King from its bag. Put it on your head.")

Wandor leaped out of his saddle, nearly turning an ankle in his haste. He tore at the lashings of the saddlebags. As he did so, he saw a faint green glow begin to swell around Cheloth. By the time he had opened the saddlebags, the glow was brightening and spreading. As Wandor lifted the helm and put it on his head, the glow spread out far enough to envelop him. He expected some feeling—a coolness, a tingling'? There was none. He tightened the chin strap of the Helm and waited.

In the hut, Gwynna leaped to her feet and dashed for the door. She was fumbling at the latch when Arlor caught up with her.

"What the devils—?"

"I must go outside. All the Khindi must see this." Arlor stepped aside at the expression on her face. A moment now, and she was outside in the cool, smoky air of the evening. She stepped out into an open space between the huts, ignoring the stares of the Khindi. A wavering green nimbus began to form around her. The huts and the Khindi crowding around began to look as though she were seeing them through rippling green waters.

The nimbus spread. As it did, part of it began to solidify and take on a definite shape.

The forest and the others of the party faded away from around Wandor. Instead, he saw a Khind village—the long huts, the campfires, the warriors pushing forward while the women and children drew back or hid. He saw Gwynna standing slim and straight in the middle. And he saw the eyes of the warriors turn toward him and knew they were looking at him.

* * *

131

Wandor sat his horse in the middle of the Khind village, and beside him stood a tall, stiff figure dressed in green except for the silver of helmet and gloves. But it was the helmet on Wandor's head that drew all eyes. A simple open-faced pointed helm, there was little about it to set it apart from all the others on the heads of Ancient Days warriors carved on tombs. But it shone golden and bore a line of shimmering green leaves in low relief across the brow.

It was the Helm of Jagnar.

Gwynna saw recognition flare in the staring eyes of the watching Khindi. She saw them going down into the cross-legged sitting position in which the Khindi did formal worship.

And then she saw something else. A faint blue glow began to wash about the fringes of the area now filled with Cheloth's green aura. Sorcery of Toshak was thrusting against her link with Wandor and Cheloth at a moment when they were all terribly vulnerable. Death pulsed in that blueness.

Now she needed to maintain one link, establish a second, and then maintain them both together. Zakonta had taught her how to do it. But *could* she do it in a moment where the magic of Cheloth, of the *Red Seers*, and of Nem of Toshak would all be surrounding her, struggling around her?

She was barely aware of stripping off her clothes, for she had no part of her mind left to spare for mere physical self-awareness. The formula for calling the *Red Seers* to her aid was also something she could go through in her sleep. But how long would she have before the sorcerers maintaining the Toshakan spell noticed what she was doing?

They were noticing it already. She felt little stabs of cold fire thrusting into her mind and saw the blueness dart and waver in more solid shafts with a silver tinge. Wandor and Cheloth were sensing what was about. She felt them pouring more of their strength into keeping their link alive. But where were the *Red Seers*? How many of them would she find in a receptive state? How long would it take them to form the massive link that alone enabled them to bring their full power to bear?

On the fringes of her mind she felt that link begin to form, small and insecure even though it was already reaching out for her. Small, insecure, and with the powers of Toshak to penetrate. She felt those powers rising like a wall between her and the *Red Seers*. Again she stamped out a swirl of despair. Emotion threatened her concentration, and there was nothing left to her but that concentration.

No—she sensed something new. Along the link from her to Wandor raw power came pouring like a river in flood. It struck the wall of Toshakan magic, and like that same river striking a village, it smashed the wall and swept it away. The link among the *Red Seers* swelled up and broke through to embrace her, swallow her up, drain her of the last of her strength. She saw the blue glow break up in a shower of blue and silver fire specks. Each of these faded. And then everything else faded away, also.

Wandor just managed to avoid falling on his face as he slipped out of the saddle. His head felt as though somebody had tried to split it open with a dull axe and nearly succeeded. He lay face down on the sodden grass, feeling its coolness against his face, until he thought he had enough control of his limbs to stand up.

As he did, Cheloth came over to him. The sorcerer was walking slowly, with a care that suggested he also did not altogether trust his senses or his limbs.

"The Khindi are yours to do with as you will. You wear the Helm of Jagnar, and you have found Cheloth of the Woods. But your enemies know this, also. They hurled themselves against us while we were maintaining the image link. But I saw the means to defeat them and used it. It was as I have done before." Wandor realized that the "before" Cheloth meant was his battle with Nem of Toshak two thousand years before. Once more he had to fight off an inner chill at the idea.

He nodded, then winced at the pain stabbing through his head. "Then the time for sorcery is past, at least for the moment?" Whether it was true or not, he badly wanted to believe it.

"For the moment, yes. A wise sorcerer will retreat from a new situation until he learns what its dangers are."

"Is Kaldmor the Dark a wise sorcerer? I never thought he was."

"Indeed he *was* not. But there is such a thing as borrowed

wisdom."

CHAPTER 17

Galkor's chamber in the seaward tower had been cleansed of the signs of the death struggle of ten days before. The bodies were doubtless now food for the fishes deep in the chill black waters outside the channel entrance. The blood had been scrubbed and scraped and even burned from the stone. And for two whole days the windows had all stood open and the sea breezes whistled chill and damp through the chamber. A more prolonged gust of salt-flavored wind came rushing in, making Kaldmor the Dark shiver. He felt cold and desperately weary in body and wretched and uncertain in mind. And he found something unnatural in Baron Galkor's calm concentration on his paperwork. The baron's calm was only a surface show, Galkor knew. The frenzied orders for the cleaning—almost the purification—of the chamber showed that. But it was an appearance that Galkor felt compelled to keep up, and perhaps he was right. Certainly few in the castle and none too many in all of Fors had nerves altogether unshaken by that night. Some indeed had already abandoned jobs, service, and at times even family and home, to flee into the countryside. They preferred to face the oncoming winter in the country or even the Khind-haunted wilderness rather than remain in a city with such sorcery looming over it. Perhaps Galkor had to preserve the gravity of a temple image, lest panic and chaos descend on the city.

But he, Kaldmor, was not stolid, stubborn, or unimaginative, or even capable of pretending to be any of these things. He was frightened. And he was going to do his best to convince Galkor that

135

there was something of which to be frightened. He cleared his throat, setting off a paroxysm of coughing. When he could speak again, and Galkor's dark eyes were finally fixed on him, he began.

"My lord baron. Do you really understand what happened the night of King Nond's death?"

Kaldmor knew at once that he could have chosen his words better. Galkor raised eyes that were for the moment too weary to be angry and said, "Stop trying to impress me with your mysterious knowledge. I understand that a considerable amount of magical power other than your own has appeared during the last ten days. Do I need to understand anything more?"

Stung by Galkor's tone, Kaldmor stopped trying to choose his words carefully. "You do. Much more. And if you do not listen now, I will find it hard to be of any service to you in the future. Until ten days ago I was certain that I had the strongest possible magic at my command. Now I am no longer certain. In fact, I would say that the odds are now against me."

He explained crisply what the intervention of the Guardian of the Mountain at Nond's death implied. He went on to deal with the moment when he felt the powers of Cheloth of the Woods flooding along the link between Wandor and Gwynna, tearing at his mind until nothing he dared use could prevent him from being driven away and back. Cheloth of the Woods, the ancient conqueror of Toshak, crossing two thousand years to ride again at Bertan Wandor's right hand. And on Wandor's head the Helm of Jagnar, so that he had only to call and the Khindi would answer and come forth to do as he bid them.

The Khindi were something Galkor could understand—a human foe. Whatever might draw them from their forests, they would come on their human feet with their human bows in their hands. Or so Galkor said.

"There will be no advance against the Marches before next spring," said Galkor with a shrug. "More than half the royal troops have left for home, so we at least have much less to fear from them. But with all the reinforcements that Cragor has sent, we still have less than thirty thousand reliable men for all purposes. And we will now need at least twice that many to take and hold the Marches. Cragor will not be very happy about that, I suspect. But he is too good a soldier to deny obvious facts."

"Then what are we going to do?" said Kaldmor sharply. "Nothing?"

"I do not know what *you* are planning to do," said Galkor. "I myself am going to prepare Fors, Yost, and the fortified towns along the High Road to stand off Khind raids. That will involve much work and take every reliable man we have. But if you wish to call it 'nothing,' I cannot stop you."

Kaldmor's jaws snapped together like a trap, and his face went hot with rushing blood. But his fury ebbed before he could find words to express it. He could not feel sorry for anyone but himself, but at times he could at least understand another's problems. Nond's death, Arlor's and Gwynna's escape, fear of the Black Duke's displeasure, the turmoil in the garrison and the town (both teeming with rumors like aged meat with maggots), these made up a burden that Kaldmor knew he could never have shouldered himself. Small surprise, therefore, that Galkor's temper had shortened. He should realize that much more arguing with the baron could lead to an open break. And then? Each of them could easily destroy or cripple the other, leaving the survivor easy prey to Wandor and his allies, now swollen to a terrifying host after the journey to the Blue Forest. No, he would have to keep his mouth shut, his anger controlled, and his relations with Galkor the best possible.

The blood flowed from his face. He turned and strode out as Galkor bent to his papers again.

Laughter sounded, wine splashed in cups, smiles crinkled faces at Castle Delvor again. A Wandor crossed the courtyard, the smell of roasting pork following him, he realized how gray and gloom-hued the castle had been before the journey. Two months ago he would have cheerfully sold his soul to bring to the castle half the life and joy he heard around him this night. Even Baron Delvor shared in the rejoicing, for all his doubts about the means Wander had used to bring it about.

A momentarily disagreeable thought. Suppose Baron Delvor had foresworn any further part in the struggle for Benzos, now that the struggle had become still more deeply enmeshed with sorcery? Wandor shrugged. That was a folly beyond Baron Delvor's powers. And even if he had done this, there was now Count Arlor to lead Nond's cause.

Count Arlor—Fear-No-Devil. The Guardian's words made flesh once again, in a way more formidable than Wandor had ever imagined possible. The count must have limits, of course, and he certainly had blind spots—Princess Anya above all. But neither had kept him from faithful service to Nond to the king's last moments. Neither would keep him from equal service to Nond's avengers. And he had begun that service very early—and very well.

Gwynna had been unconscious for three days after her part in the Showing of the Helm, at times very close to the door of the House of Shadows. But the Tree Sister and Arlor kept watch over her, and all that herbs and prayers and vigilant nursing could do had been done. In the end it was enough, and then it was Gwynna's turn to join with the Tree Sister in nursing Arlor. The tight-wound spring that had driven him from Manga Castle to the Khind camp had finally snapped. It was Arlor who came to Castle Delvor on a litter borne by eight stout Khind warriors and Gwynna who leaped cat-graceful down from her horse and flung herself into Wandor's arms.

Wandor had wept then in joy and relief. And he had wept later, without shame, as he tried to tell Arlor how much he owed the count. "Three or four times she was at the end of her strength, and if the gods had so much as blinked, she would have been gone. But the gods did not blink, thanks to you."

"Small thanks to me, Bertan. Perhaps more to King Nond. But no man can compel the gods." A pause. "Except perhaps you." And the look in Arlor's weary eyes had asked the question his lips could not shape. *Who are you?*

So Wandor told him.

"If I ever cease to do right by my guests," Baron Delvor was fond of saying, "you will know that it is time to send for the priests of Alfod the Judge to give me the Parting."

So in the high-ceilinged Trophy Room beeswax candles burned in the gilded chandeliers, reflected in the polished top of the long table. The finest wines and spirits and beers from the castle's cellars glowed in crystal and silver cups. As the last of the servants vanished, bearing the last remnant of dinner with them, Arlor drained his cup and looked around the table at the company gathered there.

Beyond doubt or dispute it was the strangest and most ill-assorted council of war Arlor had ever attended in his life. Show it to any ten Knights, and tell them it held the fate of a manor farm, let alone a kingdom, in its hands. Seven of the Knights would roll on the floor laughing, two would challenge you on the spot, and the tenth would run screaming into the streets.

Two Khind war chiefs, with a Tree Sister sitting between them as their interpreter and adviser. Three Plainsmen—Jos-Pran for the War Chiefs, Zakonta for the *Red Seers*, the Speaker of the Gray Mares for the Speakers. Gwynna Wandor, a woman, admittedly of noble birth and great war wisdom, but still a woman. The three relatively orthodox members of the council—Baron Oman Delvor, Sir Gilas Lanor, and himself. Berek, a mere freedman of Sea Folker stock, sworn to Bertan Wandor by the Oath of the Drunk Blood.

And Bertan Wandor himself. By the laws of Benzos a mere House Master of the Order of Duelists—not a high status outside the Order, though not one despised by wise men of any order. By position the House Duelist of House Delvor, leader of its scouts, son by marriage to the baron. By actual—call them "circumstances" (a word sounding more suitable for a lawyer's deposition, but Arlor could not bring himself to say "miracles")—Rider of the King Horse of the Yhangi, wearer of the Helm of Jagnar. In fact if not in law or name, supreme ruler over both Plainsmen and Khindi, and of all the people at this table the only one whose lightest word could set a hundred thousand warriors on the move.

So Wandor sat at the head of the table, and all the others stared at him, waiting for him to speak.

Arlor suspected that all the stares merely made Wandor even more self-conscious than he was already. They probably kept him silent much longer than he would have been otherwise. Gwynna, perennially restless, was beginning to fidget when Wandor finally spoke.

"We need to think of going on with the war against Duke

139

Cragor in spite of what has happened." Wandor did not mention Nond by name, out of deference to the Khindi's feelings about their conqueror. "Certainly *he* will not have changed his plans. He will be as determined as ever to conquer the Marches, now the last center of resistance against him.

"But our new allies make us so strong that Cragor will not dare attack us until his army here is much stronger. And that will not be before spring opens the Ocean to his fleets again." The Khindi smiled gravely as the Tree Sister translated Wandor's words. Their leap from despised pariahs up to indispensable allies was a great one, almost as great as Wandor's from Duelist up to—what? Wandor acknowledged the smiles with a nod and continued, more fluent now as he moved into presenting his war plans.

"This gives us six full months at least before Cragor can go over to the offensive. We can win the Viceroyalty securely in that time."

"But—" Baron Delvor started in, then stopped as Gwynna squeezed his arm gently but firmly.

Wandor nodded. "I know what you are thinking. Fall and winter are not the seasons for campaigning. But you who fought off Cragor's raiders last fall know better than I that there is more tradition than necessity behind this notion."

The baron nodded. "Perhaps."

But Sir Gilas shook his head. "It will mean waiting until the ground freezes hard enough for wagons, another two months at least. Even then we will need to pick up food and fodder along the march. How are we going to get that?"

"The peasants may be willing. In fact, they probably will be when we have a victory to show them. That makes it all the more important for us to do something new and not wait until we can make a regular campaign. I'm thinking of a quick stroke to take Yost. That will give us a seaport and leave Cragor with no good base south of Fors itself. The fortified towns along the High Road—"

"God's above!" exploded Baron Delvor. "Yost is a fortified city of thirty thousand people, with a garrison four thousand strong. And we haven't a single siege engine to our name!"

"I didn't say a 'siege of Yost'," said Wandor with mild

asperity. "I said 'a quick stroke'." He turned to the Khindi "How many fully equipped warriors, could you have within a night's march of Yost in three weeks' time?"

The Khindi consulted together in their own language for a moment. The Tree Sisters turned to Wandor. "We cannot send enough to do you proper honor. In twice that time—"

Wandor held up a hand. "For the moment, Revered Sister and warriors, I am not interested in honor. I am interested in winning a battle, for your people as much as for mine. If you can give me—oh, call it four or five thousand warriors, I will call it honor enough for now. We would be hard put in any case to find supplies for more than that."

Further mutterings in Khind, then, "Four thousand will be easy."

"Good," said Wandor. He turned to the Plainsmen. "Jos-Pran, you called for six thousand warrior's. When will the last of them be here and ready to fight?"

"A week, with good weather. A few days more if the roads are wet. But our horses are light, not like your heavy wagons for food and tents," with a sly look at Sir Gilas Lanor.

"Four thousand Khindi, six thousand Plainsmen, a thousand cavalry and infantry of House Delvor, perhaps five hundred from House Lanor—my lord count, do you think you and Baron Delvor could persuade some of the other Marcher Houses to loan us their mercenary contingents for a few weeks? We would pay adequately."

Baron Delvor muttered something like, "What with?" but nodded. So did Arlor.

"Good, again. That makes, perhaps another two thousand men, certainly fifteen hundred. So in a month we can have an army of at least thirteen thousand men within striking distance of Yost." He paused as if he were deliberately leaving a silence for somebody to fill.

Sir Gilas filled it. "But not inside Yost," he said. "How are we going to manage that?" The young Knight no longer sounded skeptical, merely curious.

"When our men, particularly the fierce Khindi and the savage Plainsmen—" drawing grins from both the Tree Sister and Jos-Pran "—march on Yost, there will be a panic in the surrounding villages and farms. Their people will try to flee to Yost and shelter themselves within its walls."

He looked around the room. "Why shouldn't we send in some fugitives of our own?" There was a moment's silence as the words sank in; then even Baron Delvor's face lit up with a slow, triumphant grin.

The gray light that comes before dawn was washing over the castle when Wandor and Gwynna and Arlor finally climbed out on the roof of the keep. Arlor sat down on the parapet. He had to fight a desire to press his aching head against the dew-damp, night-chilled stone.

"Is it wise, keeping the Marcher lords out of our council until after Yost?" he asked Wander.

"It's wiser than letting them sit on it. You know the Marcher lords, Arlor. With all thirty-odd of them in there tonight, we'd still be arguing over whether I had the right to lead. As it is, the orders are already going out." A clatter of hooves from below underlined his remarks, as two mounted messengers cantered across the drawbridge.

"Besides," added Wandor, "if we were using mostly the Marcher levies, they'd be right in doubting that I should command. There are a dozen lords with far more experience than I in fighting conventional battles with heavy cavalry and pikemen. But I know how to use the Plainsmen, and Khind archers. Probably better than the Knights and Barons. And the tribes and clans would follow me more willingly even if I didn't. We'll take Yost with what we can use best, and then we'll have a victory to present to the Marcher lords. Like the peasants, they'll be more willing to help us after that."

Arlor nodded, but slowly and reluctantly. Fatigue made his voice low when he spoke again—fatigue and memories of nightmare blueness flaring in the sky over Benzos. "Suppose—suppose someone intervenes? What then?"

Wandor took the meaning. "I spoke to Cheloth of the Woods before he went into the forest to keep vigil against any more intervention by Kaldmor the Dark. He feels that he can counterbalance any sorcery Kaldmor is capable of throwing against us, at least for the moment."

"How long a moment?" said Arlor sourly.

Wandor shrugged. "That he didn't say, I asked him the same question, but he said he was a sorcerer, not a prophet. But I think we can look forward to at least taking Yost with no magic on either side."

Arlor heaved a sigh of relief. Somewhat to everybody's surprise, so did Gwynna.

CHAPTER 18

The wind was rising as Wandor strode toward the tavern hard by the East Gate of Yost. He saw the canvas roof tear off one of the cobblestone and board lean-tos that sheltered the refugees. A woman ran out of it, chasing the canvas down the street. Her grimy feet were bare, and the cobblestones would be cold underfoot.

Wandor did not like that wind. A score of three-man teams were drifting through the city tonight, ready to create diversions in as many places. Some would inevitably start fires. And too much of Yost was built of wood. Too much of it was also packed with refugees fleeing from the Khindi and Plainsmen who prowled toward the city. Fires tonight might sweep away five thousand people and leave another ten thousand homeless.

He turned into the tavern. Light and laughter were both subdued, for lamp oil and beer were both running short in Yost. But in a swift glance around the two rooms he recognized the dozen men he had picked as his personal attack force. They were sitting as he had ordered, in twos and threes, trying unsuccessfully to look relaxed and convivial on a single mug of beer apiece.

Wandor ordered a beer of his own and a plate of thin-sliced sausage. The tavern keeper handed the mug and platter to the greasy-haired barmaid, then turned the hourglass on the counter. Before it ran out again, the battle would have started.

* * *

144

Berek reached down under the seat of the oxcart and checked the lashings. His axes Greenfoam and Thunderstone lay there wrapped in oiled cloth. The walls of Yost were barely a mile ahead. He raised his whip and flicked it lightly across the backs of the oxen. The weary beasts flinched, as much from the rising wind as from the whip. In the cart Berek drove and in the two behind him rode twenty-five of Baron Delvor's fighting men, picked for stout thews and keen wits alike. Not a one was of gentle blood, so all had calloused and work-grimed hands to bear out their tale of being masons and carpenters, coming to work on the fortifications of the city. Their hods and trowels, axes and adzes, ladders and poles, rode openly in the wagons beside them. But mail or boiled leather shirts lurked under their rough work jackets, and swords and daggers lay beneath the piles of scaffolding poles.

They were well rehearsed, and what they were to do tonight should be easy—provided that no word of it had reached Yost ahead of them. If Berek came to the city and found Wandor's head greeting him from a spike on the walls, he could take his vengeance—but not on Yost. He put the thought from his mind and laid on the whip again.

The steps up the street from inside the tavern were no higher than when Wandor came down. But there was a moment as he stood at their foot when they seemed to rise endlessly out of sight, and climbing them beyond his strength. Then he felt his sword at his side and heard the men rising from their chairs to follow him, and the feeling went away. But his mouth was dry and sour as he led the way up the stairs.

The biting wind in the street cleared the smoke and the warm fog of the tavern out of his head. The street stretched empty all the way to the East Gate. Only wavering splotches of light from occasional lamps hung on houses broke the chill darkness. There were enough shadows to hide five times Wandor's twelve men. He turned and watched carefully as they drifted off to places that offered a clear view of the East Gate.

Now Wandor's senses were too concentrated on that gate to pay much attention to the wind—its chill, its thin piping around chimneys, the debris it sent skittering past, or anything else. There was nothing left to do but watch the gate and wait for Berek. With a good hard road he should easily reach the gate before it closed for the night, but...

Wandor knelt behind a pile of firewood and stared toward the East Gate. Decaying leaves and cobwebs brushed off on his clothes. But he ignored them. He wished he could also ignore the spatters of rain blowing down on the wind. The idea of the roads turning to mud and the Plainsmen and other mounted reinforcements not getting through chilled him more than the wind. Some of the torches at the gate had gone out now, and the guards walking sentry on the walls looked more wraithlike than ever.

Then the gates began to swing soundlessly open, the squeal of their massive iron hinges lost in the wind. Wander rose to a crouch. The gates swung wide open, and four heavy-shouldered oxen drew a long-bedded cart into the street. Wandor recognized the driver in his rough brown cloak as Berek even before the man raised his left hand in the agreed-on signal. The wagon rumbled on down the street and stopped fifty feet in from the gate. Wander saw two of the sentries leave their posts and walk toward it. Then a second cart appeared and stopped squarely in the gateway.

Wandor and the two men with him vaulted clear over the pile of firewood and sprinted out into the street. As fast as they moved, the men in the carts were faster. Berek reached under the seat of his wagon, then leaped down to the street with his great axe Thunderstone dancing in his hands. The eight men in the cart behind him piled out with their own swords and axes flailing, swarmed around the two sentries, left them bloody and twitching on the stones. The men ran on toward the gate.

Now the portcullis of the gate came down with a crash audible even against the wind. But the high, stout sides of the second cart caught the portcullis, held it, kept it five good feet clear of the pavement. The eight men from that cart boiled out and joined Berek's, swarming up the stairs toward the guardroom on top of the gatehouse. Halfway up, the guards met them in a flurry of pike thrusts and sword slashes. Five men went off the stairs in as many seconds, to crash to the stone and writhe or lie still. Then more men—the disguised Khindi from the third cart stopped outside on the drawbridge—dashed in through the gateway. They stopped, turned, raised bows, nocked arrows, took aim, shot. The men swarming out of the guardroom began to fall with arrows in them. Some fell backward, jamming the door open, others fell forward, down to the stone on top of the bodies already there. The survivors of the party from the second cart swarmed over the bodies and into the guardroom. The lights there promptly went out. The Khindi in the street shifted their aim to the top of the guardroom, then to the walls on either side. More guards fell.

Now Wandor was up to the first cart and clasping hands with Berek. His twelve men were falling into a line across the street, and just in time. The uproar in the street had finally penetrated to the tavern, and the soldiers there came stumbling up the stairs, swords and pikes waving—or weaving—in their hands. There were more than twenty of them to Wandor's twelve plus Berek, but not all of the twenty-odd were sober.

Still it was a savage little exchange of slashes and thrusts for a moment as the soldier's charge met Wandor's line. He found two opponents coming at him, slowed one with a quick slash to the thigh, then met the other in a close-body grapple. No room or time or place for subtlety or style here. Wandor's left hand in its chain-mail glove clamped down on the soldier's uplifted blade, while his other hand drove the heavy brass guard of his own sword into the man's face. As the man lurched back, Wandor had room to lower his sword and thrust at the man's face, taking him in the throat. The man collapsed as he tried to turn and run.

But Wandor's first opponent did turn and run and got clean away, although his slashed thigh leaked a trail of blood as he ran. Four or five others out of the twenty managed to do the same. Some of those who remained behind were still moving, until Berek tapped each one of them on the head with his small axe, Greenfoam.

Two of Wandor's men were down and four or five more wounded. Wandor's sharp-voiced orders called the able-bodied survivors back from pursuit of the remaining soldiers. Quickly they turned the first cart across the street, then cut the oxen loose. With shouts and crackings of his whip, Berek harried the animals until they took fright and ran bawling away down the street. A dozen men then heaved the cart over on its side with a crash. As they did, the portcullis rose with a squeal, and the second cart rumbled forward. Berek was stepping up to cut its team loose when trumpets blared off to the left.

"That's the barracks for the East Gate guards," snapped Wandor. "The alarm's up."

Berek nodded and shouted to the men. "Help me with this cart!" But he did not wait for them to answer. Stepping forward, he lunged under the cart, then heaved upward, shoulders and arms coming up with every muscle in his body pushing them. The cart lurched, and Berek's side began to rise into the air. Before Wandor could shout a warning to Berek, or the other men could come to his aid, the cart rose to its point of balance and toppled over with a splintering crash. His chest heaving and sweat pouring down his face, Berek stepped back and picked up his axes. The men who had been running to give the help he hadn't needed now turned to cutting loose the oxen, bawling in panic and heaving at their yokes.

The men got the team cut loose and on its way down the street just as the trumpets sounded again, louder and closer this time. Then the clank of armor and the thud of feet rose above the bawling of fleeing oxen, and soldiers began pouring out of the street leading to the barracks. These soldiers were not half drunk, they were fully armored, and there were more than fifty of them.

Wandor took a quick look behind him and to either side. The Khindi from the third wagon and the survivors of the second were all up on the wall now, fighting their way along it with sword and axe or picking off soldiers with arrows. Berek's men had rejoined him, but that still made only about twenty men to face the attack of more than fifty.

And the attackers kept on coming, although the street was more than half blocked by the overturned carts. The advancing men were mercenaries, but if they had no loyalty to Duke Cragor except as paymaster, they had enough loyalty to their own reputation to push on. They came through the gaps around the carts at a run.

Wandor drew his dagger from his boot top and nodded to Berek. Side by side they ran to meet the enemy, their men running in a line on either side of them. The two lines met with a thunderous crash and oaths and blood spraying high, as tempers rose and weapons fell. It was total chaos, the chaos of more than three-score men desperately striving, hacking, and thrusting, and stabbing at each other with all the strength in their bodies and the fury in their souls.

Thunderstone whistled down past Wandor's ear, smashing into the face of a man coming against him. The man dropped where he stood, tangling two men coming around him to get at Wandor. Wandor had to give back only a little to meet the first one, who carried short sword and buckler. The man's buckler work left much to be desired and in a few moments Wandor thrust low with his dagger, disabling the man's buckler arm. A low cut toward the knee drew the man's sword down, and a dagger thrust into a face left exposed by the open helm finished him off.

But the other man carried a pike, and to meet that Wandor had to close, darting and weaving as the man backed off, trying to keep his distance open and his point toward Wandor. Wandor was faster, and his sword sheared down and disabled an arm. From nowhere Thunderstone whistled down again, chopping off the other arm. The man screamed and reeled back, dropping his pike with a clatter on the stone. Then an uproar of screaming and neighing, pounding hooves and scampering feet, rose from behind the carts. A man coming at Wandor froze long enough for Wandor to thrust him under the gorget. Then a man climbing up on a cart with a pike held ready for a downward thrust dropped the pike, threw up his hands, and toppled off his perch. Boiled-leather jacks would not keep out Khind arrows at close range.

From somewhere Wandor's diversionary teams had contrived to steal a score of horses and yet further contrived to drive them at a gallop through the streets into the rear of the mercenaries. The mercenaries promptly lost, if not their courage, at least their interest in continuing the attack. Those who had got past the carts tried to surrender. Some of them succeeded because Wandor and Berek were now getting their surviving men under control. The others tried to run, and some of them also succeeded. The men from the diversion teams were too few and too concerned about rejoining Wandor to spare attention for picking off fugitives. Within a few minutes about thirty men from the teams came in safely, giving Wandor nearly fifty men ready at hand to beat off the next attack.

Since those fifty now included more than a score of Khind archers with full quivers, the second attack lost more men in less time without getting as far. After its survivors retreated, Wandor had time to retrieve a good many weapons and sets of armor. And just before the third attack came in, the Khindi who had been slipping through the dark countryside arrived, more than three hundred of them. They scrambled up the outside of the wall on the ladders from the carts, taking positions on the wall and on rooftops all around the East Gate.

This was just as well; for the strength of the third attack suggested that somebody somewhere in Yost was at last taking the situation seriously. The attack came in strength along the walls, it came up the streets, and it would have come across the roofs. But the Khindi blunted the last prong by picking off the greater part of the men in it. On the walls and in the street, though, matters came to hand-to-hand fighting of the bloodiest sort. More than two hundred of the attackers were slain or maimed and more than sixty of Wandor's men likewise before the enemy's trumpets called the retreat. Another two hundred Khindi arrived in time to send a shower of arrows after the retreating soldiers.

After that, Wandor lost track of the number of men under him, the number of dead and wounded on either side, or even the number of attacks. They went on all through the hours of darkness, with the bodies piling higher in the streets and on the walls and roofs. Wandor was more conscious of his own limbs beginning to slow, his head beginning to pound, his sword and borrowed armor becoming hacked and blood-spattered (mostly with other people's blood). But there were some things that stood out even from the night's battle.

—The fire that spread from an oil warehouse until it covered an entire street. The pink and orange glow shed light across half the city.

—The report that came to him from farther down the wall. Messengers were galloping out of the North Gate and scattering into the countryside.

"They must be calling for help from the small lords and the farmers all around the city," said Berek.

"Yes," said Wandor, managing a grin, "Much good may it do them." Of his four thousand Khindi, three thousand were prowling among the estates of those same lords and the farms of those same farmers. Few of them would be inclined to spare any men to help

Cragor's commander hold Yost, and few of the men they might send would reach Yost alive.

—The time when in a rumbling of wheels and a cracking of whips, the garrison brought up an onager. Fifty pound stones and burning tar pots began dropping into the area Wander was defending. He saw men smashed into pulp, struck down by flying fragments, or screaming with hair and clothes afire. But the Khindi who held the rooftops moved forward, leaping across alleys as they leaped from branch to branch in their native woods until they could fire directly down on the men manning the onager. When three successive crews lay dead around the machine, the garrison abandoned its efforts at siege warfare.

Morning finally came and with it the Plainsmen, Jos-Pran and Gwynna at their head. Six thousand strong, they rode up to the East Gate in the teeth of a stiff wind that carried more spatters of rain. They dismounted and marched into the city on foot. Their arrival made Wandor certain of holding what he had, but the Plainsmen had neither body armor nor great skill in fighting on foot. A petty bickering of patrols and ambushes went on all morning between the Plainsmen and the garrison, while those who had fought all night ate and slept.

And then it was noon, and Count Arlor and Sir Gilas Lanor rode up with five hundred armored horsemen and more than two thousand assorted infantry mounted on horses "borrowed" from farms and manors all the way to the edge of the Marches. Mercenaries and the levies of House Delvor and House Lanor all went forward together, and against that attack the garrison chose not to stand. They retreated to the castle, setting fire to the houses all around it to give themselves a clear field of fire. Wandor's men spread through Yost. Its inhabitants hid behind locked doors and shuttered windows for several hours more. But in time the word went about that not even the Khindi and Plainsmen were running wild to rape, murder, and plunder. So the citizens came out to greet, or at least contemplate, Wandor's army. By nightfall some of those who still honored King Nond—or at least wanted to give that impression—were rolling out barrels of beer and wine and donating their firewood to build bonfires in the streets.

Wandor drifted among these fires for several hours, Gwynna on his arm. Both nodded and smiled in reply to the rapturous greetings of Khindi, Plainsmen, and levies, and to the somewhat more restrained greetings of the townspeople.

Gwynna's temper showed signs of flaring at the townspeople's lack of enthusiasm. "They should be going down on their knees to you, damn them! You've freed them from both Cragor and the garrison, and with a tenth of the damage that anyone else would have done. What do they want?"

"Mostly to be left alone," said Wandor quietly. "I know, that's impossible unless we abandon everything to Cragor. But they can't see it that way. It isn't their fight."

"Then we've got to make it theirs!"

"How, love? We can't tell them what I am and what that means. Most of them wouldn't believe it. And those who believed it would just as likely flee in horror as run to help. All the magic worked of late has a good number of people frightened as it is."

"What right do they have to fear the only force that can save them?"

Fatigue and strain and the aftermath of victory let the reins off Wandor's temper. Anger flared in his voice as he replied. "The right of any man who doesn't understand, who can't understand what thunders and roars far above his head! You've lived all your life with your own Powers and a high rank that even the Plainsmen recognized. You've never thought how the man in his shop or barn might see what we've let loose. Maybe it's time you did!" He jerked his arm free of hers, turned on his heel, and walked off.

He did not see her again until just before dawn the next morning, for the castle garrison made a sortie. It was beaten back with small difficulty and no small loss to the garrison. After counting the casualties, Wandor ordered two messages sent out. One went to the castle, calling on the garrison to surrender on promise of good treatment, with a chance for all mercenaries to join his own army. The other went to Baron Delvor, reporting the capture of Yost (except for the castle) and asking that word be sent to the Marcher lords who had been holding back their men. He did not add that they had no further excuse for any such holding back. Then he went back to the inn where he and Gwynna had taken a room.

Gwynna was lying face down on the bed, still fully dressed.

152

She rose as Wandor stepped toward the bed. He stopped, expecting her own temper to flare savagely at him, accepting it as, what he deserved.

Instead, she turned a red-eyed and tear-streaked face toward him and stepped forward into his arms without a single word. A long and wordless embrace, a long and deep kiss—they would have tumbled into bed on the instant, except that behind both stood two solid days of fighting amid blood and sweat and smoke. Wandor knew the gods themselves must be wrinkling up their noses at the smell rising from him, and Gwynna was little sweeter.

So there was a hot bath first, with much playful splashing, and then finally the long joining, alternately tender and delicate as Chongan brushwork and fierce like the fires beneath Mount Pendwyr. Finally they lay together under the quilts, and Gwynna turned a face drowsy with satisfied passion toward Wandor and smiled.

"Forgive me, Bertan. You are—were—far more right than I wanted to believe. You—you see this more clearly than I do."

"Perhaps. But I was in an absolutely vile temper. I said things I had no right or reason to say."

She kissed him on the tip of his nose. "A pretty pair we are. A fool and a curmudgeon." They both laughed. Then her expression sobered. "But I still don't see why you are always trying to bring this down to such a *human* level. You are a man chosen by the gods to fulfill such a mighty purpose, and you so often talk like a mere soldier or royal councilor."

"What else can I do, love? I am human still, whatever the gods may have to say about it or whatever they want me to do. I must fight at the human level and not think about the gods more often than I must. Otherwise I should go mad."

CHAPTER 19

Three days after the city of Yost fell, the garrison of its castle found compelling reasons to surrender. Wandor knew that bottling up the whole garrison of the city in a castle cramped with one-fourth that many inside its walls would wear down their resistance quickly. But three days was less than even he had expected.

The mercenaries spent the first two days of their incarceration glowering silently—at the besiegers, at each other, and more and more at the royal troops and Cragor's vassal levies. On the morning of the third day their officers, seeing themselves about to lose control over their men, waited in a body on the garrison commander. They asked to be allowed to march their men out and surrender to Wandor. The garrison commander refused. In fact, he flew into a violent rage and called the mercenary officers cowards and traitors.

Now there was neither military nor common sense (the two seldom being the same) in either the refusal or the rage. The castle could be held as securely as possible with no more than seven hundred men. Any more were nothing but so many useless mouths. The mercenaries were by any military standards superfluous. And it is most ill advised to abuse mercenary officers for failing to show passionate loyalties that their profession gives them no cause to develop. They are not slower to take offense or resent insults than most men.

Word of this exchange soon leaked out, and some of the mercenary soldiers attempted to storm the gates. The gate guards drove them back, and the garrison commander ordered that all the mercenaries should at once be disarmed and confined. He thereby piled one folly atop another, since there was no place to confine the entire thousand-odd mercenaries even if they had submitted peacefully to being disarmed. They did not. They came back in considerably greater force, again tried to seize the gate, were beaten off again, and then began roaming the castle, promiscuously fighting everybody they met. The garrison commander, finding the vassal levies insufficient to subdue the mercenaries, called upon the royal troops.

The greater part of these had been fighting for Cragor only because they feared for their lives if they did otherwise. They certainly had no intention of hindering anyone from leaving the Black Duke's service. They promptly seized the stables and barracks and barricaded themselves inside. The garrison commander lost his few remaining wits and ordered the royal troops burned out of this refuge.

At this point Count Arlor, watching from a temple tower nearby, judged that the confusion in the castle had risen sufficiently high. A force of five hundred picked men kept in hand for just such an occasion marched up to the castle moat. Storming parties swam or paddled on planks across the chill waters, threw grapnels over the parapets, and sealed the undefended walls. Half an hour's brisk fighting, and the survivors of those inclined to resist surrendered. The garrison commander saved the attackers some work by killing himself.

Wandor and Gwynna rode up to the lowered drawbridge just as Count Arlor was supervising the removal of the prisoners. The count was still in full armor, but his visor was up and a broad grin showed on his face as he pointed at the line of bedraggled men shambling across the bridge.

"The ones here we'll have to keep prisoner for the time being, I think. The rest—you'd best speak to them yourself, but I'm sure the royal troops will come over."

"What about the mercenaries?"

"They should join us, if we can pay them."

"We'll pay them, don't worry. If we can't pay them in coin, we'll see what we can do about billeting them on some of Cragor's supporters among the landed gentry. We'll need a garrison in our rear when we march north to Fors."

"Fors?"

"Of course." Wandor put a bit more force into his voice than he actually felt. He wanted to drive home even to Arlor the fact that he commanded. "I said we were going to try to clear the whole Viceroyalty this year, if I recall."

"You did," said Arlor. There was a note of rueful admiration in his voice.

All that kept Kaldmor the Dark from dancing on the ruins of Baron Galkor's plans and crowing like a rooster greeting the dawn was the need to stay on good terms with the Black Duke's viceroy. But he could not resist a few thrusts at the baron as they sat in the tower chamber contemplating the grim news from the south.

"You were planning for raids against Fors and Yost, weren't you, my lord baron?" said Kaldmor. "Yet Wandor seems to have snatched Yost in a single blow. The city, the castle, all the surrounding country, and the whole garrison—all gone."

"Worse than that," said Galkor. His voice was dead and flat. He was beyond trying to look or sound calm. "The reports today say that the mercenaries in the garrison and in the service of our local supporters are going over to Wandor's service by the hundreds. That's another two thousand men for Wandor. Perhaps three."

"What about the royal troops?" asked Kaldmor. In his voice was much that he preferred not to put in words. He knew no more about war than Galkor knew about magic. But he did know that if the five thousand royal troops on the northern borders of the Viceroyalty suddenly joined together in declaring for Wandor—well, it would cause difficulties.

"The royal troops in Yost have gone over. Wandor has welcomed them and placed Count Arlor in special charge of them. We shall have to keep watch on our own royalists to see that the northern garrisons do not suddenly decide to come south. That will mean a strong force in Lukaz to control the North High Road." On a map on the desk Galkor traced with his dagger the roads of the northern Viceroyalty, all converging at the town of Lukaz to meet the road running north to Fors. "At least five thousand men." He shook his head. "That will mean stripping the fortified towns along the High

Road south to Yost. There will be nothing to stop or slow Wandor if he moves north.

"And Wander will be coming north. He's building an army down there in Yost, and he is going to lead it north as soon as he has it ready. He's a gambler. Winning one roll of the dice is going to encourage him to try another. But he won't win this one."

Galkor surged to his feet, and there was a brazen ring in his voice as he went on. "Let him lead his army up to the walls of Fors! Let him! He can freeze and starve all winter while we sit warm in Fors. Then spring will come and fifty thousand of Duke Cragor's men, and that will be the end of Wander. If he doesn't retreat, he will die at once. If he retreats, he will die a little later when we march south. Yes, I think we can face Wandor's coming without much to fear."

Kaldmor managed to avoid shaking his head in alarm until he was outside the chamber door and descending the stairs. Had Galkor suddenly gone mad? No, a sudden wild overconfidence in one's own plans might not be madness. But against an enemy like Wandor it could have the same result. Kaldmor could easily foresee Galkor rushing about to perfect his plans, rushing about until he fell into some trap laid for him by Wandor. Wandor was *not* a gambler. Such did not serve the purposes of those behind Wandor.

Kaldmor's jaw hardened in determination. He himself had advised Galkor to rely on material weapons, to have no faith even in the sorcery of Toshak, not when pitted against all the powers now arrayed to fight for Wandor. But he had thought the baron would be his normal wise and crafty self in arraying those material forces. No more, it seemed.

So now he would have to probe still more deeply into the nightmare lore of Toshak, taking the risk of unleashing more than he could readily control in his search for more power. He might even have to consider the ultimate unleashing, the one he knew he could not control at all, now or ever—and the thought alone sent a congealing chill through his insides.

The northwest wind carried the smell of smoke and of oncoming snow to Wandor as he reached the top of the hill. Gazing north, his eyes confirmed the message brought on the wind. Three smoke plumes scrawled blackness across the northern sky, and beyond them a mass of slate-gray clouds loomed over the dark winter woods.

Wandor did not need word from the Plainsmen who galloped back a few minutes later to know that the retreating enemy had fired another village. Too much more of this, and his army might face trouble. The Plainsmen and Khindi were used to sleeping out in foul, even wintry weather, but what of the mercenaries, the Marcher levies, and the royal infantry?

Wandor's army was a week north of Yost now, and by and large they had found the towns and villages and isolated huts intact. Even the stored food and fodder had seldom been burned or carried off. So Wandor's stroke of taking more than twenty thousand men north with only the scantiest of wagon trains had worked so far.

Not that Galkor was suddenly being helpful or interested in winning over the peasants and townspeople. Several prisoners had explained that Galkor was leaving the settlements along the road intact merely because Duke Cragor would need them the next spring when he led his army south to retake Yost and invade the Marches.

A clatter of hooves on the hard-frozen road, and Gwynna rode up with her Plainsman escort. Count Arlor was a mile back, sharing command of the main body with Baron Delvor. And Sir Gilas Lanor was a mile back farther yet, with the rear guard and the wagons for the baggage and the sick. There was little of the former and so far, few of the latter. In an army of picked men, this was not surprising, but it was nonetheless welcome.

Gwynna still looked thinner than Wandor liked to see her. But he knew from their nights at Yost that the starved gauntness was giving way to her normal graceful curves. The frosty air had turned her cheeks almost the same color as the hair she now wore bound tight under a fur cap. She looked toward the smoke clouds.

"They must be pushing patrols farther south than usual," she said grimly. Wandor's own scouting parties of Plainsmen and Khindi made a real ambush impossible. But if Galkor could not set a trap, he could easily leave a wasteland behind him, where Wandor's fast-moving, lightly supplied army would have to withdraw or starve?

Or could it move still faster? The thought struck Wandor like a physical blow, and for a moment he could barely sit in his seat on the King Horse. Nerves tingled, his breath came quickly. Then the physical turmoil passed, leaving his mind working with furious clarity.

If he could increase the speed of his army's advance by half, he could push it to the walls of Fors before Galkor could have time to react. But he could not push the whole army along that fast, not with any amount of pulling or prodding or cajoling. What could he push to the walls of Fors?

The Khindi, of course. They could cover twenty-five miles a day without even breathing hard, and their woodscraft would provide them with much of their own food. The Plainsmen also would come. Their light horses ate little and could eat even less for a few days if by some chance fodder came up short. Wandor did not expect it to since the abundant harvest had left the farmers with an ample surplus of both food and fodder. Some had offered freely to the passing army, some had been persuaded, but all had given and given in abundance.

There was always the royal infantry, too, some fifteen hundred strong. They had their pride and confidence back now. They would follow Wandor and Count Arlor anywhere at any speed and then stand and die where they stood at the end of the march. And even some of the mercenaries could be counted on to step out with the best. Eleven or twelve thousand men in all could strike rapidly north. Meanwhile, Baron Delvor and Sir Gilas would lead the heavy cavalry, the Marcher levies, and the remaining mercenaries after them at a more sedate pace. They would have some Khindi and Plainsmen as scouts, and he would send word back to Yost and into the forests to bring up more of both. The whole rear body would make its way north in the wake of Wandor's advance body. If the advance body had to retreat, the rear would stand and support them.

But if Galkor's army clung as closely to the walls of Fors as Wandor expected, the two forces would unite outside those walls. With no siege equipment, they would have to remain outside, barring great luck or the chance for another stratagem such as had gained them Yost. But an army by then approaching twenty-five thousand men could do much to make the enemy's hoped-for spring campaign less easy than either Galkor or Duke Cragor expected.

Much would depend on speed and on all the leaders doing

159

what was expected of them, which was perhaps far too much to expect in war. Certainly Baron Delvor would tell him that, at great length. And he would listen to this, admit the baron might be right, and go on with his own plans. He would be obeyed, too, he realized, perhaps more faithfully than he deserved. Blindness to his faults comes easily to those who serve a man called on by the gods—perhaps too easily.

CHAPTER 20

Wooden shutters now closed the windows of the tower chamber. They kept in some of the warmth from the fire on the hearth and kept out some of the damp cold from the sea. If Kaldmor the Dark in his thick fur robes felt a chill, it was a chill from within, as Baron Galkor's toneless voice reported the latest news.

"Wandor has divided his army. About half of it is coming north as fast as it can set foot to the ground. The other half is coming along behind it more slowly."

"Is that all you've learned?" Kaldmor could not choose other words, although he knew he was in no position to criticize Galkor for learning little of the advancing enemy. In fact, the baron's human scouts were doing better than Kaldmor's own Powers. Cheloth of the Woods kept Barrier spells high and thick around Wandor's army, spells that had so far kept Kaldmor at a distance. No doubt it would improve Galkor's opinion of him if he tried to push a Watcher of his own through the Barriers. Perhaps he could even succeed. But his instincts told him not to waste energy or drag more Toshakan magic into the light of day merely to impress Baron Galkor.

"Yes, that is all, friend sorcerer," said Galkor heavily. At least he did not flare into a rage. "The Khindi are ranging all around both halves of Wandor's army. Any of our scouts they capture are used for archery targets or sacrificed to the High Hunter. If the scouts escape the Khindi, the peasants round them up and turn them over to Wandor."

"The peasants?"

"Is that a word in a language you do not know, Kaldmor? Yes, the peasants. It seems they are coming out of their farms and villages by the hundred, bringing food and fodder to Wandor's army by the ton. How do you think Wandor is moving north so fast? Even the Khindi can't march on air.

"Ah well," said Galkor, sipping at his cup of mulled wine. "We have Lukaz fully garrisoned and provisioned for a siege now. There was a little trouble with some of the royal troops there, but not anymore." Kaldmor sensed much left unsaid in that last phrase. "Neither Wandor nor the royalists can snatch it off quickly now."

"So nothing much has changed?"

"Nothing at all. When Wandor reaches Fors, he will still be outside the walls. We will still be inside. As long as that is the case, we have nothing to fear."

Kaldmor neither nodded nor shook his head. He did not agree in the least with Galkor's last declaration. But he also knew that he could never hope to explain the reasons why he disagreed. So it was better to keep silent for the moment.

Hard flakes of snow pecked at the sentry's face as he turned into the wind. He didn't like any part of being up here on the walls of Fors tonight, with a wind that seemed to come all the way from the glaciers to the north of the Sea Folk lands whistling past rum. He liked least of all the return leg of his beat, facing straight into the wind. And he couldn't shut his eyes, either. The stones of the parapet were slick and glazed with ice. If he didn't watch where he was going, he'd likely slip and fall right down off the wall, break a leg, and probably freeze to death before any of the other sentries came around.

He stamped his chilled feet in their stiffening boots and turned to stare out into the snow-whipped darkness. If there could only be some light out there! He had mounted this same guard during the summer. Then there had been fireflies and the campfires of patrols and the glow from cottage windows. Now the fireflies were dead, and the patrols only went out to cover a convoy for Lukaz, and the cottages were all shut up tight against the winter and the Khindi. The forest people were already supposed to be moving into the southern part of the settled area around Fors. They really must not be human, or perhaps they were just mad? How else could they move around and fight out there now?

He sensed the man appearing to his right before he turned and saw him. A big bulky figure, officer no doubt, come up to inspect the sentries. Damned officers, sitting down there with their wine and girls around the fires—!

The officer was walking toward him now. Staz, but he was a big one! Didn't recognize him, though, and that was odd. Somebody that size would be easy to remember. Long hair, too, and a big bushy square-cut beard. And treading light, too. He wasn't leaving any footprints. Wasn't leaving any—?

The sentry's mouth opened to form a scream of sheer terror. The newcomer's eyes also opened. Golden light blazed out, blinding the sentry. He never saw the brightly glowing hands that reached out and took him by the throat. He only felt them, and that for a very few seconds before he stopped feeling anything at all.

They found the sentry's body an hour later lightly frosted with snow and already stiffening from the cold. The officer who found the body took one look at it and managed to gasp out, "Send for Baron Galkor!" before violently losing his dinner. He had recovered by the time the baron appeared. But the officer and all the other sentries stood much farther back than simple deference required as Galkor examined the body.

The man's throat and neck were only scraps of charred bone and cartilage. It was as though a white-hot iron collar—or white-hot claws—had tightened around his throat and held tight, searing away the flesh until the blackened remains of the spinal cord alone kept the head from falling off. And on the man's face was a look as if in his last moments of life the House of Shadows had opened its doors to him. It was a face that made even Baron Galkor look away after a moment.

Galkor threatened dire penalties for anyone who talked, but rumors were all over the city before dawn. The fear that Fors was accursed, dormant since the events of autumn, awoke again. A number of mercenaries were stopped at the city gates. Galkor had them hanged and their bodies left dangling from the walls of the castle. The executions may have temporarily intimidated the soldiers. But they did less than nothing against the being that walked the walls by night. There was neither snow nor wind to baffle sight or hearing the second night, but not a man heard or saw the slightest sign of the intruder. Not a man, that is, except for the three who were found with their throats burned out and faces staring in agony and horror.

Galkor kept the city gates closed the next day and stationed archers on the walls to deal with any soldiers trying to leap down from the top and run. In spite of this, at least a dozen men tried to make their escape. The archers picked off some, others died in the fall, but some got clean away to spread rumors into the countryside. They missed the chance to tell tales of the third night's victims, though. Three sentries on the wall, two officers walking home from taverns, two guards in the prison. Seven men with heads all but burned from their bodies, seven men scattered over an entire mile, but all of them slain within a single space of less than ten minutes.

At this point Galkor's common sense cut through his fear and his dislike of sorcery and made him summon Kaldmor the Dark. Whatever stalked and slew in Fors now was clearly a thing of sorcery. Any chance of stopping it, or at least of discovering what it was, had to be seized on quickly before it slew half the garrison and drove the other half in panic flight out into the wintry countryside to scatter and run and fall prey to the Khindi, now beyond any doubt prowling not far south of the city.

The two men faced each other across Galkor's desk the same tower chamber where so much had happened since the summer. Both were red eyed and haggard from too much strain and too little sleep. For Galkor it was the strain of watching his perfect military solution fall apart under savage thrusts from beyond the material world. For Kaldmor it was the strain of continuous probing into what Toshak's sorcerers had learned of that same beyond-the-world, seeking any solution, whether perfect or not. As he stared at Galkor's unshaved face and red eyes, Kaldmor felt a moment of closeness and sympathy for the man greater than he had ever felt before.

"Master Kaldmor," said Galkor, "you know what I want of

you. What I must have of you. What is it that prowls Fors by night and slays like a mad beast? It must be within your knowledge, if it is within anybody's here now."

Kaldmor nodded slowly. "Perhaps. Have you thought of interrogating anyone who was near the scene of the killings, to see if they saw anything?"

That was a tactless question, as Kaldmor realized the moment the words were out of his mouth. But Galkor did not flare into a rage or grimace or even put an edge in his voice. He laughed. "I have, Master Kaldmor. That I have. Forty or more of them. And those who wouldn't talk freely have been tortured." He stopped abruptly. "Nothing."

"Nothing?"

"No one has seen anything, heard anything, anywhere near the time and place of any of the killings."

Kaldmor nodded again. "Then whatever is doing the killings, to see if they saw anything, only of its victims. At least at the level of the waking mind."

"Well, then do something to get it out of wherever else it may be if it's anywhere!" Galkor snapped, his moment's calm gone.

"I can do that, but only at the risk of killing the man," said Kaldmor.

"Go ahead," said the baron. "You can't possibly kill more men than we'll lose if this—thing—forces us out into the countryside."

"Do you think—?" began Kaldmor, then cut himself off. Galkor would not have mentioned marching out of Fors if he hadn't been thinking of it. But Kaldmor felt a sudden deeper chill at the idea, as though the tower walls around him had vanished and the bitter winds outside were blowing through him.

The winds did indeed blow hard that night, harder than before. The garrison and the people of Fors huddled in barracks and houses and listened to the howl of the wind and the crash of falling chimneys. They were listening, also, for the sound of men dying in agony and terror. They knew the deaths would come whether they heard or not.

The night's toll was ten men, taken one at a time from ten different places scattered from one end of Fors to the other. One was a guard at the treasure room of the castle itself. Though nothing was missing, Galkor flew into a rage. He swore that there must be treason as well as sorcery lurking behind all this and had the surviving guards tortured.

It was while Galkor was in the dungeon listening to the guards' agonized denials of seeing anything that Kaldmor the Dark came to him. One look at the sorcerer's face was enough for Galkor to seek privacy. He led the way out into the corridor and down to one of the unused cells. Inside, leaning against the chill damp walls, he faced Kaldmor.

"Have you learned—?"

Kaldmor neither nodded nor shook his head. His cheeks were gray and sunken with fatigue and something more, and his thick-fingered hands would have been trembling if he had not hooked them into his belt.

"I have torn the image of the killer from the minds of two guards. One is dead, the other is mad. But I have learned what we face." Kaldmor paused so long that Galkor set his jaw impatiently.

"Go on."

"What takes your soldiers in the night is—it has the image and form—of King Nond."

CHAPTER 21

Count Arlor felt a palpable physical chill breaking through his dreams of warmth and Anya. He could not have sworn which would please him more now.

His body dragged his mind into wakefulness, and he sat up. The same darkness, the same bitter cold, the same wind making the walls of the tent puff like a blacksmith's bellows. The same ragged blond beard of the commander of the royal infantry rising and falling on his blankets as he snored. But Arlor's mind also carried a message now.

Go outside.

Go outside? Now? What was outside except the cold and wind and a lonely darkness inhabited only by Khind and Plainsmen sentries who could be very quick with arrows? Too quick, sometimes. A Khind subchief now wore a bandage around a leg neatly skewered by an arrow a few days before. Short rations, hard traveling, and cold had strained people's endurance and nerves.

Besides, they were in enemy territory now. A day's march to the north the forest ended, and the cleared and settled lands around Fors began. Khind scouts were already prowling north among the farms toward the city. Soon the Plainsmen would join them to form a broad arc across the front of the army as it marched out into open country where Galkor might if he chose give battle. But Galkor was not a fool, and only a fool would give up the sure safety of the walls of Fors in return for the uncertainties of a battle in the open field.

As he contemplated the possibilities of the next few days, Arlor was pulling on his boots .and fur-lined overtunic. Then he stopped, one boot still in his hands. He realized that he was still thinking of going outside. And he was no longer wondering why. It had come to seem the natural thing to do. He pulled on the remaining boot, buttoned the tunic, pulled the hood over his head, and opened the tent flap. A blast of icy air whipped in past him as he went out, without waking the infantry commander.

Outside he turned quickly away from the small cluster of commander's tents and plunged into the forest. He passed the dark shapes of sleeping Khindi and Plainsmen curled up around their campfires in fur-lined leather sacks. Arlor shivered at the thought of sleeping in the open in weather like this. But both Khindi and Plainsmen could do it, and in weather colder than this.

Arlor kept on going, knowing only that he must do so, until he was beyond the last of the campfires. Then as swiftly as it had come, the urge to move on vanished. But neither did he feel an urge to return to his tent. To stand here in the cold amid the moaning wind in the creaking trees now seemed as natural as leaving the tent had been.

Arlor had seen stars in the sky when he first came out, but there under the trees it was as dark as it must have been before the Five Gods created light. Arlor did not have a Khind's night sight, so he sensed rather than saw the presence approaching him through the trees.

It made no sound, and for a moment it had no form, either. All that Arlor could sense was a purposeful motion toward him. Purposeful, but without menace. He felt no desire to run from it.

Then from one moment to the next it passed from formless to formed. And in the moment of passing, Arlor did feel fear, fear so great that in that moment he wondered if this was the *tselincha* of Sthi legend, if what he felt were the sensations of a man turning to stone under the *tselincha's* gaze.

As the form steadied, Arlor's fear passed, and his limbs obeyed his will. Slowly, with the grace he had learned as a page, he went down on one knee in the noble's bow to the King of Benzos. With more ponderous grace, that which had the form of King Nond raised its hand and dipped its head in greeting and response.

* * *

Wandor awoke alone because today Gwynna was riding out with the Plainsman patrols. He cursed under his breath as he tried to wedge his feet into his boots. He hadn't left them close enough to the fire last night, and they were frozen stiff. He shook his head. He had been slipping over more and more of these little details the past few days. Everyone in the advanced body was pushing onward too fast and too hard. Once they cleared the forest, he would order a halt for a day or two of rest.

He stood up and stamped hard on the frozen earth to get his feet all the way down in the boots. As he did so, the tent flap opened and Count Arlor came in. It took Wandor a moment to recognize the count, a moment when he found himself instinctively reaching for his dagger. Except for dark circles under his eyes, the count's face was the color of the snow outside. He looked as though he had not slept at all.

But his voice was steady, and he began with no effort to soften his words. "I spoke with King Nond last night." Then he must have picked out one of the several expressions that chased each other across Wandor's face. He added, "It was not a dream."

"His spirit walks?" There was more acceptance in Wandor's voice than in his mind.

"He does. And his eyes are golden now. But it is Nond in form and face and voice and manner. I cannot be mistaken."

It was simpler to believe Arlor for the moment. Simpler, and probably wiser, for why should the man lie? Wandor refused to look for either madness or treason in Count Arlor.

"Nond is prowling Fors by night in his new—form. He has new powers—"

"Given by the Guardian of the Mountain?"

"How did you know? No, you would. He has new powers, and he uses them to slay a few of Galkor's soldiers each night. They are in a panic, and there is more and more talk each day of deserting if Galkor won't lead them out of the city."

Wander stiffened at the last phrase. "Where to?"

"Anywhere out of Fors. They say it is under a curse. 'From a king I have become a mere curse,' Nond says. That truly convinced me it was Nond. The words were so much like him." Arlor shook his head and shivered with more than the cold. "He wants us to push north still faster. If Galkor's army comes south from Fors, perhaps we can get between it and the city and force him to battle. He has—"

Wandor shook his head uncertainly. "Nond was too good a general to be proposing that. If Galkor brings his army out of Fors, he'll outnumber our advanced body better than two to one. And a third of his army is heavy cavalry or pikemen. We can't fight him without the rear body, and they're already four days' march behind us."

"Nond has thought of that," said Arlor irritably. "He says he has also appeared this same night to Baron Delvor, telling him to bring the rear body along as fast as possible."

"He says," murmured Wander, looking at Arlor, fighting the wish of his eyelids to droop shut of their own weight. Then he stepped to the door of the tent and called to the two guards. "Run, find messengers, have them summon a council of war here in my tent at once. Run, I say!" Wandor buckled on his sword belt as the two guards dashed off, then turned back to Arlor. "If the council decides in favor, I will send a message back to Baron Delvor telling him to move his—"

"Damn you!" snapped Arlor. I just told you that Nond has gone to Delver and told him exactly that. He'll be on the way north already. And you want to sit around and argue it with a council!"

"Who commands this army?" asked Wandor coldly. "You or I?"

"You do," said Arlor. His voice was almost sullen.

"Yes. And I will not risk it or any man in it on tales told by ghosts and about ghosts unless every man on the war council believes it also. Do you understand me?" But Arlor was gone without even bothering to nod.

Wandor rubbed his smarting eyes. He felt like weeping or cursing his own fatigue-dulled wits. Of all the ways the strain might have pulled him, it had pulled him into a quarrel with Arlor. Faithful, gallant Arlor, bearer of a story that could hardly be anything but the truth.

There was silence in the tent when Arlor finished his story.

170

The silence was broken by a belch from the royal infantry commander. He had breakfasted too heavily on the usual dubious sausages and mealy porridge provided by the local peasants.

Silence again, with Wandor searching the faces of those seated on the furs strewn on the floor. Arlor, the infantry commander, Jos-Pran, two Khindi chiefs, two mercenary officers. Gwynna was already well to the north on her patrols. He would have given five hundred men from the advanced body to have Gwynna here where she could speak to all the council, not just to him.

To the infantry commander and the mercenaries what Arlor had just said was indeed a tale. Wandor could see them trying to keep doubt off their faces out of respect for Arlor, for him—and also out of knowledge that there had been much sorcery already in the past few months' events and there might easily be more.

The Khindi and Jos-Pran, on the other hand, clearly believed Arlor. Such things were part of their world more than of any civilized man's. Only their seeing that Wandor did not altogether believe kept them from pleading Arlor's case aloud.

Three for, three against. Even if he had believed in putting the matter to a vote, he would have found no answer. Wandor felt as lonely as if he had been standing in the middle of the northern Plains, half a thousand miles from the nearest human settlement.

He let the silence drag on, ignoring the stares that began to turn his way, while Mind Speech linked him to Gwynna.

("You have heard it, love. What say you?")

("It could be true. If it is, it is the work of the Guardian, and of him I know less than I should.")

("You have sensed nothing?")

("Nothing. No magic I could put a name to, not even a Toshakan spell. I think the Guardian keeps this—Nond—walled off from all Powers except his own. And perhaps Cheloth's.")

("I cannot Mind Speak to Cheloth, Gwynna, unless he Speaks to me first. And he has been silent ever since we left Yost.")

("I read some doubts about Cheloth in your mind, Bertan.")

Silence. He would say neither yea nor nay to *that* question.

("The gods keep you.") She had recognized that it was time to leave him alone.

171

("And you.")

Wandor's mind returned to the tent and to the seven staring faces. He squared his shoulders and took a deep breath.

"We shall go north as Arlor wishes us to," he said. "But we shall not go north until the Plainsmen and Khindi are well out in front of us. That way none can come upon us by surprise." He decided against mentioning the possibility of falling back on the rear body. This was an army and a cause not comfortable with the idea of retreat.

"What of our perhaps surprising Galkor and his army?" said Jos-Pran.

"We will not fight them before the rear body joins us unless we have to. We cannot do so wisely or safely. So it is more important for now to avoid them than to surprise them. Is this understood?" Apparently it was. "Messengers will go back at once to the rear body and order them to speed up their march in case they do not believe what Baron Delvor has seen this night. We will move north at the same pace as before."

"Very good," said the infantry commander. There were nods and smiles elsewhere around the tent. Wandor was particularly relieved to see one on Arlor's face.

The council and the dispatch of messengers and the passing of new orders took time. But the advanced body was still on the move soon after full daylight. As Wandor urged the King Horse out on to the High Road, Cheloth of the Woods Spoke to him.

("Have you chosen to order the army north as Nond wishes?")

Wandor was past such immoderate reactions as falling out of the saddle in surprise. Besides, Gwynna had said Cheloth might be able to penetrate the Guardian's spells. And why not? Had they not been, if not friends, at least allies once, two thousand years before?

("I have.")

("Arlor should be pleased.")

("He appears to be.") Wandor found it hard to keep his Mind Speech from falling into Cheloth's laconic pattern when linked to the sorcerer.

("That is good. It is indeed the spirit of King Nond that walks

172

and slays in Fors. And it is telling the truth about Galkor's plans to leave Fors if the killings continue. If he does not, he can only expect a mutiny of his army. He is not a fool, as you well know.")

("I do.")

("My Watcher will be over Fors to tell me when Galkor's army marches out. I do not wish to use it too much now. Kaldmor is delving deeper and deeper into the knowledge of Toshak. With the aid of the *limar* of Nem, he may find new powers. I wish to save my own strength for times of greater need.")

("That is all right.") Then the question that Wandor could not keep back. ("Cheloth, why didn't you speak to me of this before? Help me resolve my doubts and convince the council? You could have done it.") Wandor knew the words were ill chosen, rooted in his weariness and strained nerves, but he would not keep back the question for that.

("I could have done so.")

("Why didn't you?") If the words had been spoken aloud, they would have been shouted.

("Do you remember what you once said to Gwynna about fighting your battles as a human being?")

("I do.") He also wondered how Cheloth knew of these words, but that was a question for another occasion.

("To say that, to do that now and in the future, is the greatest wisdom for you. Always give the best of your human self and put not trust in sorcerers beyond what they can bear. A time will come when I am no longer there to aid or counsel you.")

("When?")

("I have waited two thousand years of human time for my purpose to be fulfilled. It is not a great time for me, but it is not a small one, either. When that purpose is fulfilled, I shall pass onwards.")

("Am I that purpose?")

("Part of it. But do not spend time or strength worrying. I no longer doubt your worthiness to wear the Five-Crowns, if that is what you do in time.")

("I doubt my own.")

("More proof of wisdom and worthiness.") Silence.

Wandor rode on north. By good fortune, it was more than half an hour before he needed to speak to anyone.

CHAPTER 22

Cheloth's Watcher flickered, faint luminescent green in the low-hanging gray clouds above Fors, as Baron Galkor watched his army march out of the city. Both gates stood wide open, both drawbridges creaked under the burden of men and animals and heavily laden wagons. More than twenty two thousand men here, and three thousand yet to join—a thousand from the patrols and two thousand from the garrison of Lukaz. The commander there had howled like a wounded wolf at Galkor's order, but he had obeyed. So twenty-five thousand men would face Wandor in time. Enough for victory if they could catch Wandor with his forces still divided. But suppose he found himself facing Wandor's united army?

Then perhaps he could not crush the enemy. But his army was good as well as numerous, and it should be able to more than hold its own. Cragor had not dreamed of the campaign now being waged, so he had sent across the Ocean far fewer men than he might have. But he had been openhanded enough until autumn closed the sea lanes and threw Galkor and the Viceroyalty on their own resources.

The great nobles of Benzos now largely marched with Cragor (*not* behind him); picked levies from their household troops numbered two thousand heavy cavalry and four thousand infantry. Another thousand cavalry and four times that many infantry had crossed the Ocean under the banners of mercenary captains in Cragor's pay. These were the pick of the horde of mercenaries that upheld Cragor's rule in Benzos. He had no need to disband it now that he had the Royal

Treasury at his command. Those eleven thousand men were the heart of Galkor's army, equal to any task he might set them. Two thousand mercenaries of lesser quality served Galkor himself and the Civic Council of Fors. They would be joined by two thousand more mercenaries coming south from Lukaz.

Ten thousand remained. Of these, seven thousand—too many of the cavalry on spavined mounts and too many infantrymen tramping along in worn boots and rags were the levies called forth by (or from) those lords in the Viceroyalty still loyal to Cragor. The final three thousand was the Civic Militia of Fors. Galkor had small use for or trust in them, in spite of their good equipment and discipline. Indeed, he suspected that without the curse that seemed to have fallen on their city, they would not have marched out at all. And taking them would leave Fors virtually defenseless. But he preferred to leave it that way rather than leave it held only by its own citizens. He wanted to be sure that the city's gates would not close behind him, and then open to Wandor.

Carts and wagons and pack horses were coming across the drawbridge now in a rumble of wheels and a cracking of whips and curses from the teamsters. Galkor had taken great care with the supply trains. He would not rely on foraging among the barns and cellars of the countryside. Once scattered to do that, half the army might well keep on scattering, seeking a safe hiding place where they could sit out the campaign, falling prey to cold and hunger and the Khindi.

Kaldmor the Dark came up on the parapet in time to see the last of the carts rumble out of the gates. Already the vanguard of the army was long out of sight. As the marching men breasted the top of Temple Hill, raised pikes and lances and the poles of the wind-whipped banners stood out for a moment, thin and gaunt against the driven cold gray clouds. Then they were gone.

"A good army," said Galkor to the sorcerer. "It will do all that needs to be done."

There was a note of correction in Kaldmor's voice. "It will do all that an army can do."

Stares collided for a moment. Then Galkor shrugged and wrapped his cloak about his shoulders. "Come. I have our horses ready below." He turned and moved briskly toward the stairs.

* * *

Another winter morning, gray ugliness everywhere. A message from Cheloth—Galkor's army still marching south. A breakfast of hot milk and dry bread toasted over a fire and dipped in melted cheese. Then mounting the King Horse and riding out with the morning patrols. This morning Wandor chose to ride with Gwynna and her guard of Plainsmen, adding ten mercenary horsemen to it.

They rode out of the waking camp at a canter, moving in single file. A mile north of the camp, Wandor signaled the patrol to spread out to the left and right. The hard, bare earth on either side of the road would easily support horses of any size and weight.

The scouting line formed, stretching out until Wandor could not see either end as he moved along the road. In this open country the line could stretch three miles from end to end and let nothing pass unseen. Beyond it on the left and right would be other lines, curving round on to the flanks of the advancing army. And many miles ahead the distant patrols of Plainsmen and raiding parties of Khindi would have long since broken camp to begin their day's harrying of Baron Galkor's army.

Then Wandor saw the crest of the ridge barely fifty yards ahead suddenly sprout a small dark cluster of horsemen. Mailed and helmeted light cavalry. Wandor also saw silver and orange colors he—and Gwynna even more—knew well. A trumpet call floated down to him from the ridge; then the horsemen wheeled and plunged out of sight down the far side of the ridge.

The King Horse was working up to a gallop almost as Wandor's recognition of the enemy set his blood pounding. Gwynna was hard after him, the Plainsmen on either side after her. The men ahead had a good start and a downhill slope, but Wandor began whittling down their lead the moment the King Horse mounted the ridge crest.

Hoof thunder on the frozen ground, bellows gasping of his own breath and the King Horse's, the war yells of the Plainsmen. They were nocking arrows to their bows as they galloped. One Plainsman went down as his horse failed to clear a fence, but the rest had a dozen arrows in the air in as many seconds. They would not penetrate mail at this range, but the enemy's horse's wore no mail. Two went down, spilling their riders to the ground.

Two more swerved toward a copse of pine. Three Plainsmen cut them off. A flurry of swords and lances, and of the five only a single Plainsman remained in his saddle. One more of the enemy lost his seat as his horse took a wall. Then Wandor himself came up with the last one, sword flickering out. The man threw down his own sword and lance and, raised his hands. He was a mercenary; fighting to the death was seldom part of his war wisdom.

Gwynna's eyes were cold as she stared at the silver and orange markings, but for the moment Wandor ignored her. "You follow Master Besz?"

"I do..."

"Where does Besz ride in Galkor's army?"

If the mercenary had any thoughts of telling lies or remaining silent, they lasted only until he saw the expression on Gwynna's face. Then his own face went the color of the dead leaves piled beside the fences. "Besz rides in the vanguard as chief of the scouts. In battle he will command the right wing."

Wandor nodded and smiled thinly, then turned to Gwynna. "Ride back and have Jos-Pran send a hundred more men forward to each scouting party. From now on they must be prepared to fight."

Scouts crisscrossed the chill gray-hued land all that day and far into the night, as the two armies felt for each other. Small savage fights spluttered and flared as patrols met. Galkor had no Watcher, but by the next morning he had no doubt that Wandor's army was close at hand. Wandor knew the same of his enemy.

For the next day and the next night, the two armies drew apart, and they and their commanders considered what to do next. Cheloth withdrew his Watcher to conserve his Powers for the battle of magic that he knew must accompany the battle of men.

For each army, there was an obvious strategy. For Wandor's, it was to put part of its strength north of Galkor. Threatened with being cut off from Fors, he would attack. And then the rest of the army could attack Galkor from the rear and destroy him. But this would involve a dangerous maneuver—uniting a divided—army on the actual battlefield, with one part of it already engaged. For Galkor's army, the best thing to do was outflank Wandor and separate the advanced and rear bodies. Wandor would at once be forced to fight and could then be defeated in detail. But they would have to keep Wandor's army divided.

For five days each army tried to create the conditions it needed for its own victory. Neither succeeded. Galkor was cautious and careful by nature, Wandor by necessity. Both kept their scouting lines spread wide across the armies' fronts. Neither could slip unseen around the other's flanks, neither Wandor moving north nor Galkor moving south. Wandor kept his army divided, the two halves a few hours' march apart, to tempt Galkor into an attack. Galkor kept his army united to be better able to attack Wandor if an opportunity arose.

Fires flared in the night as patrols tore up fences and barns to drive away the darkness and the cold. A steady stream of maimed and dead flowed back from the scouting lines, and a steady stream of reinforcements flowed forward to them. Where Galkor's patrols attacked unsupported Plainsmen in strength, their armor and heavier horses sometimes gave them an advantage. But more often they met Plainsmen supported by concealed Khind archers, and matters went less well for them.

Once Galkor sent a thousand picked infantry forward at dawn to drive back the Khindi. But Wandor at once brought up the four hundred heavy cavalry of his advanced body. Cavalry and infantry, Plainsmen and Khindi brawled and fought up and down a mile of countryside, and when each side drew back, nothing had changed— except for the three hundred men dead or wounded.

But there were Khindi and Plainsmen elsewhere than in Wandor's scouting line. A thousand or more of them roamed the countryside far in the rear of Galkor's army, even to the walls of Fors. Dispatch riders never arrived, flaming arrows arched into tents, pitfalls swallowed horsemen, fallen trees blocked the march of infantry, half-sawn bridge timbers gave way under supply wagons. On the morning of the fifth day the commander of Cragor's baronial levies, son and heir to the Duke of Famorin, died as he shaved himself in front of his tent, a Khind arrow through his throat. On the afternoon of that same day a column of reinforcements riding up to the patrol line was ambushed. Those who survived did not draw rein until they were halfway back to Fors. That night a barn where two hundred of the Fors militiamen were sleeping burned to the ground. Once more the survivors did not stop running until their strength was gone.

On the morning of the sixth day, Galkor gave the order to retreat. He wanted his army to walk back to Fors, not run. Much more time spent in the bleak countryside, harried by Khindi and Plainsmen, losing men in the pointless bickering along the patrol lines, and it would indeed run, and perhaps not even stop at Fors.

Even so, Galkor's army went back with more haste than dignity and with small care for its equipment. Snow swirled down on the day of the retreat, and Wandor's patrols probed cautiously forward, feeling for the enemy. Hundreds of intact tents and loaded wagons lay in camps and along the roads.

It took Wandor two days to find Galkor's army again. When he found it, it lay in a solid position covering Fors, ten miles from the city. Its right flank rested on the northern tip of Fors Bay, its left was covered by forest. Two more days of probing, and Wander knew he would not be attacking Galkor there. It was time to see if Galkor could be baited into a fight.

In another snowstorm, the world all sullen gray and swirling white, Wandor found his chosen battlefield. Tethering the King Horse in the lee of a ramshackle barn, he climbed to the loft and stared out over the countryside.

Galkor would be a fool not to attack a weaker force offering battle here. The ground stretched three miles from north to south and a mile from the base of the ham to the low ridge in the west. There were hedges and ditches here and there, occasional copses of trees, and a few farm buildings, but nothing to offer much cover to a defender or much to disturb an attacker's charge. Here Wandor's army could be outflanked at once and then hammered slowly to pieces by successive charges of cavalry and infantry. And without the scouts' and patrols and camp guards, Wandor would he bringing barely ten thousand men to the battle—at least to its opening struggle. When Galkor had committed himself to the battle, however, and his army was inextricably entangled with Wandor's, the odds could suddenly be changed.

But would Galkor give battle in the face of such an obvious ruse? Quite possibly. Even a cautious general may yield to eager subordinates, and some of Galkor's commanders would be young, fiery, eager to try conclusions with Wandor's "horde of savages" and sweep them away. There were too many of the Order of Knights among Galkor's commanders, and there were too many among that Order with contempt for both caution and irregular troops. Besides, Wandor knew that he had another ally among those with Galkor's army.

Kaldmor the Dark.

It was not just it question of the sorcerer's vanity now. If he did not use his powers in this crisis, he would likely forfeit all credit with both Galkor and the Black Duke. Perhaps Kaldmor would actually be confident in his new-won Toshakan skills. Almost certainly he would *seem* confident. He would join the commanders in urging a battle on Wandor, promising to use his powers against any traps Wandor might be planning to spring.

Wandor knew his enemy. He knew or could guess the kinds of mistakes they would make. And that was half of any battle. But did he know his own mind? Was he letting his determination to crown with victory the campaign on which he had gambled so much carry him beyond reasonable limits?

Perhaps. But the time was past when there were more than two alternatives. Retreat south, in the dead of winter, through country eaten half bare, with a revived enemy snapping at his heels. Or try to bring that enemy to battle and win a victory, and with the victory the Viceroyalty of the East.

His doubts were gone or at least controlled as he descended the ladder. Gwynna met him as he came out of the barn. He took her hand and clutched it as though he expected strength to flow from it into him. Then he said, "We are riding back and calling a council. We give battle here." He mounted the King Horse and spurred it away through the snow without looking back at the field.

* * *

"We will march to meet Wandor," Galkor had said. That had been two days ago when the scouts came in and reported that Wandor's advanced body was offering battle. "We will attack in the morning," he had said also. That had been last night, as the army camped to the west of the low ridge separating them from Wandor's army. The sky was clearing rapidly, and the brilliant colors of a winter sunset tinted clean fresh snow laying a hand's breadth deep on the ground. On the ridge the scouts of both armies moved, black stick shapes in the twilight, watching each other without fighting. With the two armies now arrayed for battle less than two miles apart, the scouts' warfare was accomplished.

Wandor's rear body had been much in Galkor's thoughts as he watched the campfires flare all across the snow. "Wandor can only want us to attack so that he can bring his rear up against us. If he thinks I cannot recognize this, be is a fool."

"He is not a fool, Baron."

"I know that! But perhaps we—you—can make him look like one. Seek out that rear with your sorcery, Master Kaldmor. Destroy it if you can—"

"Do not speak of destroying something under the protection of Cheloth of the Woods. I—"

"I said *if*, Master Kaldmor! If you cannot, at least contrive that it will not come forward to join Wandor until we have destroyed him. Contrive it so that he will have to fight tomorrow's battle with ten thousand savages against twenty-five thousand soldiers."

"I will do my best."

"That is well, Master Kaldmor. Now go about your business, and leave me to mine."

Now there was color in the sky again, the more delicate tints of a winter dawn, and Kaldmor stood under a pine tree and prepared to do his work. From the camp of Galkor's army rose the clatterings and clankings, the coughings and stampings, of an army awakening to a day of battle. The smoke from dying campfires hazed the sky on both sides of the ridge.

But Kaldmor's attention was all on the patch of ground before him. He had cleared it of snow and sprinkled it with a mixture of the four powders from his four gold boxes. In the exact center of the patch stood the *limar* of Nem of Toshak, rigid, hands at its side, eyes fixed on Kaldmor's face. On the *limar*'s chest dangled a star-shaped medallion in what looked like dirty silver.

It was a *khru* medallion, the most precious result of the recent months of delving into Toshakan lore. It had taken him many nights of sweating over molds and forges, and more than a few burns and scorches, to match formulas and dimensions and weights. But in the end he had cast the medallion properly.

What it would do, what he hoped for it, was to give almost any spell he might cast *instant* effect. There would be no need to build up the spell bit by bit, like a mason building up a wall stone by stone. Across the miles, from his place of vigil, Cheloth of the Woods would detect such slow-growing magic and counter it. But against a spell that leaped from nowhere upon its victims, like a starving leopard from the branch of a tree, not even Cheloth could act in time. And that was the way he would strike down Wandor's rear body with a sleeping spell.

Kaldmor would have struck down Wandor's whole army with that one spell if he could, but anything passing through the *khru* medallion had to be focused on a single target. The two halves of Wandor's army were a good five miles apart, too far for a single focused spell to blast them both. Not even tapping the powers of Nem of Toshak could make that possible. There was only one way of doing that, and the stakes were still not high enough to Kaldmor's way of thinking to make him willing to risk it. He would strike down Wandor's rear with one spell and then do what he could against the advanced body with a second one. That should be enough.

It was time to begin. Wincing at the bitter air flowing over his bare skin, Kaldmor stripped off his robes and began a slow walk around the patch of snow. In the swelling dawn light the medallion took on a pinkish tinge, and the eyes of the *limar* continued to stare straight at him.

Without warning, Gwynna screamed and clapped her hands to her head. Wandor sprang from the saddle and ran to her, pulled her against him while she screamed and shook, wrapped his cloak around her, shouted for hot drink. He knew what it was. Toshakan magic. Even his own head was throbbing, his vision blurring.

It passed as swiftly as it came. Gwynna sagged into his arms, and he reached for the straps of her armor to unbuckle it. Count Arlor ran up with a soldier carrying a steaming jug, and the two of them lifted Gwynna and carried her toward Wandor's tent. Wandor followed, eyes roving, trying to read the faces of the men around him. He saw shock, surprise, uncertainty. No fear as yet. There would be time for that when Kaldmor's latest effort began to show itself to the normal material senses.

It did so just as Wandor reached the tent. Beyond the ridge that concealed Galkor's army, to the southwest, a blue glow began to swell, pouring raw light into the pale sky. The blueness swelled more, wavering unsteadily like a soap bubble blown by a child, and then more still. The blueness was creeping up the far side of the ridge now, toward the crest where the patrols of both sides were scattering. Wandor ran back toward the King Horse. He reached it as the fringes of the blue flickered in tendrils and sparks over the ridge. He could see fear on every face now—and smell it pouring from every man like vapors from a swamp.

As he clasped the pommel of the saddle, he felt his arm suddenly grow enormously heavy, as though twenty pounds of iron were tied around it. Again his vision blurred, but this time there was no pain in his head. Only an enormous peacefulness and lassitude swelling up and enveloping him the way the blue Toshakan light had swelled up and enveloped the ridge. His legs, too, seemed to be hung with immensely heavy weights. He had no hope of lifting those legs to the stirrups. In fact, it was all he could do to keep his grip on the saddle. He wanted terribly much to release it, to fall down on his face in the snow, to sleep without ever again dreaming or caring about anything...

He staggered as if he had run into a solid wall and fell back from the King Horse, landing on his seat in the snow. He struggled to his feet, realizing as he did so that his arms and legs no longer seemed weighted down. Instead, they were tingling as though the blood were flowing through them at twice the normal rate. A now-familiar Mind Speech pattern began pulsing at the fringes of his mind. Cheloth of the

Woods.

Wandor could not keep the question, "Where in the name of all the gods have you been?" out of Cheloth's awareness. He felt the sorcerer stop as his probing encountered the question. Then the probing turned swiftly into words.

("Kaldmor has used a *khru*-aided spell to throw your entire rear body into a deep sleep. He was about to do the same to the rest of your army, but this I can easily fight off.")

Wandor raised his eyes toward the ridge. A green light as raw and dazzling as the blue was pouring down from the sky like rain. Where it struck the blue, sparks flickered and sprayed out in long arcs and in a hundred searing flares of incandescent colors.

("How long will the rear sleep?")

("I do not know. The spell was strong and well-wrought. I can do nothing for them until I have contained Kaldmor. Even then it may be hours before I can wake them.")

Wandor nodded wearily. Cheloth would do what he could, and there was no cause to abuse him for not doing more. And he and Gwynna and Arlor and the rest of the advanced body would do what they would have to do—fight against more than twice its numbers until the sleep-fogged rear came up to play its intended part in the battle. He swung himself up into the saddle and stared toward the ridge again. The blue glare and the green were battling each other high in the air now. Across the churned and half-melted snow, a line of horsemen was making its way. A silver and orange banner whipped in the wind of their passage.

("Galkor's army is advancing to the attack, Cheloth.")

("Then give of your best—King Wandor.")

Cheloth withdrew from Wandor's mind, and each turned aside to do his work in the battle.

CHAPTER 23

Wander had his army drawn up according to his own best judgment and the best advice from Count Arlor, Jos-Pran, and the royal infantry commander. He had kept his double purpose in mind. His army could not look so formidable as to deter attack entirely, nor so contemptible that Galkor would hold back his full strength. Drawing in Galkor's full strength was of course a far greater gamble now than it had been when he planned the battle. Now he could no longer even hope to disengage safely if luck was not with him. Whether what urged him on to give battle was wisdom or folly, care or contempt for the lives of his followers, no longer mattered.

He had about ten thousand men at hand, and of these nearly nine thousand formed a great square. Baggage was piled in the center, guarded by armed peasants who had joined the army on its way north. Next outward from the center were three thousand Plainsmen, three out of four dismounted to spare their gaunt and worn horses, Then, in a solid mass at the rear of the square, the four hundred heavy cavalry, the men likewise dismounted for the moment.

Twelve hundred of the royal infantry formed the next layer of the square, split into three equal-sized formations. Each one stood ready to support the Khindi of the outer line in any battle at close quarters. But Wandor hoped there would be no such action. There were four thousand Khind warriors in that outer line, the pick of all the clans and tribes. As long as they had arrows for their bows and a clear shot at the enemy, no army in the world could easily push home an attack

185

against them across open country.

Wandor had positioned the square so that across its entire rear ran a maze of small hedges and fenced fields, trees, and farm buildings. To add to the protection those gave, he had stationed there a thousand-odd Khindi and Plainsmen. Between natural obstacles and their arrows and lances Wandor was confident no full-scale attack could come in against his rear.

Master Besz himself led the first attack, some two hundred cavalry of his own force and upwards of three hundred in the colors of other captains. In a wide-flung triple line they trotted down toward Wandor's front. Besz would not lead any headlong charges against Khind bows. He would leave that sort of folly to the Knights.

So his cavalry divided as they came within bowshot and broke into a gallop, pouring down each side of the square. Khind arrows whistled toward them but largely fell short. The Khind chiefs ran among their warriors, cuffing and cursing the eager ones who were wasting arrows. The charge kept on until the archers guarding the rear could hit it. They unhorsed a good two-score men, and the Plainsmen rode out and lanced those who survived the fall of their horses. But the rest withdrew in good order. Wandor realized that Galkor—or at least Besz—now had a good notion of how far his opponent could strike.

As Besz's charge withdrew, the main body of Galkor's army came up over the ridge and began spreading out to the left and to the right. Galkor, it seemed, was hoping to awe his enemy by arraying his army in full sight.

But the next actual attack came soon enough, although it seemed far too long a time to Wandor's tight-stretched nerves. Trumpets blared, drums thundered, a line of mounted men began to form atop the ridge, with fifty different banners floating above them. Minute by minute they gathered until it seemed that the ridge had sprouted a solid wall of flesh and steel.

Then the drums held a single long roll, lances rose black against the sky and then dipped, and the trumpets' terrible voice rose in the call of "Charge!" The earth seemed to roll and vibrate like the drumheads themselves as the mass of armored horsemen gathered way, coming down the slope at a walk, then a trot, then a canter. The slope was on their side, the snow was too shallow to slow them, and the earth

186

was firm under their horses' hooves. Wandor swallowed and tasted blood from his bitten lips.

At three hundred yards the first Khind arrows went out, dropping haphazardly among the leaders of the charge. Then a more solid blackness flickered in the air between the Khindi and their opponents. And a thousand Khind arrows plunged among the charging Knights.

They died there, pierced through the weak spots in their rumor, hurled to the ground from horses stricken or stumbling, trampled underfoot. In a moment the first two lines among the Knights were only scattered clusters of men still plunging forward. The third line caught them up; then the second volley came down. The third line also dissolved into scattered handfuls, the fourth line closed another fifty yards, and again the arrows sought out lives of men and horses.

By now a stretch of ground more than a hundred yards deep and five hundred wide was all but carpeted with the still or struggling bodies of men and horses. Those horsemen who kept their seats passing across the death stretch could not keep their formation. But they kept their courage and determination. In half-dozens and dozens, in scores and fifties and hundreds, they plunged down the slope, lances leveled, swords dancing in the sun, banners still rising high, and war cries rising higher yet.

They were less deadly so scattered, but also less vulnerable. Some of the Knights reached the Khind ranks. Hundreds of the warriors dropped their bows and gave way or sought to hold their places with axes and knives against swords and maces and lances. Many died in this unequal contest.

But the royal infantry ran forward, pikes leveled and halberd heads swinging in a fanged line. Behind them the Plainsmen began shooting over the heads of the Khindi. More of the attackers' horses went down, more Knights died under Khind hatchets and infantry halberds as they tried to retreat on foot.

In time the charge died away, and the horsemen began to drift back up the slope to their starting place, urged on their way by occasional volleys of Khind arrows. In men they had lost nearly a quarter of their strength, in horses more than a third.

As if the Knights' charge and repulse had been a bloodletting for a feverish patient, the battle quieted for a time. Wandor rode along the front of the square, taking note of losses. Between the Khindi who had taken the brunt of the charge, the royal infantry who had helped repel it, and the Plainsmen who had run in too close, more than four hundred were dead or past using their weapons. Some of the wounded and dying greeted Wandor with smiles and waves as he rode past, but his own thoughts were too sober to let him reply in kind.

Even such a crude frontal attack had cost his army too many men. Too many of these attacks could bring defeat. And further attacks might be launched with more skill. He spared time for a glance upward into the sky above Galkor's army. Green and blue still flared and strove against each other, but was the green now flaring brighter than the blue?

As Wandor returned to his position, Galkor's entire left wing lurched and heaved like a pig climbing out of a wallow and lumbered forward. From the banners, Wandor recognized that it was mostly the locally raised levies and the Fors militiamen. But the better part of ten thousand men coming toward one is frightening, whether they are good soldiers or not. Some of the Khindi were unnerved enough to send arrows arching toward an enemy far out of range. Eventually the whole mass came to rest hard on Wandor's right flank, but for the moment still out of bowshot.

As the left settled into position, Galkor's center rolled forward, a thousand mercenary cavalry and five thousand infantry equally divided between baronial levies and mercenaries. They, too, closed to just outside bowshot, then settled into position, glowering down the slope at their enemy. Behind their ranks Wandor could see other banners against the sky, as the Knights reformed. Two sides out of three of his square were covered now. What would Galkor launch on the left?

Wandor did not have long to wait. More trumpets blared, and a long column of horsemen began creeping down the slope from the right end of Galkor's line. Well over a thousand light horsemen began creeping down the slope from the right end of Galkor's line. A thousand light cavalry, with the orange and silver markings forming a solid splash of color in the center of the line. Wandor could make out Besz himself among his men under a silver and orange banner flapping in the dying breeze.

Then the infantry came out, mercenaries and Cragor's levies in alternating blocks, in two long lines with nearly two thousand men in each line. The nearer line seemed mostly light infantry armed with short sword and buckler, but a solid mass of pikemen held down either end of the line. In the half-invisible second line Wandor saw mostly crossbowmen in cap and cuirass and stingers with nothing but boots and breeches between them and the cold.

Time passed onward, and the lights in the sky still flared. Beyond any doubt the blue was beginning to fade, driven lower and lower by the greenness slowly spreading across the sky. Would Cheloth soon have the power to spare to revive Wandor's sleeping rear body?

Master Besz rode up and down his formations with his banner bearer beside him. The horsemen largely blocked Wandor's view of what was happening among the infantry beyond. But he could see clusters of pike tips now bunching up, now spreading out. The cavalry also spread out until it formed a line stretching down nearly the whole of Wandor's left line, two or three ranks deep. As the cavalry thinned out, Wandor could see the light infantry and pikemen lining up behind them. As he saw that, he realized what Galkor (or more likely Besz) was planning.

He had no time to shout a warning even to Arlor, sitting on his horse only yards away. The "Charge" rose harsh and raw from trumpets all along Besz's line, and the light cavalry surged forward, faster than the Knights could ever have done. The whole thousand-odd was moving at a gallop before they were within bowshot. As they rode in, they spread out still more and began to weave back and forth. The silver and orange horsemen were the best at this, but none held a straight course, none made an easy target even for a Khind archer. Behind the cavalry the light infantrymen moved forward at a jog, the pikemen on either flank, the crossbowmen and slingers advancing behind them.

A good many arrows went wide before the Khindi got on to their targets. Their warrior's courage and their loyalty to Wandor the Helm-Wearer did not give them the training they needed to face Besz's charge unmoved. By the time they had steadied to their work, the cavalry line was much less than two hundred yards away. Wandor saw the Plainsmen, urged on by Gwynna, running from their horses and unslinging their own bows, adding their lighter arrows to the Khindi's. More than half the horsemen went down, dead or unseated, before the other half crashed into the Khind line.

Their horses and their weapons and their armor were all light. It was easy for a Khind to slip under their guard and hamstring a horse, for a royal halberdier to split a horseman from crown to chest, for a Plainsman to swing his heavy curved sword at an exposed calf. But while Khindi and Plainsmen and royal infantry were doing this, the enemy's light infantry were closing across the corpse-littered snow almost unmolested. Wandor could see only one way to stop them.

"Sound the 'Charge' for the heavy cavalry," he shouted to the trumpeter. He saw Arlor start, then slam down the visor of his helmet and draw his sword. The trumpet blared in a frenzy. Wandor heard the clanks and whinnyings as the heavy cavalry mounted and saw the Khindi near the left rear of the square start to scatter, to clear a path for the cavalry. Wandor waved to Gwynna, then drew his own sword and spurred the King Horse forward. Four hundred heavy cavalry plunged through the gap left by the Khindi, swept away the few enemy horsemen not already engaged, and smashed into the advancing infantry. Light infantry were never intended to stand a charge of heavy cavalry in the open field. Pikemen were. The pikemen on the near flank came running in, presenting a moving wall of bristling steel points. They drove hard into the left flank of Wandor's advancing column of horsemen. He heard the screams of horses dying on pike points as he and the King Horse crashed into the thickest press of the light-armed men.

The King Horse reared and neighed and lashed out with hooves and teeth as Wandor slashed down with his sword. Hooves crushed in one man's skull, sword lopped through another's shield arm. Count Arlor's horse bowled two more infantrymen aside by sheer weight and trampled down a third that ran in to attack it from beneath. One of the light cavalrymen rode at Wander, silver and orange streamers floating from his polished black helm. Wandor's first sword cut slashed the streamers from the man's helm and beat down his guard. The second gashed open the mail along the man's shoulder and the flesh beneath it. Then the man's horse carried him out of Wandor's reach. A moment after that, the light infantry ranks in front of him gave way. The pikemen from the enemy's other flank shouldered their way through the press, lunging hard at the end of Wandor's line.

Wandor owed his life to the King Horse. Sensing the oncoming enemy a moment before the pikes struck, it reared and twisted and, came down facing halfway from the enemy. Then it plunged among the horses behind it. Wandor was luckier than the men behind him. The sudden check to their advance piled them into a solid mass, nearly a hundred packed so tightly they could not turn their horses and barely could use their weapons. The pikemen surged forward again, the front rank kneeling and thrusting upward at the horses' bellies. Horses went down, their riders leaping or falling to the ground, fighting for their lives against light infantrymen rushing in, short-swords thrusting furiously.

But there were three hundred horsemen or more still free to move. With swords waving and oaths turning the air blue, Arlor and Wandor started pulling them back. In the moment when it began to look as though they would succeed, a new trumpet call rose. A moment later bolts from crossbows and stones from slings began whizzing and dropping into the ranks of the horsemen.

Some of the bowmen opened up from extreme range and sent a fair number of their bolts into the ground or into the ranks of their friends. But a greater number closed to accurate and deadly range. As Wandor drew clear of the head of the column, he saw Count Arlor's horse stagger, its skull drilled through by a bolt at point-blank range. The count leaped clear as his mount went down. Instantly the light infantrymen surrounded him. Wandor saw his tall figure rise above them, his sword flashing in the sun.

Arlor was not the only one, nor were all those struck as lucky as he. Some of the crossbowmen were breaking formation now, running in to fire from such close range that their bolts knocked fully armored men off their horses. Wandor backed the King Horse again to avoid stepping on still-living bodies. But he could not back much farther. To his left rear he could see that some of the pikemen and bowmen were sliding around to cut off his entire column from the main square of the army. If that happened, all the heavy cavalry would quite probably die under the bolts and pikes and stones, and the outcome of the battle would no longer mean anything. It occurred to Wandor that perhaps it was not his place to stay out here and die. But he was certain that it was not in him to do otherwise.

He looked around for a trumpeter to sound the retreat, but it was the enemy's trumpets he heard. Another call of "Charge!" and a sudden uproar of war cries and thundering hooves. Beyond the deadly grapple of horsemen and foot soldiers with bolts whizzing about them, the ground seemed to sprout a wall of gleaming armor, tall horses, colored banners flaunted against the sky. A moving wall rolling forward at a trot that became a canter. The Knights of Galkor's heavy cavalry were hurling themselves back into the battle, reformed and restored. They were eager to fight as it was proper to fight, sword against sword, horseman against horseman.

If they knew that their own crossbowmen lay in their path toward Wandor's horsemen, they did not care. In a solid explosion of sound, they smashed through the left flank of the crossbowmen, scattering or trampling hundreds, driving hundreds more back on to their fellows in panic-stricken confusion. They showed more respect for the bristling hedgehog of pikemen grappling with the head of Wandor's column, dividing to flow around it, losing speed in the process. Khind arrows began striking down men and horses here and there, but the Khindi of the left flank were weakened and shaken from the charge of the light cavalry. Hardly slowed, hardly weakened, more than a thousand of the best blood of Benzos crashed into Wandor's mauled cavalry.

Wandor saw horses on both sides flung into the air by the shock and men by the dozens crashing to the ground. The clang of colliding metal that rose into the air sounded as though someone had all at once dropped a thousand anvils on a stone floor. Once more Wandor's horsemen were so close jammed that they could not move and could barely use their weapons. If the crossbowmen had not been thrown into confusion by the Knights' charge, a single salvo of bolts could have laid Wandor and half his men on the ground.

Wandor, driven back by the shock, at least had freedom to move. With bellowed, half-incoherent orders and flourishes of his sword, he drew a dozen men out of the press, then pointed toward the mass of the enemy's cavalry. "Follow me!" he roared, and spurred the King Horse forward. Madness was on him, but only a small part of his reasoning mind was left to recognize that fact. The King Horse responded more slowly than usual; even its magnificent strength was nearing an end. But as it gathered speed, again trumpets and hoof thunder rose above other battle noises. From behind Wandor, this time. He turned in his saddle to look, and then he stared and gaped, his mouth too wide open in astonishment to cheer.

Armored horsemen were pouring out of the woods behind Wandor's square at a full gallop. They reeled and lurched in their saddles as their horses plunged forward. Almost in the lead rode Baron Delvor, shield on his arm, mace brandished aloft, thundering incoherent curses and war cries in a voice that cut through even the hooves and trumpets.

Wandor reined in just in time to keep from plunging blindly into the ranks of the enemy's Knights, so fiercely that the King Horse nearly went back on its haunches. For a moment he was a stationary target, in easy range of almost all the crossbowmen. Bolts whizzed past him, and one glanced off his breastplate with a clang and a metallic screech.

Then Baron Delvor's hurtling charge smashed into the crossbowmen. They had been rolled up from the left by their own Knights. Now they were rolled up from the right by Baron Delvor's charge, as thoroughly as any housemaid ever rolled up a carpet. Those of them still on their feet scurried off as fast as they could.

Wandor swung the King Horse around and headed back along the line of horsemen, back toward the main body of his army. The madness was gone out of him, and the danger was vanishing for the horsemen he had led out. Now it was proper and even necessary for him to return to where he could see the battle as a whole and give his orders.

As he rode, he saw that his left at least had no need for orders from him. All along the flank the Khindi, reinforced by warriors from the rest of the square, were pouring arrows into the Knights and the light infantry. Then the Khindi split apart as the whole of the royal infantry came shouldering through, advancing grimly on the disordered ranks of the enemy. Wandor saw Berek marching beside the commander of the infantry, Thunderstone on his shoulder, Greenfoam at his belt. With joy he saw Arlor emerge from the press and take position on the opposite side of the infantry commander. And a look over his shoulder showed still more cavalry coming out of the woods. Some of the Plainsmen of the rear guard had also mounted up and were riding out. Some of the Khindi ran along behind them, bows ready and shrill war yells sounding.

Wandor spurred the King Horse back through the ranks of the Khindi, toward where he had left Gwynna. As he rode, he looked toward the right, where the militia of Fors and the local levies were drawn up. As he did, he saw their formation heaving and beginning to shed men around the edges, then lurching solidly forward as, something struck it—*hard*—from the rear. Banners began to waver and go down.

Plainsman war drums sounded, and Gwynna's gold plume glowed in the bright sun as she led two thousand Plainsmen out to charge the shaken mass of levies and militia. Wandor had to ride up to Jos-Pran and bellow in his ear to keep him from joining Gwynna's charge with all the rest of his warriors.

Side by side they sat on their horses and watched as Gwynna's charge smashed the enemy apart. Most of those among the levies who died did so because they could not run fast enough, not because they stood to fight. But here and there small clusters of Knights and their retainers stood until arrows or lances or swords took them. And the Civic Militia of Fors stood in a solid mass, three thousand strong. It stood until Wandor sent out a message that they were to be allowed to withdraw. They acknowledged his clemency with sober dignity, turned about, and marched off in good order toward their city.

So much for the right. On the left there was more fighting, but in the end a victory as complete. The mercenaries had fought longer and endured more than mercenaries had ever done in all the history of Benzos. But the battle was now lost, and no mercenary sees it as his business to fight to his last drop of blood in a lost battle. Those who could make their way from the field did so; those who could surrender likewise did so. This left the Knights to fight unsupported, which they did, almost to the last man. More might have surrendered, but the royal infantry was giving them little quarter and the Khindi none at all.

"The mercenaries were too intelligent to die, so they fled. The Knights were too stupid to flee, so they died." That was Gwynna's summary of the battle on the left when she rode back to Wandor. Her leg was tightly bound in cloth after a glancing blow with a round-headed mace had cracked the bone. They both looked toward Galkor's center.

Part of it still stood, formed in a square solid and black against the snow and a sky where only a green light showed now, and even that was fading. But part of it was gone, and with it Galkor's banner.

CHAPTER 24

Fifteen men and the *limar* of Nem of Toshak rode toward Fors Bay. The men were Baron Galkor, Kaldmor the Dark, Master Besz, and twelve of Besz's soldiers.

They rode past the baggage trains of Galkor's army. Most of the teamsters and wagon guards had already fled. A few, out of loyalty or perhaps hope for loot, had not. These were now fighting Khindi, Plainsmen, royal cavalry, and each other for possession of the wagons.

Galkor stared at the shields and banners of the royal cavalry. "Where in the name of the Five Gods did they come from?"

Besz said, "I understand a force of a thousand or so found a path through the forests around Lukaz. The Khindi guided them. They slipped past your garrison and came in on your left just before the Lady Gwynna led the Plainsmen against it."

Galkor nodded, but said nothing. In fact, he said nothing for the whole hour it took them to reach the nearest fishing village on the shores of Fors Bay.

Just outside the village, Besz reined in his horse and turned to Galkor. "Here I leave you, my lord baron. You have in your purse sufficient gold to get any fisherman to take you and Master Kaldmor across the bay, to Fors. There no doubt you can find a ship to take you across the Ocean."

Galkor stared. Kaldmor looked as if he would have liked to, but be was so exhausted he could barely sit in his saddle. Then Galkor said, "You—leave me? Why? What for? Are you going to—?" His

196

face turned the same color as his fatigue-reddened eyes, and his hand went to his sword hilt.

Besz made a quick gesture, and several of his men raised cocked and loaded crossbows. "Do not think to serve me as Duke Cragor served Sir Festan Jalgath after the battle of Delkum Pass. And do not concern yourself about whom I serve after I leave you. That is not your affair." He pointed toward the beach. "Go, my lord baron. Go, Master Kaldmor and your—friend."

They went as he bid them.

The Battle of Fors, begun shortly after the eighth hour of the morning, was virtually completed by the eleventh hour. After that came the job of assembling the various forces scattered all the way from the battlefield to the city's walls, accepting surrenders, and disposing of the bodies of those who had not surrendered. Wandor said afterward that it was like trying to rebuild a house swept away by the flood of a great river, by picking up all the timbers of the house from where the flood had left them along the river bank.

This took all the remaining hours of daylight, and during those hours Wandor had many things to say to many people.

—To Baron Oman Delvor:

"Why did you charge like that? You and your men were barely awakened from the sleeping spell. It was a miracle you could even find the enemy!"

"Perhaps. All I knew when I woke was—Wandor and Gwynna need help. Ride to their aid. Kill their enemies. It looked very simple at the time." The baron shook his head, still half dazed.

—To the commander of the royal infantry and a Baron somebody-or-other, commanding the newly arrived royal cavalry:

"I cannot say how well I will be able to pay you and your men. We—Nond's supporters rule now in the Viceroyalty. But we will not bleed its people to support our army."

"We would not wish that," said the baron. "Our men will serve for their rations and clothing alone as long as necessary; even until Cragor falls. And so will the officers. To avenge Nond is more important than gold."

—To the assembled mercenary captains, except for Master Besz:

"I cannot offer more than a handful of you decent wages for entering my service. So I will not hold it against you if you wish to return to Benzos. All those who wish to do so, I will release on parole until the Ocean becomes safe for voyaging in the spring. But if any of you wish to settle here in the Viceroyalty, there are many farms lying vacant from all the years' of war. And there is enough good land for carving out many new farms. You will be welcome."

The spokesman for the captains nodded and said, "I am glad of that. I fear that many of us would find a cold welcome in the Home Lands after surrendering to Cragor's mortal enemy. He is a hard master, to say the least. I think the greater part of us will choose to settle here, at least for the time being. We ask only that if you find the occasion to raise an army some time in the future, we have the chance to serve."

—To Master Besz himself:

"I will not say I forgive or forget your treatment of the Lady Gwynna. Still less will I say that *she* will forgive or forget it. But you treated her properly, according to your strange codes. So I will not say you and your men cannot enter my service if you so wish."

"I do so wish, Lord Wandor. According to those same codes it is now proper that I do so. I think you will find my skills useful."

Then there was a long ride through the twilight toward Fors, with the sunset further reddening snow already darkened with frozen blood. The towers of the city stood black against the glowing western sky by the time they reached the drawbridge and hailed the gate guards.

"Ho, the gate! I am Bertan Wandor. In the name of Queen Anya, I ask that the city of Fors yield peacefully."

Muttering voices on the walls, the sound of footsteps and of crossbows being cocked, and a number of helmeted heads peering over the battlements. Then a single sharp barked order, the creak of a windlass, the rattle of chains, and the drawbridge began swinging down. A voice called down from the gate tower.

"By decree of the Civic Council, the city of Fors yields to the army of Bertan Wandor."

And Wander rode on across the drawbridge and into the city.

His last words of the day were to the two representatives of the Civic Council who came out to meet him as he rode up to the Civic Hall. Through teeth chattering with cold and fear, they said:

"Greetings, Lord Wandor. We rejoice in your c-c-coming. What will your army require of us?" Their faces were pale and subdued.

Wandor realized that if he had asked for a hundred virgins to sacrifice in the Civic Square the next morning, he could have had them. It was the first time he had seen free men cringing in his presence, and he did not like either the sight or the sensations it aroused in him.

The last of his strength had very nearly ebbed away now, and he had to flog his fading wits to contrive a reply. "For the moment, very little. Let any of my soldiers who want to come into the city and find a warm bed. They've been sleeping out in the cold for the better part of a month. And find me a tavern or something I can use as a headquarters." The two dignitaries scurried off into the darkness. Wandor was alone with Gwynna and her guard of Plainsmen, staring at the deserted streets and trying to keep from falling out of the saddle.

He managed to hold on until the clatter of hooves behind him heralded the arrival of Count Arlor with a solid force of both royal and Viceroyalty troops. And he even managed to stay awake until he had helped the hobbling, stumbling Gwynna to the tavern the Civic Council had offered them. But a moment after he saw the big double bed, with its ragged quilt and doubtless lice-ridden mattress, he full on it face down. Blackness took him for twelve full hours.

The castle surrendered the next morning. Count Arlor took possession of it without even bothering to awaken Wandor. In fact, Wandor did not come fully alive again until that afternoon when Arlor convened another council of war.

The council met in the chamber in the seaward tower that had once been Galkor's office, the chamber where Nond had died and Arlor and Gwynna had fought for their lives. All those who had been at the council held at Castle Delvor were there, as well as the two Royal

Army commanders. Neither mercenary captains nor Civic Councilors had a place as yet, and Gwynna at least saw small reason to give them any at all.

"Even a small council is only good for saying what can't be done," she had told Arlor over breakfast. "And a large council is good for nothing at all."

So it was a council of men and women who by and large knew each other that met in the tower chamber, and Arlor had no need to be formal. Sipping hot wine, he said, "Nond gave me no written instructions about what to do if he died before Cragor was destroyed. He said there were nine chances out of ten of my having to tear them up, anyway, so why waste paper?

"But he did say the first order of business should be to clear the Viceroyalty of Cragor's supporters. This has been done. And the second should be to appoint a new Viceroy. He gave me full powers to do that."

The gray eyes in Arlor's long lean face turned toward Wandor. For a moment Wandor had the chilling feeling that those eyes flashed gold as Nond looked out through them. "Lord Wandor—Master Wandor—will you become Viceroy of the East for Queen Anya, and rule it as she would wish until she can choose freely a man equally fit?" Now Arlor was speaking formally—perhaps to save himself from having to grope for words more suitable but less formal.

Was such a rank properly his? Wandor asked himself. And then hard on the heels of that doubt came another question. Who else could there be as Viceroy? At his orders the Khindi, the Plainsmen, and soon the greater part of the mercenaries marched or stayed at home. Any other man would be a sham figure, a puppet, both in the eyes of the world and in fact. Once more it seemed that he had no choice but to accept a burden lowered—or hurled—down upon his shoulders.

"I will."

Arlor rose and with his band on Ibis heart began swearing the oath of allegiance to the new Viceroy.

That evening Wandor and Gwynna walked on the seaward

wall of the castle. The clear weather still held—the western horizon blazed in a glory of scarlet and gold as the sun dipped into the cold blue-gray sea. Somewhere out on that sea a ship bore Galkor and Kaldmor the Dark toward Benzos and, perhaps the wrath of Duke Cragor. But for now that mattered little. The Viceroyalty was free, and until spring opened the Ocean and the roads, there would be no more war.

Wandor turned toward Gwynna and as he did so, the Mind Speech of Cheloth of the Woods came to him.

("Well, Bertan Wandor, Viceroy by public proclamation and King by rights you dare not speak of. Are you happy?")

It took Wandor a moment to decide how to answer that question. ("Not happy, I would say. But relieved. For the moment at least. And grateful to you.")

("Your gratitude is your concern, not mine. You are a *purpose* to me, a purpose I wish to see fulfilled. You seem on the road to fulfilling it admirably. I will walk that road with you whether you are grateful or not.")

Cheloth broke the link, and as Wandor looked at Gwynna, he saw that she had been hearing Cheloth's words, also. She smiled. "If I could say he had any emotions, I would call Cheloth something of a curmudgeon."

Wandor also smiled, then shrugged. "He has waited two thousand years. Why should I expect him to take much care for me as a man? If I expected him to do that after so long and with so much at stake for him, I would be getting very much above myself. I am a man, and I will be one no matter how many crowns I wear. Never let me forget that, you and all the others I call friend. And never let me make you less than what you are now. Never."

Especially not you, he wanted to add, but he knew that he could not hope to keep his voice steady while he said that, and so he was silent. If I must make you shrink away as I grow great, he said to himself, then I shall not grow great. I shall take you to a hut in the most distant forest I can find, and we shall live there as long as the gods will it, raising our children and our crops and taking no thought for the great world. For I cannot make you small without tearing away part of myself.

The sun was gone now, and it was rapidly getting colder. He took Gwynna's hand, and together they went down the stairs to the courtyard.

THE END

Continued in the next Wandor adventure: *WANDOR'S VOYAGE*

DON'T MISS ANY OF NEIL HUNTER'S
NOVELS FROM CALIBER BOOKS

Reporter Les Mason is completing an expose on the Long Point Nuclear Plant. But before he can finish he dies an agonizing death. The doctors are baffled—and there are similar cases to follow...Chris Lane, his girlfriend, and organizer of the Long Point Protestors, discovers Mason's notes, and decides to find out for herself what the plant has to hide.

2 BOOK SERIES

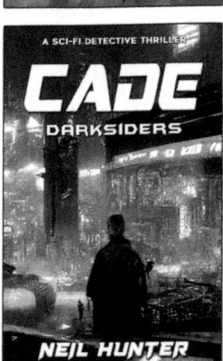

In middle of the 21st century America – over-populated decaying cities are ruled by hi-tech gangs pushing every vice and wastelands are controlled by bands of mutants. Ordinary citizens are oppressed and face a hopeless future. But Marshal T.J. Cade is a new breed of law enforcer. Teamed with his cyborg partner, Janek, Cade takes on these criminals and works in the gray areas of the law to get the job done.

3 BOOK SERIES

The village of Shepthorne England wasn't being gripped, but strangled by a winter's blanket of heavy snow and Arctic temperatures. The trouble began innocently enough with a massive pile-up of autos on frozen roads leading to and from the village. Then, from the sky, a military transport plane with its top secret cargo of devastation crashed down towards the center of the village. Hell was just beginning to touch Shepthorne and its unsuspecting citizens...

FROM CALIBER BOOKS

CALIBER
B O O K S

www.calibercomics.com

DON'T MISS ANY OF MICHAEL KASNER'S HARD HITTING MILITARY NOVEL SERIES

BLACK OPS

Formed by an elite cadre of government officials, the Black OPS team goes where the law can't - to seek retribution for acts of terror directed against Americans anywhere in the world.

3 BOOK SERIES

Armed with all the tactical advantages of modern technology, battle hard and ready when the free world is threatened - the Peacekeepers are the baddest grunts on the planet.

4 BOOK SERIES

CHOPPER COPS

America is being torn apart as criminal cartels terrorize our cities, dealing drugs and death wholesale. Local police are outgunned, so the President unleashes the U.S. TACTICAL POLICE FORCE. An elite army of super cops with ammo to burn, they swoop down on the hot spots in sleek high-tech attack choppers to win the dirty war and take back America!

4 BOOK SERIES

FROM CALIBER BOOKS
www.calibercomics.com

CALIBER
BOOKS

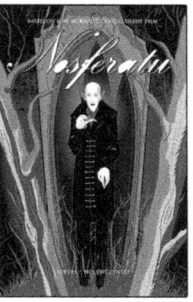